Truth Is
for Strangers

Also by Efraim Sevela

LEGENDS FROM INVALID STREET

Efraim Sevela

Truth Is
for Strangers

A Novel About a Soviet Poet

Translated from the Russian by
Antonina W. Bouis

DOUBLEDAY & COMPANY, INC.   GARDEN CITY, NEW YORK   1976

ISBN: 0-385-01704-9
Library of Congress Catalog Card Number 75–36580
Copyright © 1976 by Doubleday & Company, Inc.
All Rights Reserved
Printed in the United States of America
First Edition

Truth Is
for Strangers

Two snowplows were clearing the square outside the railroad station. The metal plows scooped up and shoved the frozen clumps of snow along the troughs of the elevators. At the top, the snow fell into the back of the trucks. In order to pull up to the station, the taxi had to go around the trucks. It came very close and several lumps of snow hit the roof with a thud. Algis was in the front seat with the driver. He glanced at the meter, unbuttoned his coat, and smiled as he took out his wallet, remembering how Rita had taught him, laughingly, that a Muscovite never gives more than twenty or thirty kopeks for a tip and that only vacationing hicks throw around rubles like visiting merchant princes. It's a marginal inferiority complex, she had said, and gets nothing but sarcasm from a cabdriver or waiter in the capital.

But Algis was alone and he gave an extra ruble tip, watching the driver's face. The cabbie lazily looked over Algis' expensive velour coat and fuzzy deerskin cap and shoved the money into his pocket without a word of thanks.

Ingrate, Algis thought to himself without bitterness. Rita was right and he would definitely tell her that, in a half hour, when she was due to have dinner with him at the station. They had agreed to meet in the restaurant and spend his last hour or so before the train together.

Now he had to hurry up about the ticket. Algis had not made a reservation at the Writers' Union. He had forgotten about it in the flurry of good-bys, but he was not worried. The soft-class cars were usually half empty, and there was no problem in getting a ticket at the station at the last minute.

Carrying his yellow leather suitcase and chic matching traveling bag, he entered the ticket office, where two long lines stretched from the two open windows. The other four were closed.

Unfailingly surprised by illogic, he thought about how people would not be standing in line angry and bored if only all six windows were open. But he thought about it calmly and cheerily, the way a healthy person listens to an account of someone else's illnesses. Sure, it's too bad . . . but what can you do? The window that sold soft-class tickets had no line, and Algis confidently headed for it. He skimmed the signs over the windows. And stopped. The electric letters read: NO SOFT-CLASS SEATS.

Algis suddenly felt tired, set his baggage on the stone floor, reread the sign, and saw that the window he had been headed for had a plywood door shut over it. It was a surprise, and so unexpected that Algis immediately lost his good humor. It meant that he would have to endure twenty hours in a crowded car, putting up with neighbors he had no desire to know and whose boring stories he did not want to hear, inhale the odor of stale underwear, and perhaps not sleep at all because of somebody's snoring.

That's great, he thought. Reluctantly he decided to look for management, pull rank, and get a soft-class ticket. It always rankled him to see people using their achievements to get privileged treatment. But what else was there to do? He couldn't travel second-class.

His talk with the duty officer led to nothing. Algis merely demeaned himself by showing his laureate book. The officer in his big red cap, young and sleepy, disinterestedly returned it to Algis and grumbled that there were no seats, the entire car was reserved for foreign tourists, and left him with his book in his hand.

Amazing. Algis was getting angry. Because of some tourists, who are harboring at least one spy and certainly people who wish us no good, I, a Soviet citizen, an honored and famous poet, and finally, a Communist, the master of my own country, am deprived of riding in comfort.

It was the same in hotels. Algis remembered the time he had found all his things out in the hall. The hotel manager offered him another room, a worse one below street level, all because some tourists had arrived and room had to be made for them. This servile pandering to foreigners and absolute disregard for one's own, considered normal throughout Russia, irritated Algis, but there was no point in getting worked up over it. Weren't there enough inconsistencies in life? He was not the only one to come up against it, and no one else was complaining. What made him better than the others? As it was, his life was full of luxuries inaccessible to most. He could overlook minor inconveniences.

Algis looked back at the billboard. There were first-class cars. It wasn't the same as a soft car. The compartment was for four people and usually full. But at least the people were cleaner than in the regular seats. He sighed as he looked at the line. There were peasants and their wives, many with sniveling kids in their arms, suitcases and sacks at their feet. As the line moved, they pushed their stuff up a foot. Algis figured them to be Russians and Belorussians by their dress and faces. The train went through Smolensk and then crossed all of Belorussia.

He could recognize the Lithuanians immediately. Even though they seemed to be dressed like everyone else, they still stood out from their neighbors. It was the different expression around the eyes, private and alien, or the cut of their clothes and how they wore them. They looked neater and more severe. And more pedigreed. That was it—Algis saw them as a different breed, set apart from the Slavic crowd. The Baltic look. Those features that

3

did not look Russian, which Russian women liked so much in Algis and which made Rita call him a Viking.

Remembering Rita, Algis anxiously looked at his watch. She was due any minute at the restaurant, and he would need at least an hour on line. Algis became completely depressed. He picked up his things and looked at the end of the line in despair. In ten minutes he would go to the restaurant to warn Rita, but he had to check his things, and first he had to take a place on line.

"Closer to the people and the masses," he thought gloomily, realizing that his farewell dinner with Rita was ruined and everything was spoiled. From now on he could not depend on chance but would plan ahead. Luckily, he, Algirdas Požera, always had the opportunity to plan in this poorly organized world.

During the last ten or fifteen years, that period when his star was rising and he was becoming a classic in his own lifetime, a major contemporary Lithuanian poet, Algis Požera had somehow become used to luxury without noticing it, become sensitive to the least discomfort. Thus the situation in which he found himself at the station completely ruined his good mood, because it made him feel like everyone else.

But fame is fame and it comes up in the most unexpected forms. Algis was recognized in the line. By a Lithuanian, of course. And he was right up at the window. He ran out of the line, this not so young, rather simple-looking man in an old coat, probably a middle-level office worker in some small town in Lithuania, embarrassed and blushing at talking to a celebrity. He offered his services to Algis; he would buy him a ticket, refusing Algis' money, saying they would figure it out after he got the ticket.

Algis was flattered and thanked the man in his velvety voice, confident once again, and thought about how his name worked for him without his willing it now; it would be that way until he died. Only one thing spoiled his pleasure. That man would travel with him in the same car and presume on their acquaintance to bore him with talk, to ask him about the life of writers. It would be improper to deny him and Algis would have to pay for the favor with the loss of peace and with false camaraderie.

Such fears were unfounded. His potential neighbor handed him the ticket and explained with undisguised remorse that he was going on a different train and would therefore be deprived of the opportunity to get to know the famous poet better. He had read Algis' work, of course, but this was his first and probably only opportunity to see him in the flesh. Algis, trying to hide the relief he felt at those words, thanked the man for a long time, probably too long, made small talk, and, picking up his luggage, left the ticket hall.

Everything was going well. Rita would be there any second, they still had plenty of time, and Algis entered the restaurant in the best of moods.

In an expensive suit with a warm sweater under the jacket, a handkerchief that matched his sweater peering elegantly from his pocket, Algis appeared masculine and intellectual. His hair was fair, sun-bleached, his eyes gray, tinged with blue, and there was a late Crimean tan on his sharp-featured face with its firm jaw. ("You're a Viking! That's just how I always pictured them," Rita used to say as she kissed him.) Algis was tall and well built; he had kept in shape even though he was forty and had begun to put on a little weight. The waiter immediately recognized a real client in him.

Even though the restaurant was full, Algis got a private table in the corner and an intimate wink and promise from the waiter not to seat anyone else at the table and to come for the order as soon as the lady arrived. The lady had not come. Algis looked around the room; perhaps Rita was early and waiting at another table. The time of their appointment had passed. She was probably held up—it was not easy getting a cab at that hour.

Algis flipped through the menu and decided to wait since he

5

was in no rush. Observing the people at neighboring tables turned out to be an uninteresting diversion, and so he fixed his gaze on the ceiling and the rough plaster molding along its perimeter. Gray, round growths near the protuberances caught his attention: they were swallows' nests. That was an unexpected discovery. Swallows had built their nests and passed the winter in comfort, here, in the noisy station restaurant, in the steam and food smells, isolated from the outside world. The birds flew from one end of the room to the other, but not with the headlong thrust that characterized the flight of their fellow swallows out in the free blue wilderness. They flew heavily, slowly. It almost seemed that they were waddling, fat with the abundance of food they picked up from the tables. They had grown clumsy—there was no danger to keep them alert, no hawk would penetrate their domain. The age-long instinct that led them south in autumn and back to their nesting grounds in spring must have atrophied with time. It was quiet and peaceful here.

The restaurant ceiling was covered with landscapes painted, like medallions, into round alabaster frames. They represented all the corners of the world: the deep forests, the plains with waving grain, snow-topped mountains, and tropical palms.

Crossing the room, the swallows saw in a condensed and convenient way all the places their brothers flew over: the forests, plains, mountains, and savannas. The difference was that they did not have to suffer and starve on the arduous journey, brave storms and blizzards and hurricanes, leave their fallen comrades behind, blindly heeding the call of their destination as had their grandfathers and fathers and as undoubtably would their children and grandchildren.

They had found their path: a peaceful and convenient one. The framed landscapes soothed them: the long-suffering route chosen by their forefathers was always at hand, visible to the birds' eye. This must have stilled their conscience and comforted them with the thought that after all they were not renouncing

6

their age-old commandments. They were doing just what their kin were doing—but they were smarter and they did it without strain or loss. True, they had become slower, their bodies covered with fat, and their instincts dulled. But it was all a question of preference.

Algis pondered in agitation, watching the ceiling and the clumsy swallows, which looked like hairy bats to him. Life was truly stranger than fiction. Chance had thrown a luscious image his way. It was so full of civic poetry. He would definitely write a poem about the swallows in this restaurant, about those who for the sake of comfort trade in the romance of travel and the heroism of struggle and mortal danger to live a sated, vegetable life within four walls.

How many people like that had Algis known in his time, and how many were around him even now. He would write a poem as sharp and stinging as a scourge, brimming with barely contained anger and pain. Its topicality would ensure immediate publication in the papers and readings on the radio. The critics would once more talk about Požera as a fighting, aggressive poet; they would remember his early incendiary verses, like the ones the Lithuanian Komsomol members couldn't get enough of. They would draw parallels between those poems and this one, and some reviewer would surely write, "There is still powder in the powder-flask."

But most of all Algis would want to see the reaction of old Jonas Šimkus to his poem, which he had already named *Fat Swallows*.

This trip to Moscow, despite the fact that he had accomplished everything he planned, left a bitter taste that was without explanation or cause. There seemed to be no reason for anxiety. A two-volume collection of his poetry in Russian translation was accepted by a major Moscow publishing house. He had gotten a big advance and had a letter of credit in his pocket that showed a figure with several zeros. He purposely did not deposit

7

the check into his account. He had taken a letter of credit instead because every self-respecting man should have an amount of money that slipped past his wife's control.

Algis had been very warmly and respectfully received in Moscow at the Writers' Union. He was offered a creative trip to Latin America. An expensive one. At the expense of the Union. They offered it, he had not had to ask. And when he magnanimously accepted, pretending to fret about finding the time, of which he, of course, had endless amounts, the directorate of the Union had expressed their joy as though he were doing them a great favor.

Who else among his writing comrades in Lithuania could boast of such position and success? He knew perfectly well the infinite efforts required for others to achieve even half of what he possessed. And everything came to him easily, effortlessly. The solid name and reputation in literary circles that he had made for himself long ago worked for him now without his active participation. The time had come for him to rest on his laurels and no matter what he wrote now, the multivoiced choir of newspaper flatterers would burn incense to his image. And if he should have a complete flop, they would maintain a discreet silence, making believe that nothing had happened.

So what was bothering him? No matter how much Algis went over it in his mind, he could remember no slight, no disrespect, no irony, no prick to his very sensitive pride. He had been cordially received everywhere, and the cordiality seemed unfeigned. Many tried to be his friends or at least acquaintances, and they did so without selfish motives, simply because they were impressed by him. Not only women, but men admired him; Algis saw the gleam of admiration in many pairs of eyes when he, tall and well built, an unaging athlete, his hair soft and shimmering like flax, was introduced to a new group. Even his slight Lithuanian accent was popular in Moscow, eliciting first kindly, and then enraptured smiles.

8

But something had happened in Moscow, something that flashed by and left a glob of tar on his pride, forcing him now to follow the tiny threads back to the cause of the unpleasant sensation that had stuck with him for several days, flaring up now and then.

Old Jonas Šimkus, Rita's father. Yes, that was it. That gnarled but still sinewy old spider with a head as bald as an egg. A Moscow Lithuanian, who spoke Lithuanian with a Russian accent, and yet was a major expert in the language, in all the niceties of its many dialects, and in the bottomless storehouse of folklore, who had a clear, youthful memory and an unpleasant, squeaky voice that blew with the cold of Siberia. He had spent an even twenty years in a camp in the North, in Siberia, where he tanned and shriveled in the cold, but managed to survive. He returned to Moscow and, like a little spider, jumped back into life as though there was nothing terrible behind him.

An optimist and a hard worker, he quickly became one of the leading translators of poetry from Lithuanian into Russian. It was he who translated and edited the two-volume collection of the works of Algis Požera. He retranslated the poems that had been done before and gave them freshness and brilliance. It was like winning a lottery for Algis to fall into his hands. He would soon be presented to the Russian readers in the best possible form. In Šimkus' translation, even the weak poems that had not quite made it took on new resonance and color and sometimes became unrecognizable, retaining only the sense of the originals.

Algis had even given some thought to sharing his honorarium with the old man—which would have been completely fair—and had even carefully hinted at it, but was met with such hostility and injured pride that he never tried to bring it up again.

He had known Šimkus for several years but it was only on this trip to Moscow that he visited his home. And not just once, but several times in the crowded two-room apartment in Novye Cheremushki, where all the houses, gloomy boxes, looked alike.

Even cabdrivers got lost in the streets and had to ask directions of pedestrians and swear. Šimkus lived here with his wife and daughter. His daughter was Rita. Algis met her in that apartment and then almost every day Rita left work at lunch and spent the rest of the day in Algis' official but rather comfortable room at the Hotel Ukraina. They gave themselves to love in his room, staying in bed for five or six hours, as though they were seventeen again. They would return across all of Moscow to Cheremushki. Sometimes Algis would walk her to the door and once or twice he went up to see the old people, waiting on the landing until Rita had gone in so as not to arouse suspicion.

He had a natural reason to visit the Šimkuses: the old man was working on his book. And they would sit up late, drink tea, and then cognac, the old man pontificating. Rita kept cool and did not let on to their relationship in any way.

Algis did not like the old man. His agility and energy at his age and after the Siberian camp seemed abnormal, a buffoon's game of cheerful bustling, and Algis would watch him secretly, waiting for him to collapse like a burst balloon, let out his air, and turn into a heap of rags. He dressed sloppily in old, worn clothes. And under the heap of rags there would be a shiny bald pate and a pair of transparent watery eyes.

Šimkus had become completely Russified, and in Moscow they called him Ivan Ivanovich and not Jonas. And his wife's surname was Šimkus and not Šimkiene, as it would have been in Lithuania, and Rita was also Šimkus and not Šimkute. That rubbed Algis the wrong way. It irritated him.

Algis was completely devastated by the old man's unfounded optimism and forgiveness. Once, before 1936, he had been a teacher of Lithuanian language and literature in a *Gymnasium* in Kaunas, was a leader of the underground Communist Party, which was so small back then that each member was allotted some ten police detectives who followed him night and day, but never did him any noticeable harm. Šimkus, a progressive, was married to a Jewess, a seamstress and designer, now the aged Rakhil Abramovna. They had a year-old daughter, a lovely child with the charming Lithuanian name Ruta, which in Russia was changed to Rita.

Smetona's regime did not long tolerate the gathering little groups of Communists in Lithuania. They began arrests. What did it threaten Šimkus? A year or two in jail, at most. But he didn't find such a future appealing and so he crossed the border with his child in his arms, ran to the Soviet Union, into the arms of the Russian Communists, his comrades-in-arms, not doubting for a second that he would be welcome.

It was 1937. Šimkus was arrested in Moscow as a foreign spy, the extreme triumvirate pronounced the then popular sentence of execution, and he spent a year in a solitary cell in Butyrka Prison waiting for his execution. His hair fell out and he became egg-bald. For some inexplicable reason the sentence was commuted to life at hard labor, and he was carted off with hundreds of other sufferers to Magadan—first by railroad to Vladivostok and then by sea, in an overcrowded hold where the living lay next to the dead. Rakhil Abramovna, as the wife of a spy, was exiled to Kazakhstan, where she stayed until the end of World War II. By some miracle she was able to locate her daughter Rita, a ten-year-old who had forgotten her parents, in a children's home in the Urals.

Only twenty years later, when Šimkus had been rehabilitated, did the family gather once again, in that crowded apartment in Novye Cheremushki.

When he talked about his suffering in the camps, about the beatings and torture at Lubyanka, the old man reminded Algis of a demented monk engrossed in his wounds, suffering and blaming no one. Algis once asked him cautiously:

"And you have no sense of injustice? They destroyed twenty years of your life, the best part. And who was it? Your own. The

Party for which you were willing to lay down your life. Do you still have your original feelings for the Party?"

"Naturally," the old man said, as though he were belaboring the obvious. He was sincere. "My dear Algis, you must understand. The Party is like a mother to me. I'm not saying that for a pretty phrase. I mean it. Now, imagine that your mother, whom you love more than anyone in the whole world, was raped and dishonored by evil men. Would you stop loving her and turn away because of that? Of course not!"

Algis was also a Communist, but of another generation. Without Šimkus' fanaticism, without his religious, frenzied faith. He accepted all the Party dogma without burdening himself with attempts at analysis, he regularly sat bored at Party meetings with an attentive expression on his face like everyone else, tried to pay his dues on time, and understood that everybody was playing the same game, which had become habitual and no longer elicited irony.

But the basic tenets of Communism were as holy to him now as they had been in his youth, when with a trembling heart he had received his Party card from the Party secretary; the card had guided him to a new turn in his life. When he spoke of "the radiant peaks of communism" or the "luminous light of October" in his poems, he was sincere and was not trying to butter anyone up.

But Šimkus' words and his blind faith, overlooking so much, grated on Algis and he thought the old man could not be completely sane. Algis was completely turned off by his folksy manner of getting down to the truth, of preaching and teaching without giving any thought to the reactions of the person he was addressing.

And so Algis uncovered the cause of the unpleasant feeling that had been bothering him since his Moscow visit. It was Šimkus' fault. That old spider, bulging his watery lobster eyes out at Algis, a doltish smile on his flabby lips, had pierced Algis' heart with a needle.

"Do you understand, my dear fellow, your entire life is in these two volumes. From the beginning—young, rosy, and very honest. To the end. The end is not very creditable. Your last works seem to have been written by someone else. I don't recognize them. The later, the worse they get. And emptier."

Algis had not replied. But Rakhil Abramovna, who was pouring out the tea, caught the guest's hostile and hurt look, and since she was more tactful than her husband, changed the subject.

Rita had been at the table, too. She lowered her eyes and blushed. Blushed, Algis thought, for her father's brusqueness. She loved Algis, after all, and it hurt her to see him demeaned. And he could say nothing in reply, because it was her father who was insulting him. But the next day in his room at the Hotel Ukraina, holding him close to her naked body and breathing warmly on his neck, she quietly said:

"Don't take offense at Father. I agree with him too."

Algis had shuddered. He wanted to hit her, to throw her out into the corridor, barefoot and naked, to her shame. But he controlled himself and took a deeper drag on his cigarette.

Basically, what was Rita? Tall and angular, like her father, and a fiery brunette like her mother. Big nose. True, she had juicy, slightly puffy lips and sorrowful Jewish eyes. She attracted Algis and yet repulsed and irritated him at the same time. Inexperienced and shy in bed, each time she reminded Algis of a girl who was giving herself to a man for the first time, and with her, Algis felt inexhaustibly young. But in everything else she was independent, even overly so, markedly her own woman in her opinions and actions, and Algis never knew what to expect from her. She did not share her father's political opinions even though she loved him in her way—brusquely and condescendingly, as she would a sick man. She was not afraid to criticize aloud anything that displeased her. And there was much in Soviet life that she did not like. Occasionally she would put Algis in a bind.

Like the time at the banquet at the restaurant of the Central House of Writers, where they were honoring a famous Moscow poet. Rita, invited by Algis, listened to the poet read his works. Her hostile sneer was apparent to everyone at the table. When he had finished to weak applause, she said to Algis so that all could hear:

"Poor fellow. How he suffers for the Vietnamese children! And yet he welshes on his alimony payments to his wife and doesn't even care what his own offspring eat!"

That evening Algis decided to stop taking Rita anywhere and somehow get rid of her. This simple affair, like the many others Algis had when he came to Moscow, was threatening to damage his reputation, and that was too high a price for a few pleasant hours in the hard bed at the Hotel Ukraina. He picked a fight on the way home. Rita listened calmly and with the same sneer to his tirades.

"Don't you think, darling, that you're defending the insulted guest of honor so heatedly because you're not so different from him?"

Algis left without saying good-by, letting her know that it was for ever. Two days later he was so upset that he called her at the institute, apologizing at length and incoherently, and Rita, laughing, responded in such a warm and friendly tone that his heart contracted from the overwhelming desire to see her immediately.

"Silly. Don't babble on. You're a Viking. And Vikings are forgiven everything. I'll be there."

"When?" He breathed impatiently into the receiver.

"Now, if you like," she laughed. "I'll get a cab."

And she really did come a half hour later. Algis kissed her hungrily, like a boy, getting in her way as she undressed. She smiled her kind smile that Algis needed so much, her deep dark eyes got murky, and Algis was losing control, even though he had a long-standing reputation as a calm, balanced lover.

Algis had not been able to meet Rita yesterday. He had been busy all day and after 10 P.M. women visitors were not permitted in the hotel rooms. The hall monitors would not let them through. In an attempt to combat vice, the hypocritical watchdogs of morality made it legal to do anything you wanted in your room as long as you did it in the daytime.

"We spend our nights during the day," she had said once, laughingly, as she left the hotel a few minutes before ten. Once she had even stuck her tongue out at the duty woman.

Algis did not want to leave without seeing Rita, so they had made a date for dinner at the station. She promised to be on time. Yet she did not come. It was time to head for the train. He realized that she would not show up. Would not come to see him off and say good-by. Not because she did not have the time. She did it consciously, to show him that the break was final.

Under the restaurant's ceiling, against the background of steppes, forests, and tropical jungles, the swallows flew—fat and clumsy, like bats.

Algis gave the waiter three rubles, apologized for holding the table for nothing, and left the restaurant feeling angry and hungry.

"The hell with her," he thought as he moved along toward the platform, his luggage weighing down his arms. "She made it easier. I won't have to lie and twist out of it to soften the break that was bound to come. It was ripening. It happens every time an affair drags on too long."

Usually he was the one to leave them. He did it elegantly, without coarseness, finding a trifling excuse and blowing it up into a tragedy. He dropped women, leaving them with the impression that he was the one who had suffered inconsolably. They even felt guilty about their treatment of him. But this time it was he who was dropped. For the first time. Gave him his

15

walking papers, and he was not even worth a farewell dinner to soften the blow.

There was no denying it: he, Algirdas Požera, social lion and idol of innumerable Moscow and Vilnius women, was getting old and the painful slap from Rita was the first reminder of that fact.

The narrow tunnel leading to the platform was filled with a motley crowd, sweaty and angry, burdened with suitcases and bundles, dragging their sniveling, cramped, out-of-scale children behind them.

The crowd spread out on the platform as though blown by the frosty draft, and meandering impatient lines were forming by the general public cars. There were fewer people in front of the first-class cars and absolutely nobody by the soft-class car, which somehow stood out from the rest, the very car in which Algis could not get a space. But who had then? Algis looked around the station enviously seeking out the people who had forced him to move from his usual car. Whoever it was had the right to do so and was, therefore, someone more important than he.

He found them. First a line of porters dressed in canvas aprons with badges, pushing carts with mountains of bright, round luggage in shapes and sizes he had never seen before. Foreign luggage. There could be no doubt about it. Then the owners of the luggage appeared—a flock of large, furry birds. In expensive fur coats, warm foreign hats, and multicolored boots with fur trim. All women. Not a single man among them. But they were as tall as men. A good half of them wore glasses on their faces, red from the cold. And led by a woman. A Russian, even though she was dressed like a foreigner. She had the same glasses. And her fur coat was no worse. An Intourist guide. Disciplined, with confident thought-out movements. Cute enough and well proportioned enough. A strict regard for what was proper showed in her eyes and in every move of her head. She commanded this group of tourists and answered for their every move. Without commotion, well practiced, like a mother hen, she

16

began loading the fat furs into the soft car, ordering them about with an imperious tone and naturally smiling as she did it, the way it is always done in the best tourist bureaus of the world.

Algis focused his envy and hurt on her and not on the tourists. That broad with her high-cheeked doll's face, confident with the power that was given to her, a sergeant major in skirts, dressed in custom-made clothes, a typical product of Intourist (Algis had met many in his day), for some reason irritated him as though it was all her fault that he could not ride in his favorite car and even that Rita had not seen him off.

She was shouting out orders in the cold in smooth quick English, without an accent, the product of a good education, the latest school in this period of increased contact with the West. Algis did not speak English. He understood a few words, and could even ask directions on the street when he was abroad. That was all he had learned in the few lessons he had before his trip to the West. And then he gave up. He usually traveled with an interpreter, who doubled as a watchdog, but who relieved him of many problems that come from being in a new place.

American tourists were getting into the soft car. He figured that out from the few phrases that reached his ears. Then he perked up when he heard something unexpected. Lithuanian. Not pure, but with a foreign accent. American. But it was Lithuanian. Familiar and dear, no matter what the accent was. And then another American, laughing, called out from the car platform in Lithuanian. There could be no doubt. These were Lithuanian Americans. Going to Lithuania. To see the old homeland, which most of them had never known, because they were born abroad of parents who had left Lithuania.

The fact that they had not abandoned their language warmed Algis' heart and made him forget his irritation with the Intourist guide. He now looked at her in a friendly way, realizing that they would probably meet at a banquet in Vilnius, as had often happened. And she was destined to take his picture back to Moscow with the usual polite inscription in Russian and Lithuanian.

She was standing by the door, counting the tourists like chicks as they climbed the steps. She had on a short brown fur coat and an elegant knit hat, but no boots; just stockings and shoes. She tapped one foot against the other to keep warm. Management and servant rolled into one. That's what the profession is. Demeaning and attractive. Attractive because you can often go abroad without a tourist visa and at company expense, and you can buy things that others can not get, with money that they stingily give you for each trip. You scrimp on food, literally starve, so that you can dress decently in some inexpensive shop in Paris or London and then show off before your neighbors and friends in Moscow.

Algis had a friend who was an acrobat in the Moscow circus. He often appeared in Europe and America and complained to Algis that his profession did not allow him to bring back too much. An acrobat can not skimp on his food. He can not save money to buy consumer goods. If he weakens from hunger he falls off the trapeze. It costs him even more then. According to the acrobat, the animal trainers made tremendous profits from guest appearances. All the circus people envied them. They spent no money on food at all, and ate their animals' rations of carrots, beets, and even oats. Not to mention meat. Animals are mute. And they won't write to the Party organization denouncing you, either. And so the trainer lives on half the animals' rations and comes back home with junk that costs almost nothing abroad but a fortune in Russia.

He watched the Intourist guide hit one heel against the other and use good English and official brightness to cheer on and amuse the foreigners who were clumsily getting into the train with their coats and boots. Algis thought she was probably an unhappy person, always at someone else's party, seeing riches she would never have, and writing reports to the KGB that were indistinguishable from denouncements. That's the work. All the young girl guides have special training, start work by signing secret documents and taking on secret duties, and they receive officers' ranks. But you'll never see them in KGB uniforms with officers' bars on their shoulders. Their lieutenants' titles figure only in payroll accounting. They're detectives with lipstick, shapely legs, and a tolerable pronunciation of foreign languages.

He went over to his own car. The small crowd had disappeared, they had gotten seats while he was looking at the tourists.

It was still early, but the frosty air had thickened into twilight, and round lights glowed along the length of the platform, turning dust silver in the arcs of their pale light.

The conductor, a warm shawl draped over her official cap, examined his ticket with a flashlight in the bare fingers of her raggedly gloved hands. He asked her as conspiratorially as possible:

"I hope the sleeper compartments aren't filled up completely?"

"You'll be alone. Going to Vilnius? Should I reserve the lower berth?"

"Yes, please."

"No one will get on in Mozhaisk. You're lucky."

"Thank you, I'll find a way to repay you."

She cast her practiced eye over his velour coat and fur hat, and sympathized:

"No room in the soft car? They're all foreign . . . Keep coming here . . . What's there for them to see? Treat Russia like it was a circus just for them."

The compartment was really empty, and it differed from the soft-class international compartments only in that it was intended for four passengers instead of two, and the berths were wooden and hard, covered with a quilted mattress and laid with sheets and a wool blanket. If they didn't put anyone in with him in Mozhaisk, he could travel all the way alone and in relative comfort, arriving home in the morning rested.

19

He opened his suitcase and reveling in the pleasure of it, began preparing for a full twenty-four-hour trip. He took out the leather shaving kit he had bought in Canada and the electric Phillips razor that was a gift from a Lithuanian emigrant in Argentina. He layed out the graceful soap dish, French cologne, brushes, scissors, files, and other minor necessities that he had managed to do without for so long and without which he could not live now.

By the time the train had started moving and was slowly floating past the lights of the platform, Algis had turned his car into a cozy den and begun getting ready for dinner. He was famished. The dining car had never been famous for its cooking, but this was the last chance to satisfy his hunger. Not by gulping down a rock-hard sandwich of sausage and hard-boiled eggs. But hot borshch, a steak, or, if worse came to worst, lamb stew. And a shot or two of vodka. Against the cold. And for his appetite.

Long-distance trains, and particularly the ones of Moscow, always loaded up on fairly good produce. Better than you could get at most restaurants. And only because tourists rode the trains. You can not feed them with consoling thoughts like: "Well, the temporary shortages in the Soviet Union have long been a constant factor." You can laugh about it among friends. But with foreigners, no jokes. Give them food. At least some Soviet passengers get to share the wealth. Red caviar or black? A lot of us don't even remember what it looks like. And the foreign asses think that all Russians eat is caviar. By the spoonful. Tablespoons. And drink tea from saucers with pointed pinkies. And definitely from samovars.

Here it is, ladies and gentlemen. They're as blind as kittens. They're led around like idiots. From black caviar they switch to red. From Georgian cognac to Armenian. They drink too much and eat too much. They don't see anything except the ballet and go back to the West with great respect for socialism.

The thoughts crammed into Algis' head as he changed for dinner. He took off his sweater and put on a soft shirt. Instead of a tie he had a bright pink-spotted ascot. He had learned that in South America and many people thought it becoming. He threw off his fur-lined shoes and slipped into suede mocassins. He rubbed cologne on his hands and face, examined himself in the full-length mirror on the door, checked his wallet, and left, locking the door behind him.

The train was rushing past village stations and little gray houses ran backward and disappeared under their heavy snow caps.

The conductor who had examined his ticket looked over his elegant figure admiringly and showed him the direction of the dining car.

"I hope it's not too crowded," she called after him. "You should have gone there as soon as you got on, to get a seat."

Algis did not want to think about the dining car being overcrowded a half hour out of Moscow. Most of the passengers had had an opportunity to dine in Moscow, particularly since it was cheaper than on the train.

He walked along the cars, through the noisy, cold, clattering doorways, from platform to platform. Cars, cars. Reserved seat cars, without sleeping compartments, the cheapest ones, which exposed the lives of their inhabitants to the casual passer-by; the inhabitants had immediately climbed up on the two-level hard shelves, sticking their stale bare feet or the dripping soles of their thawing boots into the passageway.

The last platform before the dining car contained several people heatedly clamoring in front of the locked door. Algis immediately guessed that the conductor had been right and every last seat was taken in the restaurant.

"At least half those seats are empty," sputtered the tall military man, his face red either from the cold or from the vodka he had had before dinner. "They let in the tourists and slammed the door in my face. Seems we're second-class. Us Russians! The bourgeoisie from America won't deign to sit with us. We'll spoil their appetite. That's disgusting! Who's in charge here?"

He started banging his fists on the door. A stumpy fat fellow in soft white felt boots, who was behind him, tried to reason with him.

"Really, Comrade Colonel, there's no reason to take offense. And there's no point in making noise. I haven't eaten either. But if they're not opening up, there must be a reason for it. Diplomacy. They can't explain everything to us."

"Get away from me, you diplomat." The officer snarled without even looking at him. "I want to get some chow, do you understand? And I will not allow myself, a person who has earned respect, to be kept behind a closed door in my own fatherland because of some overseas bitches. Don't you have any Russian pride? You're probably not even Russian! So don't babble underfoot!"

The short fellow in the felt boots had a broad face and narrow eyes. Obviously not Russian. An Asian. The disdainful tone of the Russian colonel, which did not hide his hostility toward other Soviet races, offended Algis. He was about to leave, preferring to stay hungry rather than be exposed to the insults of that chauvinist, who was capable of anything on an empty stomach inflamed by vodka. Algis' non-Russian background would be no mystery as soon as he opened his mouth—he had a definite Lithuanian accent.

But the colonel banged on the door in a frenzy, and the door flew open. The corpulent maître d'hôtel with a greasy Armenian face, wearing a fresh white jacket that did not quite button over his stomach, was standing in the doorway. When he saw the angry red colonel, his face melted into a pleading sweet smile. Behind him flashed the large foreign glasses and the teased, lacquered hairdo of the Intourist guide. She moved the nervous maître d' aside and walked out toward the colonel, her bosom high under her snow-white blouse and an imperious stern look behind the glasses.

"Colonel, you are to leave the premises immediately," she said quietly, but with an iron note in her voice. "You are disturbing our work." She stressed the word "our." "I will not repeat it. We will speak about this in another place."

The short fat fellow in the white felt boots backed out of the platform. The rest followed. Only Algis and the colonel remained. Algis was amused by the scene and wanted to see how the brave colonel would behave before the strong and stern little lady from Intourist. Or rather, from the KGB. Would the colonel really be scared off?

"I'm waiting," she said impatiently.

The colonel's red neck grew pale. He stepped back, spat at the floor by her feet, turned sharply, and left the platform, slamming the door.

Algis laughed aloud. He derived inexplicable pleasure from seeing a Russian officer, an incorrigible chauvinist, get his comeuppance in his own homeland. And why? Because of the Lithuanian women. The same Lithuanians that he had not considered human twenty years ago when he was conquering Lithuania with fire and sword. Of course, these were Lithuanians from America and they were protected by their Cerberus, their Russian guide. She turned her round eyes up at him and raised her thin brows over the fashionable frameless glasses. The nostrils of her pert powdered nose flared and her over-made-up lips stretched into a broad smile.

"Who are you, comrade?" she asked, no longer sternly. With the hidden female adoration so familiar to Algis, she looked straight into his eyes.

"I'm a Lithuanian, like the women in the restaurant."

"You're a foreigner?" she asked in surprise.

"No, a Soviet citizen. A starving one."

"Well, it doesn't look as though you're about to die." She

looked his athletic figure up and down. "Unfortunately, you can't go in there. However, I can bring you something from the buffet."

"Thank you so much. But I hasten to assure you that you are making a mistake by not inviting me in."

"Why? I'm following orders."

"And what are orders?" Algis was beginning to enjoy bantering with the Intourist lady, and he wanted to tease her, make her strain her not very powerful brains.

"You must use initiative. The situation is fluid and orders can't possibly cover everything."

"What are you getting at?" She frowned, furrowing her low clear forehead, surrounded by lacquered curls. Algis' confident lordly tone, his impressive body, and his manly sleek face were inspiring respect and even meekness in her.

"I am a poet," he said. "A laureate. Don't you recognize me from my pictures in the papers?"

"Forgive me," she muttered. "I seem to recall . . . I saw you somewhere . . . Won't you tell me your name?"

"Algirdas Požera. I assure you that these American Lithuanians, who are now eating with such relish in the restaurant, know my work. My name is well known in Lithuanian circles in America. And they have no inkling that their favorite poet and national hero is standing hungry outside the closed door of the restaurant."

She laughed suddenly, and a blush crept out from beneath a layer of pink powder.

"I have an idea. I will invite you to dine with the tourists, and you can chat with them at the table. Answer their questions. All right?"

"Agreed."

"But . . . I hope you know how to answer?"

"I know, I know." He smiled condescendingly. "It's not the first time."

"Wonderful. But please forgive me . . . I must, it's my duty
. . . I would be grateful . . . if you would show me your
papers."

"All that for a meal?"

"No, for our first meeting." She laughed. "My name is Tamara.
Tamara Georgievna."

She gave him her hand, and when he would not release it
quickly, blushed and lowered her gaze.

"Let's go. I don't need your papers. Do you speak English?"

"No."

"Then how will you converse?"

"In my native tongue. They're Lithuanian, you know."

"Ah, yes, I had almost forgotten. Are you a Party member?"

"Obviously, Tamara. Any more questions and I'll be a former
Communist who perished from starvation. And you will be the
cause of my ignoble death."

She looked into his eyes softly, womanly, and it seemed that
she would meekly put her hands on his chest. Algis knew that
look was total capitulation.

"Let's go, I will introduce you, Comrade Požera."

She turned to the Armenian, who modestly awaited them,
plump hands folded across his stomach. "One more setting. At
my table. Put it on the general account. Don't open the doors
again."

"Welcome, dear comrade," the maître d' said, spreading his
arms as gracefully as a ballerina and looking at Algis with his
languid, olive-black eyes. "You will be the only man in the entire
restaurant. Like in a bouquet of roses."

They went down the narrow passage past the kitchen; sharp
exciting smells wafted out. Tamara was in front, swinging her
hips in the tight skirt, and he followed, slightly tense, as he always was before a public appearance, annoyed that he had
agreed to turn dinner into a press conference, where he would
have to repeat banal phrases under the watchful eye of the stu-

25

pid woman from Intourist and not even notice what he was eating. Thank God she did not know Lithuanian, or he would have to weigh every word as at an interrogation.

"By the way, Comrade Požera," she said without turning back, as if she had guessed his thoughts, "I don't speak Lithuanian, and I would like to be part of the proceedings. Could you translate for me . . . in general terms?"

Algis did not reply, controlling himself, so that his tone would not betray his mounting irritation.

The dining car was divided by a carpet runner into two long rows of tables. The Americans, like children, occupied the left side. The right side was empty. Except for the center table, which had a solitary setting with a steaming bowl of something red. It had to be borshch. That was Tamara's place. Like an observation point, from which she could easily see all her charges and answer questions from any part of the restaurant.

While Tamara introduced Algis, relishing the English words, the waiter set a place next to hers.

"Dear ladies. Allow me to introduce a gentleman who is of extreme interest to you and who happened to be on our train purely coincidentally. The pride of contemporary Soviet Lithuanian literature, laureate of the State Prize, Comrade . . ." Here she paused uncomfortably, squinted at Algis, and asked him out of the corner of her mouth to repeat his name in Russian.

"Požera . . . Algirdas . . ." he whispered back, and blushed, feeling like a schoolboy. He looked at the faces turned to him, which were young and old, but all with the single Lithuanian look.

"Algirdas Požera!" Tamara announced loudly like a circus ringleader, and Algis shuddered to think that maybe she was reaching for circus applause.

But, luckily, everything went smoothly. They merely smiled politely, their eyeglasses glinting. Over half the women were wearing glasses in frames of the strangest shapes and colors. And

Algis was struck by the thought that people abroad suffered from poor vision much more than they did in the Soviet Union. That's if you judge by the number of people who wear glasses. Of course, his ophthalmologist friend in Vilnius had his own opinion on this aspect of Soviet life. He felt that so few wore glasses, not because the rest had good eyes, but because there were so few regular checkups of the population.

The appearance of Algirdas Požera in the restaurant did not create a sensation among the American Lithuanians. They looked him over kindly and with curiosity as he bowed, as though on stage, and continued eating and conversing in low tones.

Tamara led him to her table. Red borshch was steaming in his bowl too. He spread the napkin in his lap, took a piece of bread from the platter in the middle of the table, and began eating, his eyes on the empty row of tables, at the end of which stood the maître d'hôtel in the tight white jacket, a towel over his arm, his beady eyes approving of the heads bent over their plates and the chewing mouths.

Every table had a glass dish with glistening red globules of red caviar. The caviar that the Soviet man on the street could not find in the stores. It was only for export and high officials.

Tamara spooned a thick layer of caviar on her bread and bit deeply, careful not to smear her lipstick. She had an unpleasant plebeian manner of eating and talking with her mouth full.

"I don't like groups like this," she confided in Algis. "Besides English they also speak their own gibberish. And I have to stand there like an idiot and blink my eyes. Maybe they're laughing at me or saying horrible things about our country. They all hate us Russians, you know."

Tamara had forgotten that Algis was not Russian, either, and talked to him as if he were one of her own, seeking sympathy. She reminded him amazingly of the colonel who had tried to get

27

into the restaurant in vain. The same chauvinism. Arrogant and disdainful. At best, patronizing.

Algis had encountered this even among intelligent people who did not accept the corny official patriotism. And even these people, well educated, confused Latvia with Lithuania and Lithuania with Estonia, and could almost never be sure which city was capital of which republic. It was that special brand of chauvinism, uncaring, patronizing, and semidisdainful.

"But, thank God, I don't have long to fuss with them," Tamara said as she pulled back her lips and bit into her caviar sandwich. "In Vilnius I turn them over to the Lithuanian Intourist and go home."

Algis saw a tall young woman in a tight sweater stand up in the row of tourists and, smiling from ear to ear as only Americans can, head toward them, brushing her bell-bottoms against the tables.

A grumpy grimace appeared on Tamara's porcelain face, but she quickly replaced it with her practiced official smile.

"Hello, Mr. Požera." The American extended her hand and Algis noticed that her eyes with blue makeup were slightly crossed, lending her a very feminine and pretty air. "I'm an old fan of yours. I heard you read in Pittsburgh two years ago. Right?"

"Yes, yes." Algis nodded, pulling up a chair for her and motioning for her to sit. "I was in the States. And I appeared in Pittsburgh."

They both spoke Lithuanian, and Tamara's face became inscrutable. She was furious. You could tell from the way she tore into her sandwich, staring into the space above their heads.

"I'm so pleased to meet you. I'm writing my dissertation on Lithuanian poetry. Of the Soviet period. At the University of San Diego. Everything written by you that our libraries have, I've read. In the original. Is my Lithuanian pretty bad? No? I'm a third-generation American. Joanne Mage. My father was Mage, too. But my grandfather was Mažeika. I know it's a very common name in Lithuania. Like Smith in America. Perhaps I'll meet some relatives, what do you think?"

She spoke with a rounded funny accent, as though she had hot potatoes in her mouth. She looked at Algis with her gray eyes without coquetry, very openly, and he immediately liked her.

"Will it bother you, Mr. Požera, if I ask them to serve me here, so that I can have the opportunity to talk to you in unconstrained circumstances? Who knows if there'll be another opportunity like this one? And there's so much I want to ask. I don't even know where to begin. I don't want to start with compliments, but, in my opinion, you are a star of the first magnitude in today's Lithuanian literature. If you don't mind, please ask the waiter to bring my setting over here—he doesn't speak English."

Algis was sincerely pleased that she would be dining with them. He winked, called the waiter over, and had him bring everything to the table. He did not ask Tamara, he simply forgot about her. But as soon as the waiter had moved Joanne's things, a portly tourist with thick glasses got up from another table and carried her soup over in outstretched arms, letting out little cries of fear of spilling. Laughing, she sat down next to Joanne and introduced herself in good Lithuanian and a deep voice. She was a schoolteacher from Chicago and taught Lithuanian children language and literature at Sunday school. Several other tourists moved their plates from surrounding tables.

Then Tamara stood up and clapped her hands to call for silence.

"Dear friends," she said in English. "I appreciate your interest in this famous Lithuanian poet. But so as not to tire our guest with excessive questions, I suggest the following procedure. Whoever has a question tells it to me, I translate it for Mr. Požera, and he answers you. That way we will save time and learn much that is interesting and beneficial. So, who has a question?"

"Is Mr. Požera married and how many children does he have?"

Tamara translated the question and added sympathetically, as though apologizing, "That's how they all are. Not serious."

Algis smiled and replied that he was married and had two children. He even took out a photo of the family from his pocket and the snapshot was passed from table to table to the accompaniment of oohs and aahs and noisy compliments. Tamara took a quick look at the picture as she returned it to Algis and asked:

"A blonde?"

Algis did not reply.

Questions showered from the tables. He had to describe his house and tell whether it was rented or his own, and explain what a co-operative apartment was and how much it cost. The price seemed low to the Americans. However, when he falsely added an extra room and told them that he had five in his apartment, none of them was impressed. A Volga car in his own garage had no effect either. Of course, Joanne did note how expensive and difficult it was to purchase a car in the Soviet Union. Tamara swooped down on her like a hawk, calling the remark hostile propaganda and saying that it did not correspond to reality. According to her, she had a car and the waiter who was serving them also had a car. He had told her that earlier.

Tamara's pushiness was the final straw. Algis addressed the Lithuanians in Lithuanian and told them to ask questions without the interpreter.

"Then, let's do it this way. Each of us will ask only one question. Otherwise we'll exhaust Mr. Požera and he won't think kindly of us. All right? I'll go first. Please tell us, Mr. Požera, how accurate is our information on the fact that there is no freedom of speech in the U.S.S.R. and that artists and writers are expressing not their own ideas, but those that they are told to express by the Communist Party?"

And Joanne smiled prettily, her gray eyes gleaming as though she had just told him something complimentary.

The question was not new. All foreign delegations to the U.S.S.R. invariably asked it and, whenever he was abroad, Algis heard the same insistent question at every meeting, press conference, and even private gathering. He found it incongruous that gray, wise people could pose questions with such naïveté, as though they did not realize that a dictatorship, a totalitarian regime could tolerate no such freedom. Perhaps they derived sadistic pleasure each time they made him lie without blushing and repeat the nonsense that set his teeth on edge. And not one of them, people of the truly free world, where you can chew the fat about any old thing, not one ever took pity on him, the way decent people do when they see their opponent is unarmed.

Each time Algis would put on a serious look and lie. Tastefully, well, in a beautiful voice. He would prove that black was white and vice versa. Brazenly, without shame. Following the rules of the game and mocking his listeners the way they mocked him.

And this time in the dining car, looking straight into Joanne's gray eyes with a fatherly smile, he said that only socialism gives the artist complete freedom. No one applies any pressure. No one can buy his soul, the way they do in the West. And as a Communist, his heart belongs to the Party. In fulfilling Party commissions, he is exerting total creative freedom that is his heart's desire.

The tourists listened to him cordially. Most were ladies far removed from the arts and understood nothing from his complex construction, but nodded in agreement just in case, so that he would not think them ignoramuses.

Only Joanne looked away and said,

"You haven't convinced me."

Several older Americans shushed her immediately, and one reprimanded her.

"Mr. Požera is chatting with all of us, Miss Mage. And we appreciate his generous consent. Your remark borders on tact-lessness."

She said it in English and gave Tamara an excuse for butting in.

"Ladies"—she nervously jumped from her chair—"we are not letting our guest eat in peace. I suggest we put off our conversation until we get to Vilnius. We'll have better facilities for such an interesting talk."

"Tamara!" Algis shouted at her in Russian. His angry tone set everyone on edge. "You are not intelligent enough to teach me how to behave with foreigners. I have more experience than you and I have never once taken a false step. You make one with every word. Your behavior is compromising not only yourself, but the country you unwittingly represent. Is that clear? Shut up, I ask you. If you value your job."

Under the powder, Tamara's face colored in a motley way, her nostrils whitened, and her lips compressed into a thin worm. But Algis' cold, merciless gray eyes made her give in, look down at her plate, and make believe the only thing that interested her was eating.

The Americans were clearly pleased by the scene. Joanne more than the others. Even though they did not understand a single word of Algis' harsh reprimand.

Tamara did not interrupt again. Algis continued answering questions and told them about the economic upswing in Lithuania, citing statistics on the growth of industry, the number of students, and the women who have important positions in public life. He knew it all by heart since his first trip abroad, when he studied it all carefully and memorized a lot of statistical data.

The figures were not invented. But they did not give an accu-rate picture of life in Lithuania, just of the side that was good for a demonstration. The true life, with its passion and drama, Lithuania's true fate, a country of complexity and tragedy, would be carefully hidden from the tourists by the powerful and watchful apparatus in which dumb Tamara was only a cog. And so was he. Didn't his smooth patter lead them away from the truth they had come to find, traveling far and at great expense? Not all of them were rich.

On the other hand, why disclose the truth to them? So that they could rub salt in our wounds? Start barking to the press? And on the air? What for? Who would benefit? Lithuania? The Lithuanians, of whom so few are left in the homeland? Bring on another uprising? Egg the people on to suicide?

No, let somebody else do that, but not Algirdas Požera. He loves his people. More than a lot of bleeding-heart do-gooders. He lauds his people. And is appreciated by the people. And he will not rub their noses in it. He sees things in perspective. He'll show them the way toward the light and happiness. Not an easy path. Through suffering and gloom. The new is always born of suffering.

Joanne asked another question. Everyone grew still, because they would not have dared to ask it. She repeated it in English, so that Tamara would know, too. Tamara stared at Algis with a sneering scrutiny behind her glasses: let's see you squirm out of this one.

Joanne touched a nerve that was carefully and deeply hidden from the West.

"Please answer one question, Mr. Požera. If for some reason it is not convenient, I won't insist.

"Lately the Western press, particularly the newspapers of the Baltic emigrants, have been carrying frightening information about what transpired in Lithuania right after World War II. It seems that the Russians, in order to pacify Lithuania, in order to force her to submit after the loss of autonomy, committed mass murders on the scale of the killings sanctioned by the French in Algeria about the same time. How accurate are these rumors? If I'm not wrong, Mr. Požera, you were grown by then and taking

33

your first literary steps. Your poems dating from that period are devoted to the class struggle and the courage of the Communists. Therefore, they in some degree must reflect those events, unless it is all lies by the enemy. In those years you wrote about young Lithuanian girls going off to die with their heads held high. This was after the war, in peacetime. Whom were they facing and who was threatening them?"

Listening to the long, endless question, Algis nodded his head automatically. Neither Joanne nor the émigré press knew a tenth of the truth. It had been so terrible that even to talk about it now, twenty years later, to open scarcely closed wounds, was cruel and heartless. Algis knew much too much to lay out the profound sorrow of the great martyr, Lithuania, before these well-to-do little ladies from America!

There had been a war in Lithuania then. Undeclared and unnoted in history texts. Cruel, uncompromising, occasionally taking on unheard-of barbaric forms. The war was waged without any rules and was especially inhuman. Neither side took prisoners, and if they got someone still alive, he only lasted a few days until they beat the necessary information out of him. Then he was buried, like an animal, without a cross or any marker.

Little Lithuania had been in flames, bleeding to death. And this went on for many years after World War II while the rest of the planet was coming back to its senses, healing its wounds, and seeking the pleasures of peacetime, the way it always is after a bloodbath. And no one knew—not in the West, not in Russia— that blood was flowing at every step in Lithuania, and the losses of that little nationality overshadowed its losses in the great war. The population dropped catastrophically, visibly, threatening monthly to erase Lithuania from the list of world nations.

The pathetic news that did leak out from a Lithuania completely surrounded by Russia, closed to foreigners (and even Russians needed special permission to go there), was not believed, people waved it away, as they always do when they want to protect their peace of mind and not add other people's troubles to their own.

Particularly since the Moscow papers pictured Lithuania as a prosperous region of lakes and amber that exported products unseen in Russia, like smoked hams, delicious cheeses, and pink bacon five fingers thick. The Lithuanian resorts of Palanga and Druskininkai were becoming fashionable. Lithuanian ensembles were appearing in Moscow, and the fellows and girls, rosy-cheeked, fair-haired, tall and slender, all handpicked, amazed the Muscovites with the whirl of national dances and the patterns and shapes of the new national costumes.

Even in Lithuania, the local press made no mention of this war. They spoke of class struggle, the creation of kolkhozes (collective farms), of combatting the kulaks—the usual bull that concealed the reality. Prize-winning Lithuanian dairymaids, swineherds, and tractor drivers smiled from the pages of the newspapers, but the smiles stayed on the pages. Your picture in the paper and a complimentary article were a death sentence that could not be commuted. The Forest Brotherhood would find the man no matter where he was hiding and there was only one way out: death. Many of the people Algis had written about in the papers met this fate. One of them was Brone Didžiene. She was on his conscience.

The Soviets avenged the death of activists. They rounded up everyone who lived in the district and sent them off in echelons to Siberia. Resisters were shot on the spot and relatives were not allowed to bury them.

At the end of the 1940s, Lithuania was the Soviet Vendée. It fought alone, refusing to surrender. Without any hope of success. And was bleeding to death, because the blood of a small nation is not limitless. No one has yet figured out how many thousands were killed and who was left in the cold Siberian ground.

Stalin acted on the principle that the end justifies the means. And therefore, in order to cut off national opposition, heretofore unseen and sure to set a bad example, Stalin's orders were to destroy it at the root by destroying its nourishment—the people. Every area where battles had flared up had its entire population, from infants to old men, sent to Siberia. Thousands of farmhouses stood empty, windows boarded up. Bushes were overgrowing the fields, and stray cats wandered along the deserted countryside.

Freight trains traveled in endless convoys from Lithuania to Krasnoyarsk Krai, on the banks of the Yenisey River in Siberia, loaded with people like cattle cars. They were headed for the cold, hunger, and death. So many were shipped to Siberia that Krasnoyarsk Krai was called Little Lithuania—Mažoji Litueva.

In this slaughter, Algis was on the side of the powerful, of the occupiers. Not because he did not love his people; just the opposite. There were many like him, who were ready to destroy their people out of love for them. He believed, without a shadow of a doubt, that Communism was the only true path, and no one could or should stop its triumphant progress.

But the people, his people, were dying, refusing to take the path, hating their Russian guides. Algis suffered, trying to comprehend his compatriots' stubbornness, impressed despite himself by their courage and heroism, more thorough and massive than any other nationality could muster.

There was so much heroism among them, that heroism became a natural phenomenon for many years, the norm of life. The heroism of thousands of solitary people, which will never be sung. The heroism of the Communists, who did not think about fear when they crawled into empty farmhouses, changing their sleeping place nightly, sleeping with pistols under their pillows, and dying of a bullet in the back or an ax blade in the forehead. The heroism of their enemies, the Forest Brotherhood, pursued through the thickets of the forest like animals and finding their death from a grenade in a forest bunker under the roots of ancient oaks. These bunkers, blown up and collapsing on top of them, became their graves.

Now Algis often suffered from heart pains. Unexpected. Not an attack, yet. A gnawing, nagging pain. It was his youth resounding in a heart spasm, a youth so horrible that even now he would not wish it on his enemies.

The memory of those times lives in his heart like a splinter.

Looking at the waiting faces of the American women, the first pictures of that period's courage that came to Algis' mind were of women. They had perished alongside the men. And just as bravely.

Three women's faces. All with the subtle Lithuanian beauty. Young and sorrowful. As if they had foreseen their fates. Oh, how I'd like to tell you those three stories.

The district authorities could be pleased—this was the first area in Lithuania in which order had been restored. The district was famous for its rich chernozem soil. The Lithuanian Ukraine they called it in the newspapers. The local peasants were sturdy and well-to-do, their neighbors no match for them. Stone houses with metal roofs stood in beet fields like manor houses, surrounded by gardens and apiaries. There were few forests here, they cut into the expanse of the rich black earth like islets, and nothing here resembled the usual Lithuanian landscape.

All this simplified the authorities' task. They treated the rich muzhiks, land-owning peasants, unceremoniously—five echelons from the district left for Siberia. The district was depopulated and pacified. The Forest Brotherhood swooping down from other forests could not set to work here. The sparse groves did not offer shelter from search parties, and the farmhouses were empty and boarded up, with no one there to give shelter for the night, hot food, and a trusty guide.

The Communist enforcers in the district were joined by a Russian regiment from the regular army, disciplined and with heavy artillery. Together, they initiated roundups according to the rules of military science: they blocked roads and surrounded the forest groves after combing every inch. Bloodhounds led the soldiers to the best-hidden bunkers, and the soldiers would drop a few anti-tank grenades into the air holes. The explosion would rip the trees out by the roots, and the soldiers would move on without even looking to see what was left of the inhabitants of the underground shelter.

They cleaned up the town, too—they deported hundreds of families and settled approved people into their houses and farms. Their shirtless brothers. The new settlers were from other, poorer districts, where there was little land and it was like sand in comparison to the land here.

The district was the first to report 100 per cent collectivization; there were kolkhozes in all the villages and spring sowing was done on time and at a high level. Of course, each sower was guarded by a soldier with a machine gun, so that he would not run off in fear or be shot by a sniper in the bushes. The reports did not mention this fact.

The time had come for the authorities to reap the fruit of their heavy labor. The district was not only pacified. There was another achievement, of the most delicate nature, that crowned their triumph.

They had created a dance group at the local high school. The dancers were almost professional. No expense was spared, they had bright national costumes, *klumpes* (native wooden shoes, necessary for folk dances) of the best wood, and a whole orchestra of *kankles* (a Lithuanian folk instrument). When the dancers were sent to Vilnius for a republic-wide competition, they brought home first prize and all the other awards.

The authorities were unable to dig up anything in the other districts, where people were afraid to stick their noses out the door, but this district demonstrated a full flowering of culture, national in form and socialist in content.

The authorities were looking forward to their rewards: orders and certificates. They made up lists of candidates. One of the first names, right after the authorities themselves, was Genute Urbonaite—the high school teacher who had taught the dancers and trained them for their victory. Genute was not a Komsomol member and was not a joiner, but she had performed such a valuable service that now they could not pamper her enough. There was one more point that was an important factor. Genute Urbonaite was so beautiful that while it was possible to find another like her in Lithuania there were certainly no others in the rest of the world. Her picture in the Lithuanian national costume was printed on the cover of a Vilnius magazine and, if they had held a beauty contest then, she surely would have been crowned Miss Lithuania.

The authorities—middle-aged men, worn by duties and tied down by Party discipline and wives and families—grew young at the sight of Genute, fell into unaccustomed flurries of activity, remembered that they were men and that life was short and who knows what lies ahead?

The first secretary of the Party committee, the chairman of the district executive committee, the head of the division of state security (and the terror of the district), and the head of the local MVD (Ministry of Internal Affairs) all licked their chops, made discreet hints to Genute when they were alone with her in their offices, and promised her mountains of gold.

She only laughed, baring her moist white teeth, looking at them with her big gray naïve eyes as though she did not understand their hints, but leaving room for hope nevertheless.

When each of them received an individual invitation to Genute's house for her birthday, all the authorities' wives were told that there was an important meeting and not to expect their husbands until morning.

The wives did not see their husbands in the morning or at noon. They were found the following day in the teacher's apartment. The four bodies were under the table laden with cold food and half-filled glasses; they had been machine-gunned. The beauty Genute Urbonaite had disappeared without a trace.

This was the greatest blow of the Lithuanian underground and it had been delivered in the only pacified district, where Soviet power was triumphant. For their loss of vigilance and moral turpitude the murdered men were buried without any honors, and even their wives, hurt by their infidelity, did not come to accompany them on their final journey. Troops were brought back into the district, patrols covered the roads, the forest was combed, and the district became like all the others in Lithuania.

They could not find Genute Urbonaite for a long time.

But her cover picture in the magazine was her downfall. Someone recognized her on the street and led the police to her small apartment on the outskirts of Kaunas, where she had been hiding for six months.

She was brought back to the scene of the crime for the trial. The military tribunal in closed session sentenced her to death by hanging and stipulated that the sentence be carried out publicly in the town's main square on Sunday and that the whole population be there.

Algis arrived Saturday night to cover the story for his paper and managed to get permission to see the condemned woman.

"That's right," said the mayor, who was in charge of the execution, "talk to her. And write it up. We need to know the enemy's psychology."

The mayor was short and wore wide blue jodhpurs. He spoke in a dull everyday tone.

"Be careful with her. She's a dangerous bitch. She put away four men. That's no joke."

The master sergeant, who had a Kalmyk non-Russian face, threw on his greatcoat and took Algis to her. It was mid-November and at night the cold made itself felt. The puddles on the stone street were covered with a layer of ice. The ice cracked under the officer's dry boots. Algis followed in his footsteps, cutting diagonally across the cobblestone square.

The town slept. Here in the center, the hulking Catholic church with its sharp Gothic spires rose above the square, spotlighted by the vague, cloudy contours of the moon.

Everything seemed dead, like the scenery for a medieval play. This feeling was reinforced by the sounds coming from the edge of the square. Several dark figures were hammering nails into a beam laid across two stout poles. Other carpenters were building steps to lead up to the wooden scaffold. The people were invisible, mere shadows. Some distance away, a bonfire crackled loudly, and a watchman was warming himself, his collar pulled up like a monk's hood. Algis' heart contracted as he drew the parallel with the Inquisition. The gloomy cathedral, towering over the cobblestone square, the dark figures on the scaffold, the smoky fire, and the hooded monk. The only dissonant note was a portrait of Stalin, smiling slyly into his moustache, that hung over the entrance to the committee headquarters in a red frame decorated with pine boughs.

The condemned woman was spending the night not far from the execution site, in the stone cellar of a one-story house with dark windows. The cellar was deep, and Algis counted twelve cement steps before reaching the narrow corridor that led to a single door, heavily padlocked. The officer said something to the guard, who was armed with a machine gun, and opened the lock with much jangling of keys. He pulled the door, which did not have a peephole like most jail doors, toward him and silently let Algis in. Shivers ran down Algis' spine when he heard the door squeak shut behind him, slam with an iron thud, and the rattling of the key in the lock.

A single bulb in a metal cage burned in the low ceiling that had rusty beams. Algis saw her in the dull light.

Genute was sitting on the far end of a bench, a shawl around her shoulders and her feet tucked under the bench. It was cold in the cellar. Algis' hands were cold and he put them in his pockets.

"You'll catch cold," she said, quickly looking at him and succumbing to a long fit of coughing. "I have pneumonia."

"Oh-oh," Algis said, at a loss for words. "Didn't they give you a bed?"

The bench was bare, and he could not make out anything else in the cellar.

Genute did not reply. Cuddled up in her shawl, she sat resting her chin in her hands, her elbows propped up on her knees. Her big eyes were raised up at him. He could not see their color in the dark, but he knew they were gray from her cover portrait.

Algis introduced himself, embarrassed and uncomfortable in her presence. But her face came alive, some interest glowed in her eyes, and even a slight smile crossed her lips.

"Thank God, you're not an interrogator. I know you . . . I've read your work."

Her lips were set in an ironic smile and her eyes narrowed as she examined him.

"I did not expect to meet an author . . . the rising star . . . of Lithuanian poetry. Have a seat." She looked over at the other end of the bench. When Algis gingerly sat down at the very edge, she smiled at him, almost cordially.

"You have talent, Požera, you know . . . Even though you write all the wrong things. It supports my theory that our people are endlessly talented if there is enough to go around for the likes of you. Please don't take offense, we are enemies, on different sides of the barricades. But you are also a talented Lithuanian, and I cannot help being proud of that . . . because I am dying for Lithuania."

She said it simply, without a hint of complaint in her voice, and she looked at him without hostility, even gently, like a mother at a wayward son. Algis knew that she was three years his junior, and he was crushed by her wisdom and calm and by her smile, all-comprehending and all-forgiving.

"Don't ask me questions. I'm tired of them," she said with that same sympathetic smile. "I'll talk to you whichever way my mind takes me. Let this be my confession. They refused to send a priest. They don't believe in God. You be my priest . . . You have kind eyes . . . and I'm glad that God sent you. How long will they let you stay?"

"I don't know. We didn't discuss time."

"Good. It'll be easier for me to make it till morning, conversing with a man who loves our language. Right?"

Algis nodded and coughed. She joined him with a hoarse long cough.

"Put on my coat. You're cold."

She shook her head as she coughed.

"Forgive me . . . Why warm up a corpse? . . . Tomorrow my pneumonia will be gone . . . And I'll stop coughing . . . You, Požera, you'll live a long time. Guard your health. This regime will stay in Lithuania for a long time, maybe a hundred years. They won't kill off all the people, some will live and bide their time. You know, you won't be alive then, either . . . But they'll remember us both. You—for your talent, which served the wrong people. And me—as one of the victims. The same blood flows in our veins.

"We're a handsome nation. Right, Požera? You have a good face . . . Our knights under Prince Vitautas looked like you. Pedigree lives through the ages. They say that I'm not bad-looking either. What do you think? How many generations passed, leaving the best traits, drop by drop, to create you and me? Do you have children? You will. But I'll leave no one. It makes me sad. Not everyone has eyes like mine. Or my waist and my legs. My ancestors saved it for me, and I won't be able to pass it along to anyone. And there will be fewer beautiful Lithuanians in the world."

Algis listened to her, looked at her, and only then compre-
hended with icy fear that tomorrow she would die, that she
would no longer exist, and beauty such as Lithuania would not
soon see again would disappear. Not only Genute Urbonaite
would be killed. Lithuania would be losing part of its riches and
its beauty.

She guessed his thoughts and gave a sad little laugh.

"At the festival they called me the symbol of Lithuania. Your
people like inflated verbiage. So, tomorrow brings the end to
Lithuania. But I'm not Lithuania. I'm not taking that much upon
myself. I am Genute. Genialie . . . that's what Mama used to call
me. I'm twenty years old. And I'm not sorry for what I did. If
not me—then it would have been another. Our people are not
cowards. Right, Požera? Tell me, but be honest. If you had met
me earlier . . . under different circumstances, would I have ap-
pealed to you?"

Algis hurried to nod yes and felt completely inadequate and
pathetic before her.

"Would you have married me?" Her eyes glistened slyly.
"Don't worry, I'm only kidding. Gallows humor. Isn't that what
they call it, Comrade Požera? Literally and figuratively. You can
tell your friends about it some time. I trust they're all intelligent
and you'll laugh, not heartily, but sadly. Because you are a
Lithuanian and there are so few of us on this earth. And with
your help there will be even fewer.

"As a writer, you want to understand why I did it? Right? I
could have had a marvelous life . . . with my looks . . . life
promised much. And I'm ending up in the noose. Of my own vo-
lition. I'm not hoping to be saved. Your side has the power. But I
don't like you . . . I mean, I despise you . . . and there was no
other way for me. I'm no hero. It's just the way I understand
honor. And one must pay a terrible price for it—one's life.

"You love Lithuania, don't you? I can see it in your poems.
And you have the face . . . of a decent person. I love Lithuania

44

too. And we are enemies. Požera, don't you see that that is the tragedy of our nation?

"You and I would have made a magnificent couple and have given our children to the world. The most beautiful. The most graceful. With gray eyes. And flaxen hair. And the world would have been awed—how beautiful Lithuanians are.

"Why do you smile? Those children will never be. And no one cares."

She fell silent, her chin nestling in her knees, and then she looked up at Algis meekly and beseechingly.

"They're saying all kinds of things about me in the district. That I was the mistress of the authorities. That I used to hold orgies. I confess to you: I'm a virgin. My word of honor. I have never known what they write about in novels. Because I waited for love. And it did not have time to come into my life. My body was never touched by a man's hand, and that must be very pleasant if the hand belongs to one you love. No one, not a single man, has ever seen me naked . . . Many have dreamed about it. Would you like me . . . to undress for you?"

Algis shuddered and looked toward the door. The heavy solid gray door was shut tight. There was not a single crack in it.

"It's cold here," he said, trying to stop her. She had already gotten up from the bench.

"Cold doesn't exist for me anymore." She smiled. "Neither does heat. Do me this one favor, Požera, look at my naked body . . . I don't ask much. Just sit and stare. And then perhaps, I won't take everything away with me into the grave, something will remain in your memory."

She undressed quickly, with brusque nervous movements, as though afraid that they would come in and stop her from doing what she wanted.

The pale light streamed from overhead, and Algis thought that a halo flared up and shimmered around her head, her flaxen hair in a tight braid on her breast. Light fell on her forehead, the tip

45

of her nose, her chin, her breasts, where the braid lay silvery, and on her round, firm belly. Everything else was in shadow, but he could guess at the milky whiteness of her slender, flawless, female body.

She was like a maiden from the ancient legends, and her shaded eyes glowed with a mysterious otherworldly light. The smile on her voluptuous, unkissed lips was triumphant.

"Get up," she said. It was barely audible but masterful.

Algis stood.

"Come here."

Algis took one step and then a second.

Her eyes were directly before him, big, translucently gray, with long fluttering lashes. Her eyes moved in, widening, filling up his view, dissolving. Algis felt the cold touch of her lips on his left eye and then his right eye. Then her lips touched his forehead, slid down his nose, and lightly pressed against his mouth. She blessed him with a kiss like a cross.

Her hand pushed against his chest, moving him away.

She was standing with her eyes closed, her hands flat on her hips.

"Go now," she whispered. "That's all."

Without realizing what he was doing, Algis tore off his coat, threw it over her shoulders, even buttoning it in front, and backed away toward the door.

She did not move from her spot, and her lids were shut like a dead woman's.

They opened the door when he knocked and he ran up the steps, across the square, past the cathedral with the sharp spires, to the sound of the carpenters driving in the last nails into the scaffolding.

Algis did not wait for morning. He left on the night train, without explanation. It goes without saying that not a word flowed from his pen. The newspaper filled his space with an official, one-paragraph statement that the captured bourgeois nationalist and murderess, G. Urbonaite, agent of a foreign power, was condemned to death and that the sentence was carried out.

Should I tell you that story, American ladies? Algis thought angrily, looking into the simple, curious faces of the tourists. It's all past and forgotten. Lithuania has regenerated. A new generation. They'll take you to see schools and universities. You'll see healthy and attractive boys and girls there. But the most beautiful and handsome one will not be there. The son or daughter of Genute Urbonaite. And so what? Who'll notice it? Nobody even remembers that Brone Didžiene ever lived. Of course, she left children behind. But do they remember their mother? They were just tots when they stood in the crowd that damp night and saw their mother's body dangling in a noose from the old tree that grew in their yard. Her hands were tied and there was a sign around her neck. They couldn't possibly remember what it said, because they did not know the alphabet.

There was no one at the office of the Victory Kolkhoz except for a very young woman, citified, with mascara and bright lipstick.

"Could you please tell me where the chairman of the kolkhoz is?" asked Algis, without expecting an answer, since she was obviously a visitor like himself and might even be looking for the chairman.

"I'm the chairman of the kolkhoz," she said, blushing deeply. She extended her firm strong hand. Her handshake was like a man's.

Algis was taken aback. Here, in this turbulent area, where people went to sleep every night to the sound of gunshots, where people were being forced into the kolkhoz, much later than in other villages—all business was in the hands of this compactly built yet fragile city coquette, who blushed at the sight of a man and flirted with her bedroom eyes. She was very feminine and

47

pretty. She was wearing a flowered silk kerchief, fashionably tied in a careless knot under the chin, a short wool skirt that did not cover her inviting round knees. They showed through her nylon stockings, which had a fashionable black seam along her firm calves and a high black heel. Algis had seen women like that on Laisves Street (Freedom Street, the main street in Kaunas; it was renamed Stalin Prospect, then Lenin Prospect; now it has the original name). They were blood and milk. Saucy, seductive, attracting men's eyes like magnets, and most of them not available.

"They called to tell me you were coming," she said, mumbling and blushing. "I've been waiting since morning."

What had brought her here?

Without waiting for his questions, she quickly and joyously gave him the information. She turned out to be from Kaunas. She had worked as a weaver in a factory. When the Party called, she came out here, over a year ago. She had three children, still tots, and she had brought them with her. Her husband? He was against it, an irresponsible person. She left him and took the children. And was very happy. Felt like a person for the first time in her life.

She took him to her house, a simple village hut with a painted wooden floor and potted geraniums on the windowsills, fed him a huge and delicious meal, apologizing that she did not prepare something better. This was not Kaunas, where you could pick and choose. Stimulated by the presence of a guest, she rushed around the room, taking care of her chores swiftly and neatly. The children were clean and well behaved, the house in order, and there was no trace of tiredness in her face.

"If you write about me for the paper," she asked embarrassedly, "please don't mention my husband. Let him be. He's a fool and drunk. He didn't understand the new life. And to tell the truth, I feel sorry for him. His ignorance will be the death of him.

"What can I tell you about myself?" she mused, chewing her lip, painted just for him. Algis was charmed by her. She had an excess of femininity, no matter how she tried to hide it. In every movement and look, in her smile and her pensiveness.

"Judge for yourself. Who was I before? On the go day and night. No time to think of myself. And now there is equality. All paths are open for women. I'm needed. Some like me, others would like to destroy me. I'm alive. And before? Never heard a kind word from my husband. Gimme, get me. And—to bed. If he wasn't too drunk . . ."

She burst into a blush and turned away.

"Now I want to organize a nursery and a kindergarten here. To free all the women. The women give me a lot of support here. I beat it into their heads: you are equal now. My whole economy here is based on them. As for the men . . ." She waved the thought aside. "They drink moonshine and keep looking at the forest, hoping for a chance to join the Brotherhood."

Algis listened to her and was amazed that she never even hinted at the danger that awaited her at every step. Or the difficulties of country life, the agricultural problems of a kolkhoz that could stump an experienced person—and she was a city girl and a newcomer who just recently learned the difference between rye and oats.

Everything was clear and her life was carefully mapped out. Set the kolkhoz on its feet, then go get an education; they had already promised it to her at the district committee headquarters. The children? Take them along. She would get by. Difficulties only exist to be overcome.

She spoke sincerely, with relish, and Algis envied her confident outlook that brooked no doubt. You could only be happy here in this dead hole, Algis thought, if you had her physical and mental strength to live far from everyone, with no one to talk to. That was why she rushed to pour out her soul to him, a chance visitor from the other world where she grew up. Then she would fall

49

back into her work and worries, performing all her duties lightly, without complaint, confident that everything was before her and that her life was only beginning.

"Well, judge for yourself. They don't like Soviet power in Lithuania. Why hide it? I'll tell you why. Our backwardness. Was life so good under Smetona, the President overthrown by Soviet troops? One was rich, the other poor. The villages were unenlightened. And now? Everyone can become a person if he wants to. That's what you have to beat into those thick Lithuanian skulls. They'll thank us later. Honestly, for a mission as holy as this I would have given up not only my husband but my children as well."

She was not trying to paint herself in better colors for him, she truly believed in this. Late that evening as Algis was going to sleep in the next room on the wide wooden bed with an eiderdown and the fresh city sheets she had taken from the trunk, he kept thinking about how he would describe her for the paper. To present her as she really was would make her unbelievable; people would take it for propaganda. But she actually was like that. The Soviet slogans were an absolutely clear life's plan for her and she sacrificed herself for the future the slogans promised, without even considering it a sacrifice. For such people, the power and attraction of Communism was as simple as two times two. The bloodshed and echelons transported to Siberia would be redeemed by the results.

He undressed as he listened to her moving around the kitchen trying to be quiet, placed his pistol under the pillow, and relished the feeling of the soft blanket and the rustle of the starched sheets on his chest. He lit a cigarette, blowing smoke up to the ceiling. His head was spinning. From exhaustion. He had spent the entire day going from farm to farm with her, looking at the agriculture she showed him with concealed pride, as though it were her own: rusty plows and harrows piled up in sheds, skinny dung-covered cows herded under one roof and still mooing their complaints for the tender touch of their former mistresses. She had given him rubber boots and wore a similar pair. The mud was knee-deep. He could barely move his legs by the time they got back. But she was still fresh and firm as a winter apple, quickly changed back into her nylons and high-heeled shoes, freshened her makeup, and started on her household chores. She made dinner, fed the children, washed them and put them to bed, had dinner with him, and put a bottle of real Armenian cognac on the table. He had spent the day with her, and yet he did not know when she had had an opportunity to get it.

They drank the bottle between them, equally. She drank with pleasure and without covering her glass when he poured. But he got drunk and she did not show her liquor. She made his bed and cleared the table with the same lightness and was now bustling in the kitchen.

The cognac was interfering with his thoughts about her as the heroine of his next article. In his clouded brain she appeared with her round knees in the stockings' net. With her soft delicious neck, a soft vein throbbing in the hollow by her collarbone. With her playful eyes, enticing and mysterious. Just try touching her, just hint at it. She could be capable of punching you and writing a complaint to boot. She was too idealistic and straight. But she was a dream woman. If she let you, you would not forget her for a long time.

"Could she have really suppressed the female in herself?" thought Algis, tossing in bed and listening to the sounds coming from the kitchen. "A year without her husband. She could not permit herself anything here with the local peasants. And so nothing. She bears it. In the name of what? She's crazy. Saintly stupidity. She'll wither away here. When she catches on it'll be too late. She got her equality. Alone, without a husband or caresses. In this mud and dirt. In her other life there was asphalt, avenues, bathtubs, theaters, and restaurants. I'm going back tomorrow, and she has to molder here. And she's got no regrets. She seems happier and more confident than I.

The hell with her, Algis decided, and pulled the covers over his head. But he heard things quiet down in the kitchen and bare footsteps creep up to his door.

"Brone," he called hoarsely.

And she came in. In a short nightie, barely visible in the dark, she stopped at the head of the bed and bent over him. He saw the contours of her breasts, falling out of the lace bodice, bobbing before his eyes like overripened pears.

"You won't chase me away?" her nervous voice whispered. When he put his arms around her and masterfully pulled her toward him, she said:

"I can't go on . . . Don't condemn me . . . It's stronger than I am."

He could not remember a more intoxicating female sweetness, guileless and abandoned, than the one in which she drowned him that night. Slowly cooling off, her insatiable, heated body quivering, she pressed herself to him and whispered in his ear, softly touching it with her lips:

"Take me with you, take me away . . . I'll wash your feet and drink the water . . . I'll carry you around in my arms . . . I want to live some more . . . I appeal to you . . . Take me away . . . I can't anymore . . ."

She cried, convulsions racking her body, but tenderly caressed his cheeks, his nose, his chin, as though soothing him and not wanting to frighten him. Algis was perplexed and tried to calm her with the very words she had so bravely told him during the day. About equality, the holy goal, the sacrifices we all make for the future. He bulled his way through, knowing that he was saying the wrong thing, that she was waiting to hear something else. He did not know what. He was sorry for this woman, a good warm woman who got into a field she did not belong in without thinking, merely because she was looking for her piece of happiness. If her husband had been a bit better and kinder, she would not have gone. And now she was paying for it. She opened up to him like a woman and poured out her soul, hoping for nothing. Just for a little tenderness, which she needed more than anything.

Algis' empty words sobered her up. She shut up and stared at his profile in the dark. Then she sighed and in a calm steady voice, as though there had been no tears, said:

"Well, my friend, you're right. Everyone has his cross. It was all nonsense what I said. A woman's always a woman. Forget it, all right?"

Algis nodded.

"Should I go back to my room?" she asked, her expectant eyes glistening in the dark.

"Why?" Algis put his arm around her neck. "Stay here."

She removed his arm, sat up, her feet dangling over the edge, and turned to him.

"Where do you keep your gun?"

"Under the pillow."

"I'll go get mine. The night is long, and who knows who'll drop by. Protection should be right at hand."

She brought her gun and stuck it under the pillow with his. Then with a merry despair she threw herself into the bed and grabbed Algis with her naked arms.

"It's only one night, but it's mine. You're not married, are you, my friend? Let's live it up. There is no God, and there's nothing to be ashamed of."

Like the first time, she drowned him in insatiable caresses, touching and kneading him, trying to satisfy her female hunger for the year ahead.

Algis awoke late, daylight streaming into the window. She was not in the bed. He could hear her hearty quick voice and rather happy laugh as she busied herself with the children, humming to herself.

He breakfasted alone. She served him and behaved just as she had the day before. As though the night had not happened. Occasionally there would be a glimmer of sadness in her slightly mocking gaze, but she would immediately put it out.

Then a man came with the wagon she had ordered to take him to town. She said good-by to Algis in front of the man, shaking his hand. She said dryly:

"Write the truth about us. The kolkhoz farmers don't believe the papers."

Then Algis remembered that he needed a picture for the article, and he asked her for a good photograph.

"I have a photo, it's up to you to judge if it's any good."

She went into the house and brought him a card with ripple edges and a mat finish, as they make them in fancy photography studios in the city: three-quarter view, earrings, sly eyes, and as much smile as the photographer had demanded.

"Will it do?"

Back in Vilnius, when he had to give the picture to the retouch labs, Algis saw that she had written on the back, hurriedly and with grammatical errors: "To Algirdas Požera from Brone Didžiene. To remember me for a long time. Let this dead copy always remind you of the living original."

Algis roared with laugher, imagining the scene if he had turned in a picture with that inscription. He taped up the back of the photo, took it to the lab, and sat down with his article. It was hard writing, he did not bring out too many interesting facts, and he could only remember her eyes, her warm firm breasts, her salty kisses when she cried and begged him to take her away. He could not write about that in the newspaper, and what he did come up with did not please the editor. He cut the article to a one-hundred-line filler and decided against the photo, saying that one like that belonged in a photographer's display case and not in a newspaper and that little ladies with eyes like that do not work as chairmen of kolkhozes.

Algis did not argue and soon forgot about Brone Didžiene, remembering her only six months later when he again went to Saulja.

He wanted to see her and, if possible, to repeat that night. He remembered the night in all its details. And he was drawn to it again. But he was not allowed to go there alone. It was spring. The roads were flooded and the authorities gave him a guide—an instructor at Party headquarters, a pale young fellow in high swamp boots. They set off by foot, because wagons could not get through. In the lowlands just before the village, their path was blocked by a huge puddle. The pale blond instructor told Algis to climb up on his shoulders. Algis rode slowly through the cold murky waters that reached the instructor's waist.

He felt uncomfortable, being carried on someone's back, and he said in an apologetic tone:

"When we get to the village, we'll warm up. I remember that the last time Brone Didžiene had some excellent cognac."

The instructor stopped, turned back to look at him, and asked mockingly:

"Brone Didžiene?"

"Isn't that the name of the chairman here?"

"Brone Didžiene isn't here. She'll give you some cognac . . . over there, in the cemetery."

He nodded in the direction of an empty hill sparsely covered with crosses. She had been killed the month before, Algis subsequently learned. The Forest Brotherhood came at night and took her asleep. They herded the kolkhoz farmers to her yard, read a sentence in the name of the Lithuanian people, and hanged her from the tree in front of her house, a sign around her neck that said "TRAITOR." They did not touch her children and her husband came from Kaunas for them. He buried her in the village cemetery, absolutely refusing to put up an obelisk with a red star as a headstone.

The white cement cross towered over the fresh grassless grave.

There was a portrait of her on the cross—the same photograph she had given Algis transferred into an oval piece of porcelain. Three-quarter view, with earrings, Brone Didžiene smiled down at Algis with her victorious eyes—a marvelous, excellent woman, such as he would never meet again, and he was the last man to whom she had given stormy and carefree happiness.

Well, would that be enough? Or give them more? Algis mockingly thought as he stared at the American tourists. That's the true Lithuania. And all you'll be shown is pictures from an exhibition. And you'll go back to America conquered. And the Soviet regime will seem a benefactor to you. Lithuania flourished under it. But I know whose blood nourished the flower. And I can't tell anyone. Even though I want to. I want to very badly.

Algis remembered another woman's fate—a nameless one, because Algis did not know her name or even how she looked. He encountered her in a situation where he could not look at her face. He often thought of her and of the man who was directly connected with the event and who came up in Algis' sights quite often later.

He was the junior lieutenant of the Ministry of State Security of the Republic of Lithuania, a young skinny Jew people called Motya the Rabbit. Algis never knew his surname, only his nickname, which was used by all the regulars of the Versailles and Metropole restaurants in Kaunas. He did resemble a rabbit in profile. He was not particularly dashing in his uniform and epaulets; he was a heavy drinker and debaucher, always in debt to waiters and lunch stand operators. But in the forests he was a daredevil officer who did not know the meaning of fear, and many bands of resistants searched for him long and fruitlessly.

After the war, Rabbit ended up alone, having lost his large family that used to live in Kaunas and dozens of Lithuanian hamlets. He survived because he had fought in the Russian army. He returned to Kaunas with several medals and a tic caused by a concussion. In Lithuania Jews were not killed by the Germans; the dirty work was done for them by Lithuanians from the police battalions. Rabbit, seeking revenge, joined the Ministry of State Security, the punitive division of Soviet power. He let himself go wild. When he returned from the forest operations he drank steadily, becoming more and more satanic. His front teeth were knocked out in some fight and he refused to get false ones. He took on the look of a pathetic, crumpled gnome, lonely, embittered, and dangerous to those around him.

But the Ministry of State Security apparently valued him highly and forgave him his orgies and scandals, knowing that he was matchless in his work.

Rabbit hopped along until he got his. The Forest Brothers captured him alive and in a completely impossible way he managed to escape. This was a unique occurrence. No one from the MGB had ever managed to escape from the Forest Brotherhood. The Brothers took care of you swiftly and ruthlessly. But Rabbit got away—thereby creating a mess of trouble for himself and completely ruining his career as an officer.

Algis heard the amazing story from him at a dirty table in a railroad station lunchroom. Rabbit, lisping toothlessly, no longer in uniform but wearing an ill-fitting civilian suit, gulping and rushing as though he were afraid Algis would not believe him and leave before he finished the story, told him:

"Obviously, there is a Jewish God in heaven. Somebody of my people has to stay alive. And here I was sure that it was all over, the end of my family.

"Here's how it happened. They sent me to Šakaia to the operative point. Some band was making trouble, we had to give them a scare. We chased through the woods, couldn't find anybody. The bastards were all in their bunkers. Go find 'em.

"So I'm sitting in Šakaia, going crazy from boredom. Not a decent restaurant in town. The sticks. And it's Sunday. A holiday.

57

You could really hang yourself. Why don't I go visit this woman? I noticed her at a farm. Could see by her face that she didn't lead you on. And, as you know, women like me. I put on all my medals, my epaulets sparkled gold, my boots were shiny, stuck my cap on the back of my head, and I was off. About three kilometers. A warm sunny day. I'm walking along, no sense of danger.

"The path first goes through a meadow and then into the forest. There's a man mowing hay in the field. One of ours. A local Communist. Last name Gedris. I remember names, it's my job. You can count the Communists in Šakaia on one hand. The rest are enemies.

"Gedris is mowing away, and his little daughter is playing nearby. He had taken her out with him. I have to tell you that Gedris was a big fellow, twice my size. This is important for what follows. Gedris was the only witness who could support me, to prove I'm telling the truth. But he's dead, I saw them finish him off with my own eyes.

"But listen. I said hello to Gedris, he waved to me. The meadow ended, the path went into the forest, bushes taller than me all around. I'm walking along whistling. I hear someone say in Lithuanian:

"'Hands up!'

"And four machine-gun butts pointed at me from the bushes, from all four sides, straight at my head. I couldn't even raise my arms, I had to squeeze them between the butts. They jumped out on the path. The Forest Brothers. I figured my time had come. They took away my gun, watch, Party card, and MGB identity papers. It was stupid of me to have taken it all along.

"They recognized me. One even winked and said, 'Gotcha, pal, we've been looking for you a long time.' It was clear. Bye-bye, Mama. Even though I don't have a mama anymore. They tied my hands behind me with a leather strap and one of them held the other end of the strap. They led me far away. Into a big field.

58

There's about ten of them there. And Gedris, our Communist. And his daughter. At first I thought he was a traitor. He set them onto me. But then I saw his hands were tied, too. They got him like me.

"They weren't very interested in Gedris but were very happy to have gotten me. They were roaring with pleasure. Planning how to execute me. I heard everything, they weren't embarrassed. I was already a corpse in their eyes. They were afraid to shoot because it would be heard at the operative point. They'd cut me. It was quieter. The knife was all right with me. You die all the same.

"You understand, Algis, the little girl screwed up their whole party. Gedris' daughter. She started to cry at the top of her lungs. One of the bandits gave her a shove to shut her up. And Gedris, the father, could not allow that. His hands were tied, so he kicked the one who pushed his daughter. The Brother flew off the handle and let loose with the machine gun, right into Gedris. But he stood there, without falling. And shouted. And the daughter began screaming. Algis, I've seen many men killed, but I've never seen anything like this. He was as long-lived as a bull. They were all shooting him. And he stood there and shouted. He was riddled with bullets. He finally fell but jerked around and went on shouting. They kept firing into him, row after row, like a sewing machine. And he went on shouting. There's a man for you. Never seen anyone like him.

"Well, they finally killed him. They were in a panic. They had raised such a ruckus that they had to get out of there. They shouted: 'Finish him off.' That was me they meant, of course. One of them got a gun, the one they took away from me, and stuck it at my forehead. This is where they made their mistake. Another of them holding my strap behind me. If you shoot wrong, the other one gets it, too. He kept trying to find a good spot on my head. I hunched up my shoulders and backed away from him, knocking over the one behind me. He fell into a ditch.

I realized I was free, though my hands were still tied. I jumped over the ditch and behind a tree.

"They shot. I ran. Between the trees, like a rabbit. I'm not called that for nothing. They all missed. I ran all the way to Šakaia with the strap still on my hands. I brought soldiers back to the spot, but there wasn't even a trace of them. They only found dead Gedris and his daughter crying over him. That's all.

"Instead of rewarding me, at least for keeping my wits about me, they kicked me out of the MGB and the Party. Everything I had done for them, forgotten. I no longer inspire confidence. It had never happened that one of our men returned alive from capture. Therefore, there was something wrong about me. I tried everybody, even the president; I had been in his personal guard. No one listened. And now it's over for me. They don't pay me a pension, I have no profession, all I do is drink, if someone pays for it."

Algis did not pity him. He gave him some vodka and quickly got away. But he thought about Rabbit's fate often. After all, Motya was doing the same job he was. Each in his own way. And his sad end might become Algis' at any moment. They could throw him out at his first mistake, without even a thank-you for everything he had done.

And besides, Motya the Rabbit had somehow impressed Algis. A drunkard, in his rare sober moments, he was witty with that special Jewish black humor that smells of tears.

Once they were sitting in some dive and a little peasant in a torn fur jacket was dozing at the next table. He would fall asleep, his head on his chest, and he would wake with a start and a yelp.

"He's dreaming of his taxes," Motya the Rabbit said without a smile.

Algis laughed long and hard. It was true, with a sniper's accuracy, and brought sadness to the heart even though it was funny.

Algis ran into the Rabbit several times. He would have drunk

himself to death if a fat Jewess had not married him, borne him
a bunch of kids, and found him a job as a salesman in a hard-
ware store. Many years later, Algis learned that they had managed to get out to Israel. Motya sent pictures from there to
Kaunas. The Rabbit, neat and clean, leaning on the hood of his
new Mercedes, surrounded by his well-fed children and wife.
Many envy him in Kaunas. Even Lithuanians.

Thanks to this Motya the Rabbit, a junior lieutenant of the
MGB, Algis was witness to an event he would remember to his
dying day.

It happened in Pasvalis, in the North. In winter. Algis was
there for the paper, and met Motya in the town's only restaurant.
He sat at Algis' table, dressed in his military greatcoat and cap,
babbling on drunkenly. He suddenly asked:

"You want to smell gunpowder? Come with me. Not far from
here, they've surrounded three bandits on a farm. We'll take
them tomorrow. They're surrounded by the strike battalion. It'll
be fun. With smoke. And fire."

Motya the Rabbit helped himself to a bottle of cognac and
filled his flask with it.

They went to the farm in the morning.

The fields were covered with heavy snow. There had been fog
at night, and it froze over in the morning. The snow drifts were
encrusted with shiny ice that shone like Christmas lights. The
bared birch branches drooped icicles and shivered. It was easy
to breathe and the bright light made you squint.

The farm, or rather the red brick shed with a high straw roof,
capped with several feet of snow, stood alone in a large, smooth
field, gently blanketed with white snow. It stood unprotected. As
in the palm of your hand.

The three that were in there were trapped. There was no path
of retreat. The perimeter of the field on which the shed stood
was surrounded by men in black uniform jackets of fur and
quilted cotton. Several jackets showed dark against the snow

closer to the shed. They were corpses—the result of the first unsuccessful attempt to rout the three.

The battalion was hidden in the snow now, shooting at random. Machine guns rang out once in a while. Pieces of brick flew off from the shed walls, red dust shot up like a fountain and the snow was powdered with the red dust for several feet around the shed.

Beyond, framed by the rime-covered birches, other farmhouses cowered. Without a single smoking chimney. Like a ghost town. Only the anxious mooing of the cows, frightened by the shooting, was a reminder that the houses were inhabited and that people were watching an entire battalion deal with three brave partisans.

Answering shots came from the shed. Rarely. In brief, economizing spurts. And each time someone in the ring cried out in pain and crawled back toward the ravine where the horse-drawn sled and green first-aid tent were set up. Others would cry out and lie where they fell, doubled up, their guns at their sides.

"They have a great view from the roof," Motya the Rabbit whispered hoarsely into Algis' ear, burrowing into the snow near him. "They pick out their targets as if they were hunting. But they won't get away, the bastards."

The commander of the strike force was an MGB captain, a Russian who knew no Lithuanian. The soldiers did not understand Russian. Motya the Rabbit served as the captain's interpreter, shouting out his orders in poor Lithuanian with a marked Jewish accent.

Bottles of moonshine were passed around the entire ring. The soldiers would take a swig and spit into the snow. Rabbit and the captain were applying themselves to Motya's flask, and the captain fastidiously wiped the flask's mouth with his sleeve each time. Rabbit drank simply. Algis turned down the cognac.

"We're going to attack now," Rabbit told Algis. "You lie still, this is not your business. The captain is a jerk, he didn't bring along a mortar. We'll lose people needlessly."

The soldiers grudgingly got up to follow the Rabbit, who ran out in front. They shouted with rheumy, hoarse voices. They were simple Lithuanian country boys, drunken and doomed. The captain in the long overcoat climbed out of his hole when the cordon had moved toward its goal and followed them without rushing, his pistol aimed at their backs, dragging his boots in the snow.

Three long, gasping rounds from the shed's roof flattened the whole cordon. The soldiers crawled back, their panicked faces powdered with snow. The captain, crawling on his elbows, led the way. The dead lay still like dark bundles of rags against the snow. The wounded shouted and rose to their feet only to be felled by more shots.

The attack did not succeed. The captain was swearing in Russian, and Motya the Rabbit was cursing, also in Russian and with the same Jewish accent.

The machine guns went into action again. With tracer bullets this time, multicolored dotted lines streaming toward the roof.

"Now we're moving." Motya slapped Algis on the back. "We'll smoke them out."

The bullets knocked off huge clumps of snow from the roof and they fell into the red brick dust. The gray straw of the roof came into view and soon blue smoke rose to the sky from several points. It grew and crawled up the steep slope. It billowed out of the tall dormer window, as tall as a man. Flames reached up and the whole roof was blazing. Tongues of fire stretched toward each other from either side of the house and met in a high bonfire, shooting sparks into the sky with a great crackle and howl, like fireworks.

The shooting from the shed stopped. The cordon around the field also stopped shooting. The soldiers stuck out their noses from the snow and squinted at the fire.

63

The fire raged and howled as it consumed the shed. Algis had only thought of the three burning to death behind the brick walls when a woman appeared in the dormer window, her smoldering clothes silhouetted against the red flames. Algis was close to her, within two hundred meters, and he could see clearly and painfully that she was young and coatless, and her pale flaxen hair was being buffeted about her face by the wind, which was drawing the burning flames from the shed, their purple blue tongues licking at her body.

Algis could not see her face. Her hair was in the way. But he heard her voice. All the men did.

"Goddamn you!" she shouted in her high-pitched maiden's voice.

And she began to sing. She sang loudly, not in keeping with the melody, which was the old Lithuanian anthem. She shouted out each word at the men lying around her in the snow. Her voice penetrated, drilled into their ears. The soldiers, weapons at their sides, sat hypnotized, eyes riveted on her. The lads' faces were contorted. They looked as if they were about to cry.

Motya the Rabbit pulled up his collar, as though to drown out the song, turned away, jerking his head more than usual.

The captain, drawn to his full height, smoked his cigarette gingerly, as if it were burning his lips with every puff. He cast his nervous glance from the mesmerized soldiers in the snow to the fire and the small figure surrounded by flames in the window.

She was not singing, she was shouting. The dying scream that way. She could be heard not only in the neighboring farms but probably at the end of the world.

Algis groaned and buried his face in the snow, and did not see her fall into the fire. He only heard the silence and the fire's roar. And Motya's surprised voice.

"That's some broad. You couldn't find one like that if you tried."

Algis lay in the snow, deafened and numb, not daring to lift

64

his face and a single thought, clear and shining, throbbed beneath his skull: We are a great people. Unequaled. That girl was more powerful than Joan of Arc. The fire carried her up to the sky. . . . She'll become a saint . . . And I . . . I'm nothing but shit . . . I'm nothing . . . Everybody is nothing . . . Russia, which is killing us . . . and America, which keeps silent . . . They are all shit. There is only . . . my suffering Lithuania . . . my crucified homeland . . . under the knife."

Tears burst from his eyes, and Algis felt them burning holes in the snow.

"Are there tears in your eyes?" Tamara asked anxiously. Worried because Algirdas Požera the famous poet was brought to tears perhaps through some fault of her own—after all, she was held responsible for practically everything—and also because it had happened in front of the foreign visitors, Lithuanians at that, and she did not know what the reaction in their press would be.

"Have you remembered something very sad? Yes? Your difficult childhood in a bourgeois regime?"

The last question Tamara asked in English, solely for the benefit of the tourists, since she knew that Algis spoke no English.

Algis did not want to be angry with her. He tried not to notice her. His eyes were brimming, he felt it and blushed slightly.

Joanne and her friends politely averted their eyes, giving him a chance to compose himself. He smiled at them, sadly. He had to say something, to explain to them. And to calm down the dumb Tamara.

"I was sad," he began quietly, and at all the tables the women hushed and strained to hear. "I remembered three women . . . from my youth. They were all different but they were Lithuanians and they loved little Lithuania . . . and gave their lives

65

for her . . . One day, I'll write about them . . . A requiem, perhaps . . . for perished beauty."

Tamara understood nothing of what he said, and bent over to Joanne, who translated. She nodded at Algis approvingly and gratefully, her glasses glinting in the light, and began to develop his thought, loudly addressing the tables.

"Dear ladies! Our dear guest reminded us in his introduction of those who laid down their lives for the happiness of the people, for the triumph of immortal ideas. There were many women among them and our people hold their names holy. Schools, streets, and kolkhozes are named after them."

While her English flowed on, as smooth and soft as puréed peas, Algis called the waiter over and asked him to treat the tourists to some good Caucasian cognac—at his expense, of course.

"Yes, we have some. Georgian . . . three star," the waiter whispered understandingly, and closed one eye to take a head count. "I don't recommend the Moldavian."

"Fine, the Georgian then. And cut up some lemon. And sugar."

"There's no lemon."

"For shame. We're losing face before the West," Algis chided him, laughing, and the waiter giggled like a buddy.

"Ah, they're tourists, they'll drink it this way, too. As long as it's free. They like bargains. I know them like the back of my hand . . . I've been feeding them for years."

"Forget them," Algis sprang to their defense. "Everybody's got his own weakness. Serve them properly. I won't forget it."

"You'll need ten bottles. No less." The waiter thought deeply. "Remember, we're not inexpensive. One hundred per cent restaurant surcharge, and the railroad gets as much, too . . ."

"You won't bankrupt me." Algis dismissed him with those words.

Tamara was still telling the tourists about Soviet women, and they were obviously bored, squirming in their chairs, playing with their paper napkins, and looking hopefully at Algis. Particularly Joanne. Her eyes were devilishly sly. Her whole face radiated dimples that appeared and disappeared. She liked Algis. She did not try to hide the fact. Even from Tamara, who looked from Algis to Joanne with all the disapproval of a mother hen. And she pursed her lips, making it clear to Algis that she would not allow any hanky-panky in her group.

"Well, screw you, you KGB hypocrite," Algis muttered to himself, and took a full glass of cognac from the waiter.

The plentiful amounts of cognac on the tables created a lively stir among the Americans. They sniffed their glasses and smacked their lips, bulging their eyes as a sign of approval of the cognac and the man who so generously treated them.

The waiter gave Tamara a full glass, too. She raised her thin eyebrows over her eyeglasses and said to Algis in Russian: "You shouldn't have spent so much. They'll get drunk now, and I'll have to answer for it. Do you know what kind of morals they have? None. They do what they feel like. And if this many drunken women get something into their heads all at once . . ."

Algis did not listen to what would happen if that many drunken women wanted something. He stood with his glass in his hand, rolling on his spread legs with the train.

"I'll be leaving you soon, my chance but very dear fellow travelers . . . my compatriots, separated from your people by the ocean . . . but who remember their roots. Let us drink a farewell drink for our Lithuanian women. A sip for each of the three fates. Believe me, they were beautiful people and any nationality would be proud of members like them. Let's drink to them by name . . .

"Genute Urbonaite . . ."

"Genute Urbonaite," they repeated with an American accent.

"Brone Didžiene . . ."

"Brone Didžiene," the Americans echoed with a majesty befitting church.

"And the obscure woman, whose name I do not know."

"And the obscure woman, whose name I do not know."

Tamara, who did not understand what was happening, thought at first that they were praying, but calmed down when Joanne explained to her and drained her own glass, immediately coloring pink under her layer of powder and rouge.

The tourists got up noisily from their tables and felt duty-bound to say good-by to Algis and shake his hand before leaving the dining car. Joanne did too and asked in a low voice:

"What car are you in, Mr. Požera? It's still not late, and I would very much like to see you one more time, if it would not be too inconvenient."

"Mr. Požera is very tired," Tamara interfered brazenly, her cheeks flushed from the cognac. She stood between Joanne and Algis. "We have taken up too much of his precious time as it is. My dear ladies, say good night to our guest and go to your compartments to rest."

Tamara stuck to Algis' side, and Joanne made a face at her behind her back and went past the tables toward the exit, looking back regretfully several times.

Algis controlled his mounting anger. The cognac, and he had consumed an entire bottle, had gone to his head. He hated Tamara, that hot, little Intourist number, scrubbed and starched, her hair teased and lacquered. Her hairdo, covered with a stiff crust, irritated him and he wanted to stick his fingers into the mass of hair, muss it up, pull it apart, so that her porcelain face, half masked by her foreign glasses, would contort with pain and all its layers of powder and paint would crumble.

They were left alone in the dining car, except for the waiter, who was making up the bill and preparing it for Tamara's signature. She leaned over the table, her back to Algis, and her black skirt crept up over her firm calves and rounded thighs, showing him a glimpse of her appetizing rear end.

Algis, drunk, let out a low whistle. Tamara looked back and

started to straighten up, but the train lurched and Algis caught her, pressing his hand over her high, cushiony breast, that was like a balloon.

"Walk me back." Tamara closed her eyes under her glasses. "Your cognac has gone to my head . . . I shouldn't drink."

The waiter gave Algis a conspiratorial wink as he led Tamara toward the door. She leaned heavily on his arm and complained, stumbling over her words:

"If only you knew, how . . . difficult it is with them. Especially the women. They have no morals. All they care about is money. And they buy men with money, even with cigarettes. Shame! We still have some lowlifes around who nibble at their bait. And I have to answer for everything. Write reports, give explanations.

"Would you like to come in? I'm alone in the compartment. I'd like to talk to a Soviet man, relax a bit . . . I can't stand foreigners . . . You'll come in? It's no trouble?"

Tamara had the first compartment in the soft class, after the conductor's section and the toilets. They had not been seen by any of the tourists, and Tamara shut the door behind them. Algis sat down on the soft berth and sank into its soft back. He usually traveled in this kind of compartment. Now he had been pushed out by the tourists and he was doomed to spend the night in a hard compartment. If he was very lucky, he would not have any neighbors for the night.

Her compartment was for two. Two cozy sofas, covered with beige slipcovers, were separated from the window by a table. Their knees met stirring up an unhealthy, angry excitement in him. Over everything that had gone wrong that day. Because Rita had not come and he had waited in vain. Because he had to travel in the wrong compartment. Because Joanne, that American Lithuanian, a pretty and promising creature, had been taken away from him. And by whom?

By this Party hypocrite, drooping from the cognac she had

consumed, with a feminine ass and disturbingly firm legs, who had stuffed her still young and greedy body into a corset of rules and taboos. Guardian of the law, overseer of others' morality. What about her real self? What about HER? She stared at him through her glasses like a cat at cream, and she did not know what to do, how to behave now that they were alone. And Algis felt a tremendous desire to humiliate and insult her. To trample and crumple that well-to-do, proper shell she hid herself in.

"Have some." Tamara offered him an unopened pack of Camels. "I have plenty."

"I prefer my own, Lithuanian ones."

"You know, their way of life is foreign to us, but their cigarettes are good. That's true. Once you get used to them, it's hard to change."

"Are you married?"

"Why?"

"No reason. Just asking."

"Yes. Does it matter to you?"

"No. I was under the impression that you were a virgin."

Tamara laughed, parting her colored lips just a little more than necessary and showing her even, small teeth.

"I look that young?"

She leaned over to him, and her eyeglasses gleamed before his eyes.

Algis carelessly tore off her glasses and discovered to his surprise that her face lost much when they were removed. It even looked less feminine. He set them back on her nose, intentionally gruff and familiar, and she fitted the earpieces herself, having taken no offense.

"Never take off your glasses, even in bed with a man. They make you sexy."

"You think so? Many people have told me that."

"Do you mean that many have seen you naked in your glasses?"

70

"Why do you put it that way? I could be offended . . ."

"By me? It was you who invited me into your compartment. Why?"

"Well, to talk . . . to sit around . . . You are . . . such an interesting . . . man and . . . poet."

"Stop the nonsense, Tamara. I don't have much time. Take off your pants."

He expected her to become incensed, to set up a shout for the whole car to hear, to chase him out. He was hoping for that so that he could tell her everything he thought of her and those like her as he left.

But she just quieted down somehow and looked up at him meekly:

"Someone might come in . . . I'm on duty . . ."

"I don't give a damn about your work." Algis pressed hard on her knee. "Take off your pants . . . or I leave."

"Don't get excited . . . We'll . . . take care of everything right away. Lock the door."

Algis reached over toward the mirrored door and saw his reflection. His face was red and angry, and he almost broke up into laughter when he saw himself. But he regained control, turned the lock, sat back down on the couch, and began unbuttoning his pants slowly and demonstratively.

"It's too light in here," Tamara muttered helplessly.

"Are you used to the dark? Like a thief? Hiding?"

"No . . . Why are you so angry? I'll do whatever you want."

Her voice was full of docility and readiness for anything that he might want. There was no trace of the proper severity and unapproachability that she exuded in public. That spurred Algis on.

"Which couch do you want? Yours? Or mine?" she asked humbly, her voice and expression letting him know that he was the master and his word was law.

"No couches! Get up! That's right. Turn your back to me. Fine. Bend over. More. Lean on your arms."

He raised her skirt, pulled it up over her waist, unfastened her garter belt and tossed it down toward her shoes, pulled down her white-white panties, exposing two soft white semispheres, which were immediately covered with goose bumps.

Tamara shuffled from foot to foot, helping him undress her, but when he fell on her with his full weight and she felt his hot body against her naked flesh, she turned her face in her large glasses back toward him and asked:

"Comrade Požera, what are you doing?"

"What does a peasant do to his wife? You don't know? Now you'll learn! You stupid broad! Spread your legs! Wider, I said!"

He listened with malicious pleasure to her muffled groans as she felt him enter her painfully and when he grabbed her hair, breaking the lacquered crust, and pulled her toward him.

Tamara moaned, twisted her head, banging her glasses into the wall, and he went on, didactically whispering in a hoarse voice:

"And don't teach morals to others! Do you understand? You're no better! You have a husband—he's probably a Party member, like you—and you offer your ass to the first guy who comes along after a glass of cognac. You bitch! Know this—I'm going to sleep with Joanne today. I like her better. Consider this a bribe so that you will leave us alone. Understand?"

He was shaking her, pushing against her, slapping his stomach against her buttocks. She was barely standing, her face in the wall, but she did not throw him off. She sobbed, her thin shoulders heaving under the nylon blouse, and her tears made uneven tracks in her heavy makeup.

The car was swaying and the wheels clacked rhythmically under the floor. Beyond the wide, chrome-framed window, frosty around the edges, the dull wintry countryside rushed past. Dark naked groves alternated with snow-drifted meadows. Empty, locked-up dachas, gray and uninviting, with empty birdhouses on their roofs, flashed by. It was cold and lonely, and the cold crept in through the rattling window.

But it was warm in the compartment. Waves of heat rose from the hidden ventilators. Tamara's fur coat, swaying on its hook, rubbed its soft nap against Algis' face. He was in frenzy, feeling a will-less female body, obedient to his every move, shamelessly exposed to him and given to him for his pleasure and its humiliation—whatever he wanted. Tamara was no more capable of resisting him than a stray bitch could resist a pedigreed mastiff.

Finally, he straightened up and felt for his zipper. The mirror reflected Tamara's naked, drooping buttocks as she stood on her knees. He could hear her quiet, whining cry. Only now was there something human about her, and Algis felt a stirring of pity for her. He found the hem of her skirt on her back and pulled it down over her nakedness. He left the compartment without a word, squeezing through the half-open door. There were tourists standing by the windows in the corridor, their backs to him, and he hurried out to the platform, his head lowered, averting his eyes. He wanted to run.

He felt mean and vile. As though he had been smeared with something viscous and sticky that would require a lot of scrubbing to remove before he could cleanse himself. He even had the sensation that it had all happened to someone else. He was just a chance witness who could not get rid of his feeling of disgust.

He crossed a few public cars on the way to his, and their fetid air stank of underwear and diapers. In between cars streams of frosty steam blew up between his feet, trapping his legs and body with cold air and cooling his hot face.

He did not feel like going to his compartment. It would be stuffy. He stood on the cool platform, which was empty, and leaned his forehead against the frozen, icy glass.

Someone passed from another car and the open door let in the rumble of the wheels and the blue gray cloud of cold air. The

73

frosty window, like an old, dull mirror, showed the reflection of an old woman, wrapped in several scarves, with a simple, calm peasant face. She was leading a young fellow, twice her size, who was hatless and shaved bald. The man stared straight ahead and stepped carefully. Algis looked around. The old woman was leading a blind man who had empty eye sockets and long-healed scars on his forehead and cheeks. Like all the blind, he had a senseless, alienated expression. Even though he was almost thirty years old, he must have been blinded as a child and the stamp of underdevelopment remained on his face. He was wearing a quilted country vest, and a country accordion, with chipped paint and patched bellows, hung on a worn strap across his shoulder. The old woman carried his flapped hat upside down to collect alms.

They were beggars. A blind man and his guide. They were probably mother and son. Algis had not encountered beggars in a long while. The conductors did not let them into the sleeper cars. Their only places to make a living were the suburban electric trains and the public cars on long-distance trains, where the travelers were simpler and more generous and the conductors did not care about anything, including their jobs that required them to keep out ticketless beggars.

The couple distracted Algis from his unpleasant feelings, and he followed them into the stuffy, smelly car. He stopped in the doorway, under a pair of dirty feet that were hanging down from the top shelf.

The blind man smiled an eyeless smile, exposing his large equine teeth, felt for his strap, and put it on his other shoulder, stretching out the accordion and creating a moaning sound. Someone moved over to give him room on the bench, and the old woman seated him, wiping the sweat from his forehead and nose with the corner of her jacket. She wiped his face with the soft, habitual movements that only mothers have. Algis felt a stab in his heart. He imagined the war, so many years ago, blind-

74

ing the woman's little son, and how she saved him and nursed him until he grew to be twice her size, and needed by no one but her, spending his life holding onto her.

The other passengers made room for her opposite him. She threw one scarf after another off her head onto her shoulders, exposing her gray hair and wrinkled, frostbitten face with its faded gray eyes, full of meekness and patience. She put her son's hat on her lap, neatly smoothing out the fur flaps and strings.

Passengers from the entire car had gathered there—it was a diversion from the boring monotony of the trip. Besides, for centuries Russia has harbored a weakness for beggars and tramps and their heartrending songs. Something brought the audience and the performers close together. There was even something similar in their faces.

The blind man pulled at the end of his accordion, ran his fingers along the buttons of the keyboard, and began to sing. He sang nasally, pointing his pug-nosed face, with its flared nostrils and empty eye sockets, up toward the ceiling, where somebody's bare feet dangled.

> "Do Russians want war?
> Ask the silence."

The old woman took up the second phrase. And then together, blending, complaining in two voices like beggars on church steps, they sang:

> "Ask those soldiers
> Who sleep under the birches
> Ask their mothers . . ."

Algis caught his breath. God only knew how the words of this song, written by Yevgeny Yevtushenko, the young Russian poet —whom Algis did not like—sounded so amazingly right in the swaying stuffy car and blended with the image of the performers, so that he understood that this was true art. Who but this fellow deprived since childhood by the war of light, and, therefore, of life, who but this mother, who suffered with her blind son, who had more right to ask:

"Do Russians want war?"

Ah, Yevtushenko, Yevtushenko. If only you were in this car now, to hear with your own ears how blind beggars sing your song and stir up people's souls. They are singing your glory. Without knowing you. Thank God they don't. That they don't see you changing your foreign suits every day and spending thousands in the most expensive restaurants. Many don't understand you, fortune's pet. So progressive and daring in one poem that it seems the KGB will arrest you that very night, and so toadying and devoted in another that it's hard to believe the same author wrote both.

Algis did not like him as a person. For his posturing, for his love of cheap and noisy scandals, for his obvious moral uncleanliness. And now Algis was keenly jealous of him. Before his very eyes Yevtushenko was turning into an anonymous national poet, whose songs blind beggars sing in trains for alms. It was a poet's highest reward, and if it had happened to him, Algis Požera, he would have thought his wildest dreams had come true.

Why did Algis have such a squeamish dislike for the well-known, and, of course, not untalented, poet? Because he had settled himself so cozily at the authorities' buttocks, which he kissed and sometimes bit? But Algis was sitting in the same place. And also kissing. But not biting. One must choose: either kiss or bite. One must not make a principle out of unprincipledness. Algis was a Soviet poet, born of this regime and singing its praises, sincerely, at the top of his lungs, without grimaces or obscene gestures in his pocket. It was more honest that way. And no one could snicker about him the way they did in literary circles in Moscow about Yevtushenko, as though he were a soccer player who kicked equally well with both feet: "Lefty, righty, just mediocre."

All this was true. But the beggars were singing Yevtushenko and not Požera's. Algis transferred his hostility for the author to the innocent singers. He pushed his way through the crowd of passengers in the corridor and stepped out onto the cold platform, where he could feel the pounding of the wheels. Kitchen smells reached him. The dining car was ahead, and in order to reach his compartment, Algis had to go through it.

He was full, he was no longer high, and the only thing he wanted was to get to his compartment as fast as possible, undress, wash at least one part of his body after the unfortunate business with Tamara, and go to bed, stretch out on the soft mattress, on the crisp white sheets. He did not want to see anyone. They remembered him in the restaurant. The waiter with his sly understanding grin and the maître d' in the white jacket that did not meet on his broad stomach, with his sorrowful Armenian eyes.

But before he ran into them, he saw Joanne as he passed through the half-empty dining car. She was sitting alone at a table, and there were no other tourists around. There was a bottle of champagne on the table, and she was sipping it gently, meekly, from a tall glass, staring out the window, where it was dark and fleeting lights rushed by once in a while.

Algis was happy to see her alone without the guide and even thought that perhaps she was waiting there on purpose. She was hoping to run into him. He went up to her table, collapsed on the chair opposite her, causing her to look up with a start and laugh joyously, for she had indeed been waiting for him.

"Joanne, I am all yours, now," he said as though they were old friends.

"So am I," she said smiling.

77

"What's to stop us? We are finally alone. There is no one in my compartment except me. Let's take the champagne with us."

"All right. Let's. But not right now."

"Why?"

"I'm an American, my dear and respected poet. Business before pleasure. If I go with you now, we'll forget the business. Right?"

"What business?"

"I'm interested in more than your body. I have a professional interest, too. I want to write about you and I have many questions. Privately, without extra eyes. And ears."

Algis was disappointed.

"My poor Joanne. You really are an American. If there was anything Lithuanian left in you, you would prefer going off and forgetting your work . . . if only for an hour."

"You're too quick to judge me. We will go off and I'll show you how wrong you are."

She laughed, leaned across the table, and touched his hand with her fingertips. Intimately, tenderly. Algis softened, grabbed her fingers and kissed them. She pulled away lightly.

"I asked you to wait till later. Let's talk now. Rather, I'll ask and you answer. If you find it necessary. I know quite a bit, my dear poet. You are not always free to answer. Don't think that we are so naïve in the West. I won't write anything that could cause you unpleasantness. Let's get started."

Algis nodded and caught her hand once again. She did not pull away.

"Of all the things of yours that I've read, there is one poem I love the most. It is very popular among the Lithuanian émigrés in America. Do you know which one I mean?"

"N-no."

"Obviously you like everything that you've written?"

"Oh, no, far from it."

"All right, I won't bore you. You have a little piece. It's small, but it contains all of Lithuania. The landscapes. The air. The poem brought the smell of home to us émigrés. It's great lyricism. Our Lithuanian lyricism. Incomparable. 'My Lithuania, with dewy smile.' Remember?"

"Oh," Algis laughed. "To tell the truth, I like that one, too. Is it really well known among you?"

"Yes. Children learn it in Sunday school in order to taste the joys of their native tongue and to love and have a whiff of the air from their faraway homeland."

"Thank you. I'm touched. There is no higher reward for a poet . . ."

"And for a literary critic, there's no better coup than an interview with an author."

"We're even. Ask away."

"So, back to 'My Lithuania, with dewy smile.' How did it happen? What led you to sing the praises of the Lithuanian countryside so three-dimensionally and lovingly? As though there was nothing else in the whole world. The poet and nature. No ideology. Pure art. How could you find such an unbiased point of view in our stormy times? Was this the most peaceful period in your life?"

Algis grinned wryly. Joanne was watching him with her crossed eyes and waiting for an answer. God, what if I told her the truth? Impossible. What then? Lies again? And how did the poem come about, what prompted me to write it?

The battered old Willis, with the tarpaulin pulled back, leaped and jumped like a goat over the ruts and potholes in the road, which was surrounded on both sides by the fencing of old trees, their crowns cut off for spring. Young juicy leaves showed green in buds on the stumps of the clumsy branches. Rooks squawked in the plowed fields along the road. The earth was rich and dark and fresh. Salt breezes came from the Baltic Sea.

Algis was bounding on the hard, torn seat, holding on to his

79

companion whenever the Willis lurched. A healthy, irrational joy was upon him. Like a child in spring, he was happy to be alive. He forgot the sad nighttime thoughts that had not let him sleep after the meeting with the city committee of the Party. He did not notice the gloomy faces of his traveling companions. He was breathing deeply, swallowing the springy sea air, and the first line of a poem, light and translucent, like the countryside around him, was arising in his head, by itself, as though he had long carried it around in his heart and it was now bursting out.

That night in Kleipede, he had spent a long time tossing and turning in the hotel to the snoring of his unknown neighbors. He did not really have to come today. He was on a business trip and did not answer to the Party here. He had attended the committee meeting only as an observer and correspondent. But when First Secretary Gineika asked him, before the meeting began, to join the Party operation the next day, calling on his sense of duty as a Communist and explaining that there weren't enough men, and making it a personal favor, and so on and so on, Algis agreed without giving it much thought. They put him on the list.

What had been called a military operation at the meeting was later presented in the papers as a national holiday and a demonstration of the patriotism of Soviet people. Actually it was a military operation, and in Lithuania, where a civil war had been going on for several years and was being carefully covered up, it took on a particularly cruel and dangerous aspect.

Every year the government announced the great day for signing up to lend money to the state for the development of the U.S.S.R. Each worker in the city had to give the government no less than a month's wages, which was then taken as an extra deduction during the year. This did not create any particular problems. The worker never saw the money, paid nothing, only signed up at the office and missed a certain amount each month.

It was much more difficult in the villages. Peasants do not receive wages and there was nothing from which to make deductions. That meant that the farmers had to pay out of their own cash in a single day whatever sum the state decided for them, and got nothing in return but the state IOU, which was not worth the paper it was printed on. A general sum was set for each village and then divided up over the households on the basis of wealth.

The Prekule District, where they were headed in the Willis, had to contribute twelve thousand rubles. And not a kopek less. By midnight the money had to be on Gineika's table.

"If you don't deliver," Gineika said to the three of them, including Algis, "you'll pay with your Party cards. The plan must be fulfilled. At any cost. Is that clear? Don't namby-pamby around and don't pat anyone on the head. Remember, whatever you don't collect of the twelve thousand will come out of your own pockets. I will only accept twelve thousand. I don't care where you get it. Have a good trip."

They were given a machine gun, pistols, and grenades for the trip.

Algis had not slept after that meeting. But the May morning stirred the poetic strings in his soul and somber thoughts were chased out of his head. His companions in the Willis were not poets. They squirmed from the cold and squinted in the wind. Gladutis, the instructor at the city committee, wrapped his leather coat around himself tighter and held his pistol in his lap. The one sitting next to the driver was a Russian, Vasya Kuznetsov. He was puffing away nervously on a cigarette. The wind blew the ashes on Algis and Gladutis and died immediately.

The spire of the church was a beacon leading the way to Prekule. As they got closer they saw the little houses scattered around the church. This was the district center, where they were to carry out the operation. The other villages were scattered in the fields and forests and they had to get to all of them today.

The town looked dead. The shutters were closed in most of the houses. The Willis made a U-turn on the cobblestone square in

81

front of the church, frightening a bunch of chickens, and stopped in front of the round cement well. Its wooden handle was in the left hand of a scrawny, unkempt person. He was waving a welcome with a revolver in his right hand. He was the only Communist in the district, Kliukas, secretary of the district committee, whom they had come from Kleipede to help.

At first, Algis saw no significance in the fact that Kliukas, the district's only Communist, was standing by the well brandishing a gun on that day of all days. He was struck by the man's appearance more than anything else. A pathetic scrawny creature, very removed from bellicoseness. His gun looked ridiculous. His thick rumpled hair that had not been washed in a long time and his sloppy worn clothing made him look like a local drunken accountant, who was harassed by the neighborhood wives and despised by their husbands. But first impressions can be very misleading. Kliukas was a hero. A fanatic madman who did not know the meaning of fear.

He had been there for a year with his old police revolver, the only representative of Soviet power in the district; he carried out all his orders, and campaigns, forced the locals to obey—and he did it all completely alone in a hostile environment where he had no friends, no acquaintances, no wife, no children. What he ate and where he ate only God knew. He slept in sheds, moving each night so that he could not be found; he would disappear whenever the Forest Brotherhood came roaring through the district, and reappear when they had gone, and take up his duties once more.

That day he was signing up his district for loans. Algis, Gladutis, and Kuznetsov had been sent from the city to help him.

"You're late, comrades," he greeted them, for some reason not letting go of the handle. "Work is on in full swing."

They got out of the Willis, stretching after the journey.

82

"Where's everybody?" Gladutis demanded in an official tone, stung by Kliukas' remark.

"They're gathered," he giggled, his beady eyes glimmering under his bushy eyebrows with what Algis felt was an unhealthy glow.

He pointed his gun at the sturdy stone building, shutters closed, that stood opposite the church. The heavy door was barred with a metal bar. Only then did Algis make out the indistinct rumbling of numerous voices coming from the stone house.

"I have my own method. Tried and true," Kliukas explained. "All the poorer farmers who have to pay twenty-five rubles, I rounded up at dawn into the house. To meditate. They don't have much money, they need to work the land, and here they are locked up. Their whole day is gone. I let them figure it out: it costs more not to pay. As soon as you pay, you're free to work to your heart's content.

The guests looked at each other. Algis squinted at Kliukas, at the fine features on his unshaven face, at his shiny, evil eyes, and Algis became even more wary, as one does when facing a not completely sane person.

Gladutis was the senior member of the group. He saw nothing abnormal in Kliukas' behavior.

"What results?" he asked, businesslike.

"Over a thousand." Kliukas proudly patted his pants pocket with the gun. "And the accounts. Everything in order."

"Not bad, not bad," Gladutis approved. "Why are you standing by the wall? Let's go somewhere and discuss our plan of action."

"I can't leave," he replied, turning the crank on the bucket line. "There'll be victims."

And he beckoned them, ready to show his major surprise.

"Down there, look down." He pointed deep into the well, where the taut chain disappeared.

And when Algis carefully looked over the cement edge he saw

in the damp darkness, far below, a man in a crumpled peasant hat, his gray bearded face turned up toward them. He was tied to the bucket and waist-deep in water. The old man stared up at them without blinking.

"Let 'im soak. Kulak!" Kliukas' triumphant voice sounded behind them. "I won't pull him out for less than two hundred."

Algis' heart shrank. He straightened up and angrily confronted Kliukas.

"Do you realize what you are doing? If he had not been our enemy before, he will be now."

"No, he won't," Kliukas soothed, and waved his gun. "What for? I'm developing his Marxist thinking."

He said it without a trace of humor, and Algis was sure that he was dealing with a loony who derived some childish pleasure from all of this.

Kuznetsov puffed silently on his cigarette, and Gladutis, surprised by nothing, gave Kliukas an approving slap on the back.

"Fine! We'll go eat, and then we'll finish up."

Kliukas, encouraged, lowered the crank a full turn, and the peasant was up to his neck in water.

"Aren't you tired yet, brother?" he called down cheerily. "The bosses are here. No more bathing, you'll develop a cough."

An indistinct "blub, blub, blub" floated up from the cold depths of the well.

"He's ready," laughed Kliukas. "You can write up another two hundred. Come on, comrades, lend a hand. I can't pull him out alone."

Gladutis grabbed the handle, and they began hauling the squeaking chain, rolling it up on the wooden crank. A blinking bearded face appeared over the cement edge, the man's soft hat pushed into the crank. They pulled him out by hand from there. The four of them lifted the shivering wet man and the bucket to which he was tied. Over his thick knit socks, the old man was wearing *klumpes*, the age-old wooden shoes of the Lithuanian

84

peasant. The shoes, the crumpled hat, and the wet pants clinging to his legs—everything about him smelled of poverty and gave no hint of the kulak, wealthy landlord, that he was supposed to be.

"Cough up the dough, old man," Kliukas laughed as he untied the old man from the bucket. "I'll bet you sewed it into your sock. Once you help the government strengthen its power you can go dry out on the oven."

A flock of rooks flew like a dark spreading cloud over the church steeple and noisily began settling in the trees.

That was the last thing Algis could recall clearly later. The rest came back in bits and pieces. He did remember that for some reason the first line of the poem he had begun in the car kept running through his mind: "My Lithuania, with dewy smile . . ." He muttered the line to himself as he followed the old man to his farm and as the old man shoved the money at him without a glance. The fellow refused to sign up for a receipt and finally his fair-haired nephew, with a runny nose, signed for him. And while the peasants left the district committee office one by one, arguing with the guard before going back home for the money, Algis repeated "My Lithuania, with dewy smile . . ." over and over, in order not to hear the young women's cries and the bitter grumbling of the old women, in order not to see the frightened children's eyes.

He also remembered how Gladutis had told him, as though Algis had insulted him somehow:

"Intellectual flimflam. There's not a proletarian vein in your body. It's easy to write verses. But who's going to take care of this? We Communists, that's who. We do all the dirty work without flinching because we have a long-term goal. For the good of these very people. They'll understand later and they'll thank us. And don't start drooping and pouting, you're no fine young lady."

And he also remembered Kliukas' joyous cries.

"Half the work is done! We have six thousand! I swear to God, we'll be the first ones to report back to headquarters!"

They reported back without Algis. And to this day he did not know whether they had reported or not.

Sometime around noon, Algis got overpoweringly hungry. He forgot the strict orders not to touch any food, and asked for some food at one of the houses. They later told him that he was lucky he ate near the town square and not at some distant farmhouse. The driver saw him running out of the house, doubled over in pain. He began to vomit and fell on the cobblestones. A thin line of vomit dribbled from his mouth.

Everything else was done without him. He did not know how they got him to Vilnius or how they put him in a private room at the special polyclinic of the Central Committee.

He spent seven days, a full week, unconscious, grinding his teeth from the fire that was consuming his guts. The doctors had diagnosed it as acute poisoning and just when they had given up all hope of recovery they called his father from Panevezys. So that he could be with his son in the final hours.

The first thing that Algis saw when he came to was his father's face behind the window, his gray moustache and his nose flattened against the glass. Algis did not know where he was. He jumped up, threw off his covers, and sat up, only to fall back from weakness. He was wearing white shorts and a shirt covered with official black markings.

His father on the other side of the window saw him and blinked in confusion. Algis saw the tear make its way slowly down his father's brown, wrinkled cheek. It was murky. And very large. Then Algis started to cry. Bawling. Like a child. With a flood of tears that cleansed his soul. He must have cried aloud because the nurses and doctors in white coats came running, scurrying, exclaiming happily and putting him back to bed as if he were a little child.

Much much later, when he was on the mend, they brought

him the newspapers that he had not seen while he was sick. He read the accounts about the successful spread of the loan system among the population of Lithuania. The papers also carried letters from peasants who expressed their pleasure on this account, in the official newspaper language, and each letter ended with a toast to the honor of the beloved leader, Comrade Stalin.

In the stack of newspapers he accidentally came across a black-bordered obituary that described the heroic death of Vasili Kuznetsov, a Communist from Kleipede port, who had been vilely slain by kulaks. Straining his memory, Algis realized that this was the very same Vasya Kuznetsov who had been in on the operation in Prekule with him. It could have been the wet peasant from the well who had chopped him to death with an ax. But no matter how he tried, Algis could not picture his face. All he could remember was the cigarette and the sparks blown by the wind in the Willis.

Six months later, when he was fully recovered, Algis wrote the poem. It began with "My Lithuania, with dewy smile." It was a lyric poem, as transparent as the tears he shed in the hospital. It was praised by critics and read in concert performances by many actors. It did not have a trace of what he had lived through in Prekule; it only had the freshness of the May morning that Algis had perceived as he bounced along in the Willis gulping the salt air, the freshness that can only be in Lithuania.

Joanne was waiting patiently for an answer, taking tiny sips of champagne from the high-stemmed glass. Algis was looking into her close-set gray eyes, her firm unnaturally white teeth, and the warm hollow in her neck. He wanted only one thing: not to talk about anything with her. Just to get up from his chair and go to his compartment. And for her to follow docilely.

Algis told her what he wanted. Frankly. Even the part about not wanting to talk about anything and wanting her to follow him in silence. Because another such opportunity would probably never happen for either of them. And they should hurry to take advantage of it.

"O.K.," Joanne agreed. "Let's finish the champagne and go."

"Don't be hurt, Joanne," he tried clumsily to smooth over his refusal to talk. "You're a smart girl. There's a saying in Russia: 'My tongue is my enemy.' Please try to understand everything without words."

"All right." Joanne looked sensuously into his eyes. "Your words make me want to cry. To your success, Mr. Požera. God watch over you, our Lithuanian God, in this land that is foreign to me and to you, too."

Algis drank his glass of champagne in a single gulp, like a shot of vodka, and the bubbles stung his eyes.

The train had been standing for some time, and through the blue twilight of the early winter evening he could see the station's yellow walls, the spotlights of the lamps, each surrounded by a frosty nimbus, and people scurrying to and fro, carrying their bundles and luggage, whipped into a frenzy by an unseen hand, almost as though each was sure that he would not get a seat and that the train would leave without him, even though he had the ticket he had fought for in the long lines.

Algis glanced over at Joanne and realized that she was noticing everything. The shabby clothing, the public's hunted look, and their antediluvian luggage, which could be seen only in Russia. But he did not feel like distracting her with empty chatter, as he would have done before, defending the honor of his uniform. The Soviet uniform. The most spotless one in the world. Let them see the truth and draw their own conclusions. Why let in tourists if you don't want the world to know anything? Ah, for the money, the hard currency. Well, you have to choose—if you want the profit then don't put rouge on the facade and camouflage an unattractive appearance.

Then he remembered the conductor's words: no one will get on in Mozhaisk. He would have an entire night with Joanne

Mage, an American Lithuanian, a marvelous travel companion given to him by fate, if the conductor had been right and they weren't going to stick him with some lousy native of Mozhaisk.

"Shall we go, Joanne?" he said, tossing some money on the table to pay for her order in Soviet rubles.

"Yes, let's." She was suddenly in a hurry, too. "Our guide could return at any moment. I feel like a schoolgirl and she's the dean of girls. Intolerable bitch!"

They left the dining car under the all-knowing, cynical stare of the waiter and the sad, oily eyes of the white-coated chef. Algis felt them staring at his back and realized that either one of them, and maybe both, would run for Tamara in a servile rush and tell her that the tall Lithuanian with the light hair, well, that . . . poet took the American tourist to his compartment. She would start looking for them. And find nothing. Because she did not know his compartment. Even if she looked into every one, which was unlikely, she would not find them because he and Joanne would lock themselves in and answer to no one until morning.

Spurred on by a childish desire, he briskly made his way along the narrow corridors, turning sideways to pass other passengers. Joanne barely kept up with him, not understanding his rush, but attributing it to his flaming desire for her. It flattered and excited her. Everything around her was unusual. The train rushing past the frozen, poverty-stricken country, where people dare not speak frankly. The beautiful poet with a world-famous name, whom she really did love as a lyric poet, and who had lost his head over her and was rushing like a teen-ager to be alone with her.

Algis was losing his breath from rushing. Finally he reached his car. There were new faces in the corridor, but the door to his compartment was firmly closed. Thank God! The train was speeding out of Mozhaisk and he had been left in peace. He tugged at it. In vain. The door was locked from the inside.

"Please wait. A woman is changing inside."

It was said in Russian, but with a clear Lithuanian accent. A tall man, about Algis' age, in a jacket and tie but wearing, for some reason, jodhpurs and boots, was standing by the hall window. The mixture of civilian clothes and uniform was beloved by petty officers in the rural areas of Lithuania. He had a peasant face, too. Rough and wind-blown. But his eyes, under his low brows, gazed out confidently and even brazenly.

"There's someone in my compartment?" Algis asked in an irritated tone in Lithuanian. An offensive, brazen smirk was his answer.

"First of all, the compartment is not yours, but the state's. Secondly, now it is full: you and the three of us."

His smirk softened and turned into a gentler, friendlier smile.

"It'll be a Lithuanian compartment. Nobody to feel uncomfortable before. All four of us are our own people, Lithuanians."

The man had long, equine teeth stained by tobacco.

"Sigita," he called softly, knocking on the door. "Are you ready? People are waiting out here."

Another Lithuanian-looking man stood behind him, older and shorter and also wearing an old-fashioned jacket and navy jodhpurs and boots.

"Algis." Joanne touched his sleeve. "Let's go back to the dining car."

"In a minute," he replied irritably, feeling his plans falling apart and the unpleasant sensation creeping up to his heart, as he did lately whenever he worried or got angry. "I want to see whom I'll be spending the night with."

"As far as I could understand, it's a woman," Joanne said, a mocking tone creeping into her voice.

"Some woman," the tall man laughed. "She's just a girl. The milk hasn't even dried on her lips."

"Your daughter?" asked Joanne.

"Daughter or not, why do I have to give you a report?"

"Don't talk to her that way," Algis cut him off. "That's no way to talk to a woman. And to make sure you stay careful, let me tell you that this is a foreigner, an American Lithuanian."

Surprise and then anxiety showed on his long wrinkled face.

"Forgive me, if I behaved badly. Forgive me. If you don't mind, could I speak to you . . . before we go inside?"

And he beckoned Algis away from Joanne. Algis followed him for a few steps, glaring severely and with hostility.

"Here's the problem," he whispered, looking over his shoulder at Joanne. "Me and my partner are from the Kaunas police. And the girl we're transporting is a criminal. We have to take her back to trial. Get it? So, if it's possible, it would be better not to involve the foreigner in this. Please keep her out of the compartment."

"What the hell is this?" Algis muttered, wincing with a toothache-like pain. "It's some sort of plague. There are two policemen in my compartment transporting a criminal. Under armed guard. And I have to spend the night in such pleasant company. I'm definitely moving. Help me move my things."

The door was opened by then, and when Algis looked in, he could see no one. Then he heard rustling in the upper left berth. A curly towhead leaned down. Pug-nosed, full-lipped, a child's face. With big gray eyes. Wary and surprised. And a soft, melodious voice:

"I know you. You're Algirdas Požera!"

And when he nodded, her eyes lit up with such unfeigned pleasure that Algis unwillingly smiled back and shook her proffered hand. He saw the Komsomol pin with Lenin's profile on the lapel of her jacket and became even more confused.

A criminal. With that trusting child's face. She couldn't be over sixteen. And a Komsomol pin. And the two guards. Are they just having a tremendous practical joke at his expense? Did someone put them up to this?

"Algis, why don't you invite the little girl to join us?" Joanne

91

said behind him. "You're so popular. Even children recognize your face."

"No, no," the tall man in jodhpurs said. "She must rest. She has a heavy day tomorrow."

"Are you traveling with us in the same compartment?" she crooned. "No one will ever believe that I traveled with you. Boy, am I lucky."

Algis suddenly felt that he did not want to leave the compartment. The girl's face and her manner of speech seemed familiar to him. He had to figure out what was going on. And in order to do that—he had to rid himself of Joanne, send her back to her soft-class compartment. He had suddenly lost all interest in her. He told her to get back to her compartment and that he would look in later. He went into his own, sat on the lower berth, threw back his head, and made contact with the gray smiling eyes.

Both policemen stayed out in the corridor, discreetly turning toward the window, probably watching them in the reflection in the glass. He did not care. He watched this girl Sigita and her smile and tried to remember whom she reminded him of so poignantly and painfully. He strained his memory, stubbornly searching its deepest reaches. More and more clearly, each time with separate frozen images, like snapshots, the same angular virginal figure, the same smile on the same puffy, chapped lips, and the same slightly wild look of the gray eyes under knit brows. The wary look, ready to rebuff at any moment, of an immature person who had already learned that this life can bring trouble from any direction.

For a second it seemed to Algis that he had already met Sigita, knew her, and had memories of her. A sixteen-year-old country girl, shy and clumsy, at that period in her life when, like a wild apple, she was filling with the sweet juices of ripening maidenhood. Neither the poor, overwashed dress long outgrown and splitting at the seams; nor her long, scratched legs with scabby knees; nor her windblown, peeling nose could dim the quiet charm with which she glowed and which filled her every movement in repose and in sudden anger.

Of course, it was not Sigita who welled up in his memory. Algis had been young himself then, and Sigita was not even born or was at best an infant on her mother's knee. But the one who passed through Algis' memory was the same age and could have been Sigita's twin. Maybe her name would come to him. It was on the tip of his tongue. Dana . . . Danute! It all came to him from the depths of his memory, piercingly clear. Algis sensed the smell that permeated this memory. The smell of blooming clover. Sweet, damp, like honey. He remembered the clover blossoms. The fuzzy white and purple blossoms among the dewy, ornate, rounded leaves.

It was a small railroad station, lost among the fields and forest groves. And the train was small, like a miniature toy set. A narrow-gauge track led to this place deep in the provinces; the little engine, shiny new and black, puffing and whistling like a teapot, named "cuckoo" by the locals, pulled seven or eight tiny cars. It lost steam on the inclines, angrily hissing, and the passengers, usually peasants from the surrounding villages, would get out before they got to the station. It was closer to home anyway. They would walk alongside the train while their bags and packages were handed down to them through the windows.

The cars reeked of makhorka tobacco, sweaty feet, and sour sheepskin jackets. The passengers crowded together, sharing their sandwiches of fatback with onions. The gulped moonshine from dark bottles, spreading the smell of raw alcohol. The bottles were stoppered with twists of newspaper.

Algis was not distressed by proximity to the people in those days. On the contrary, he ate fatback and onions with them, drank moonshine, and listened greedily to their leisurely peasant conversation, impressed by their accurate and sharp observations. He tried to remember them. He used to say that he was inspired by their attitude toward him, that they considered him an equal and listened to his opinions.

He loved these people. They were the true Lithuania. With her troubles and cares. They did not read newspapers and thus did not resemble the people described in them.

In those days, he felt that he was just one of them who had managed to get ahead a bit. And was embarrassed by it, as though he had been dishonest toward them.

He was young, naïve, and as pure as a maiden, and he accepted the whole world wide-eyed, feeling its pain and sorrows, sincerely hoping and believing that soon, in just a little more time, everyone would be happy and well off, and all the misery of the world would disappear.

That was the Algis who arrived one raw morning at the little station and jumped off onto the wooden platform, still dewy and showing dark footprints of bare feet stretching across the boards. Algis followed them and found two solitary females at the end of the platform. Both barefoot. An old woman and a woman-child, about fifteen.

That was when he memorized the wild look in the gray eyes under the furrowed brows, the lanky scratched limbs, and the scabs on the knees. That was Danute. The Danute who was to cross his path often while he was living at the kolkhoz. For some reason he could not forget her.

Danute and her mother had brought milk cans, cucumbers, and radishes, in large wet bunches with clumps of earth on their long tails, to the train.

"Who'd like milk? Who wants radishes?" Danute called out, her bare feet slapping the wooden flooring as she pushed her wares through the windows. She offered the produce, unwillingly, even angrily. She had reason to be angry. In all the time the train was in the station, not one person bought anything. Obviously this happened often. The passengers were primarily peasants, and they were not buyers. They were taking the same products to the market themselves.

The engine whistled, the cars jangled and seemed to float away. Algis, with his suitcase, and the two women were left on the platform. Danute walked past him toward her mother and looked him over quickly. Algis gave her a simplehearted smile. She glowered at him, knitting her brows. There was so much anger in her look that Algis was dumbfounded. He only later realized that she had taken his smile for a jeer.

Danute went up to her mother, placing the basket at her feet. The woman started to scold her. Algis could not hear their words, but he could tell that she was blaming the girl for the lack of sales. She slapped her face.

Danute leaped away from her mother like a goat, cursed at her, and ran off the platform onto the path, her heels flying in the air. She ran without looking back until she disappeared behind the bushes in the ravine.

Algis would have probably forgotten her if their paths had not crossed again. It happened that very evening.

Algis set off for his destination from the station. He was going to Rodina Kolkhoz, which was under the direction of a marvelous woman, Ona Saulene. Algis had written about her many times for his paper and felt at home in her kolkhoz.

Saulene's life was good advertising for the benefits of Soviet power in Lithuania. She, and others like her, had gotten what they could never have dreamed of before. Before Soviet power she huddled in a pathetic little hut with her husband and three children. She had no land and worked for rich peasants on their farms. She was illiterate, poor, and embittered. Tall and heavy, like most Žemaite peasant women, she was a harsh, severe person with a firm masculine personality and a quick native intelligence.

She put all her talents to use when Lithuania was annexed by Russia. The Soviets, without giving it much time, started forming

95

kolkhozes on the Russian model. Take away the peasants' land and cattle and unite everything into one large farm where everyone is equal. No more rich or poor men. It was easy to deal with the rich—they were shipped off to Siberia. The poor had nothing to lose—there was no difference between breaking your back on someone else's farm and doing it on a collective farm.

This was Ona Saulene's finest hour. She was reborn. She put a pistol in her coat pocket, the very first coat she had ever owned, issued to her by the state after the kulak properties were confiscated. And she traveled around the farms, sending the rich to Siberia according to her lists. Rounding up plowshares, sowers, horses, and cattle to a common yard. Showing no mercy to the rich, but being fair and honest with the poor.

She paid dearly for it. The Forest Brotherhood that had survived the roundup to Siberia and had hidden in the woods got its revenge. One night her hut went up in flames. The doors and windows had been sealed from the outside by some steady hand. Her husband and three children were inside. She had escaped miraculously, attending a meeting in the district capital that night. She came home to a heap of ashes. Silently, without a single tear, she rummaged through the rubble, gathering the charred bones. She buried everything herself, in a common grave, and then went on fiendishly building the kolkhoz.

The peasants, long oppressed and frightened by everything that was happening, were happy when she became a candidate for chairman and gladly voted for her. Ona was one of them; no one could doubt her integrity, and they had hope that this woman with a man's personality and strength would hurt someone only out of sincere feelings and would protect them from the district authorities, who were spreading like mushrooms after rain.

Ona turned out to be exceptionally gifted. Illiterate and oppressed, she understood the economics of farming and knew better than anyone how to make people work. Not only the women, but the men, too, feared a scowl from her. When she drove past workers in the fields, they all bowed low, the way they had long ago to their masters. The people respected her. The peasants prospered and the farm moved forward. Hidden behind her broad back, the people had no fear of the devil himself. She did not take excess profits for herself. She lived like the rest.

Algis observed her with undisguised interest and awe. She had aged early. Big-boned and heavy in the last few years as a result of heart trouble, she was unattractive. A flat weathered face, a bulbous nose, and beady, penetrating eyes under bushy brows. Yet her little eyes could be kind.

Algis noticed that her gaze melted when she talked to him. She confessed that he reminded her of her oldest son and every visit of his was a quiet holiday for her. She would sit deep in an old battered armchair by the fire, smoking her cigarettes, hand-rolled in newsprint, and spend long hours talking to him. One night at her house, he awoke from his sleep to see her standing over him, searching his face. Women like Ona embodied the new life that had come to Lithuania with Soviet power. She was that power, truly of the people, never sparing herself for the general good. She had quickly learned to speak out at meetings without embarrassment, to argue crudely but wisely with the authorities. Even visitors from the capital learned to fear her tongue.

Once Algis ran into her in Vilnius. She was there for a conference. She was sitting in the half-empty Bristol Restaurant, under the crystal chandelier that hung heavily from the ceiling and was reflected on all sides in mirrors. The parquet floor was covered with red carpet runners. Knitting her brows, she was giving her order to the waiter, who was respectfully bent over her. Algis joined her. She was wearing a black wool dress, a city dress, with a deep décolletage. Algis was stunned to see the pink silk of her slip pulled up to her throat. Embarrassed, Algis tried to explain that underwear should not be visible. It was worn under the dress. Saulene was not impressed.

"Let them all see that we don't go around in burlap sacking," she said proudly, looking around the restaurant with a chip on her shoulder, ready to do battle with anyone who did not show enough respect for her.

Back on the kolkhoz, Ona lived alone in a large house, confiscated from rich people, filled with antique carved furniture. She only used one room; the rest was in disrepair, as was the estate with its sheds and barns. The only remnants of the past riches were the two peacocks that had come with the house and refused to leave. They awoke her at night with their harsh, piercing cries.

Toward evening, his business finished and with nothing to do until the train later that night, Algis went for a walk.

The evening was blue and transparent. The pale moon was creeping out from the distant hills, dissipating the twilight. You could see for miles. You could even make out a slow river, winding its way through the hazel groves. Raw freshness and the first strands of mists meekly crawling along the lowlands toward the meadows were blowing from the river.

The clover along the sandy road was steeped in moistness exuding such a honeyed sweetness that you wanted to drink in the air, instead of merely breathing it, to store it for a future day. Algis was in the peaceful exalted state that usually portended the birth of a new poem, and enjoying the anticipation, he wandered along the sandy path, thinking of nothing.

Visiting Ona Saulene gave him spiritual peace. Lithuania had been pacified for some years. The shots had died down, the patrols had disbanded. The former empty farmhouses had lights in their windows once more, fearlessly and cozily, and homey smoke rose from the chimneys. The meadows, overgrown with weeds during those years, were neatly cared for once more; they were blooming joyously, as though to make up for lost time.

That meant that it had not been all in vain. Peace and comfort had come to Lithuania, and the people who had survived greedily reached for a life of work and cares.

That was what Algis thought, and Saulene's kolkhoz was the best example for his philosophy.

Whenever he went there, Algis did not question anyone or make any plans. He observed the life around him and that gave him plenty of material. This time too. Early in the morning, he climbed up into the two-wheeled cart, hitched to a frisky gelding. Saulene heavily sat down next to him on the seat stuffed with clover hay and took the reins like a man. They went off, swaying gently along the dusty road. He had decided to accompany her until he got tired of it. Follow through on all her daily duties, without even taking notes, trusting his memory.

The gelding trotted smoothly across the hilly plain, and when Algis asked her why she did not get a car, since several kolkhozes already had them, Saulene only gave a short laugh in reply to what she considered a childish whim. Cars stank and there were enough tractors fouling the air as it was. Soon there would be nothing to breathe in Lithuania. Horses had their own homey smell.

She was in a good mood that day, perhaps because Algis was there. She was even mischievous and youthful, revealing a new side of herself to Algis.

The fields were full of thick, bearded barley, which had whitened considerably, and clover, which covered most of the land and was ripe for harvesting. It stood knee-high and even at midday it was cool in the dark thickets. A gray hare, its ears set apart, jumped out into the road, scaring the gelding, and hopped off to the other side and the coolness of the clover.

Algis did not notice when Saulene smoothly pulled a gun out from under the seat. Without taking aim, she shot into the clover, stopped the horse, and said:

"Go, pick up the game."

99

Algis was amused. He was sure that she could not have shot the hare, but he did not argue. He decided it was a game, and, to humor the old woman, he got down and went into the clover. His pants soaked through immediately. He looked down earnestly, making believe he was looking for it.

"Left . . . And a bit over."

He obeyed, laughingly, and found the hare on the crushed clover, its fur stained with blood and its eyes shut. Her aim was true; the hare was shot in the head. It was impossible. An old, sick woman, without taking aim, her horse at full speed, had managed to down a hopping hare. And it was no accident, because she knew precisely where to send Algis after it.

"We'll dine like hunters," she joked, hiding the hare under the straw, and shoved her pistol there too. The weapon was a trophy —a German Luger.

The peasants were mowing clover on top of the hill and the wonderful spicy smell of sun-warmed hay wafted toward them. Three horse-drawn mowers moved noisily through the field, piling up juicy heaps of clover. Women were in the iron drivers' seats. Saulene trusted them more than the men. Further up, a chain of colorful scarves. Women raking yesterday's harvest.

"Watch." Saulene winked at him. "As soon as they see me, they'll start singing."

Sure enough. He could hear a song, low at first. Then the others joined in. Not one had raised her head, all making believe that they did not notice the arrival of the cart.

"Those are my orders. When I have a guest, they have to sing. Let the visitors see how happy we are. What do you mean, it's just for show? Do they live badly? Look at the neighbors. They were poverty-stricken before, and they still are, but now it's collective poverty. That's because no one is in charge. Everyone steals what he can for himself.

"Use your head. Who got rich and became a master in Lithuania before? Hard-working, sober peasants, who saved every crumb. They were all sent off to Siberia. That's a mistake, I think. Lithuanian land is left without a master. A poor peasant will never become a master, he's not used to it. So they need strictness. They need to be afraid. You have to drag them by the ears to the good life."

Algis knew from his previous trips how much the people in the kolkhoz feared her. This trip provided another example. She drew up to a tractor parked by the side of the road. The trailer held two reapers, the wooden blades outstretched like wings. The workers, snoozing in the hay, jumped up and rapidly explained, afraid to anger Saulene, that the babbitt had burned out and the tractor driver had gone for a new one.

"How long ago?"

"About two hours . . ."

"Maybe three?"

"Maybe, three . . ."

"He's out drinking, the toad!"

She took the reins and urged the horse on. Saulene complained to Algis as though he were one of her own:

"There's never any peace with those menfolk. I've trained mine to stop drinking. But the tractor driver, he's from a machine training school. I wish the children in school would grow faster. I'll train my own workers, then I'll have no headaches."

The horse was racing down the hill toward the Šešupe River and the bridge made of freshly cut wood. A dirty, smeared little peasant, barefoot, his boots over his shoulder, was riding toward them over the bridge on an unsaddled piebald mare.

"There he is. Sobered up." Saulene pulled up the horse and squinted meanly.

The peasant saw her and slowed up. He shielded his eyes from the sun to look and make sure that it was Saulene. He jumped from the mare onto the railing, tossed his boots under her feet, and fell ten feet into the river, shooting up a shower of splashing water.

Saulene pulled up in the middle of the bridge and shook her head disapprovingly as she watched the driver dog-paddle away from the bridge.

"He had plenty of moonshine. He was afraid to breathe into my face. Pick up his boots," she ordered Algis. "He'll be back."

The gray spire of the church, surrounded by an overgrown park, towered in the center of the settlement. The main street, ten houses long, led to it. The church was small and decrepit. Cracks snaked through the natural stone of its walls. Grass-green moss grew in the cracks. A reedy birch tree yearned for the sky. The sun played on the fine old stained glass in the narrow windows. It was the windows that had saved the church from being closed.

"Some big shots came down from the city. There sure are lots of them nowadays," Saulene complained to Algis. "'Close the church,' they shouted. 'You can incorporate it into the kolkhoz as a warehouse.' There had been an incident, the priest got mixed up with a forest band. They sent him to Siberia and closed the church. I was sorry. Where will the old women go? I thought. They'll drop like flies from boredom. I didn't let them. I said the church had historical value. You can't destroy it. To tell the truth, I wore out my knees there in my time, too. It's a pity. So they sent another priest. Meek as a lamb. Works with me."

Algis had meant to examine the church anyway, so he asked her to let him off.

"Wait, let me drive past," Saulene said, and urged the gelding on. "The people watch me from their windows. They'll think that Saulene has got religion in her old age."

Algis got off around the corner, promised not to be late for dinner, and followed the grass-covered street back to the church.

Its walls reeked of the ages. Inside, in the colored semi-darkness, it smelled of the damp. It was pleasantly cool after the heat on the street. Several old women, their backs to Algis, were kneeling. There was no one else. Quietly, stepping softly, Algis went from window to window, his face turned to the soft light streaming in in a dusty column.

He heard steps of bare feet scurry past him. Algis turned. He recognized Danute from the back of her cotton dress, its seam split, and by her long tanned legs. He remembered the station, the old woman who slapped her, and the wild, hostile look he got in return for his smile.

Danute tiptoed up to the old women, got on her knees, and whispered her prayers, swaying head and shoulders. Then she rose, bowed to the tall dark crucifixion, the paint flaking on the Christ's body, and, looking down at the floor, walked past Algis into the blinding sun.

At dinner, Algis remembered Danute and told Saulene about the station, the slap, and the church.

"Doomed people," she sighed bitterly. "They have nothing for Caesar or for God. The mother and I were once friends. We used to work in the peat fields together, ulcerating our feet. She was a woman like any other, but she got stuck with a lousy man. During the war, he joined the German *Polizei*. And not a word from him since. They wanted to ship her and the daughter to Siberia. I wouldn't let them. Unenlightened poverty, that's all. She's no enemy. Now I'm sorry. She's a viper. Refuses to join the kolkhoz. I took away her land and tax her to death, she still won't go. She lies like a beggar, steals here and there. No matter how hard I fight with her—she's like a rock. The girl, too. Fruit doesn't fall far from the tree. The kids go to school, but not her. She sells milk at the station. Is that anything for someone her age to be doing? . . . My heart is heavy."

Saulene looked closely at Algis, to see if he understood.

"You want only good for people, and they don't understand. They're like infants. I swear. If you don't lick them, you can't teach them. And yet, God only knows who's right. I don't read books and only spent two years in school. That's my degree. I hold the people through fear, not wisdom. I don't know how long I'll be able to do it. And there's no one to ask for help and advice."

She was like a sultan. She loved the people. In her own coarse way. She knew how to hold them in her power. And was like a mother to them at the same time. She was particularly anxious that the children study, all of them. She interfered in every family's private life. To make them live well as she understood the term.

The men stopped drinking. Except on holidays. And then they took turns inviting her to their homes, to have a ceremonial toast, drinking moderately, so as not to incur her wrath. In one family, she chased out the drunkard husband, who went to the city to work. She put the eldest son, Vitas Adomaitis, a fine fellow, in charge. He was a demobilized soldier, and he became the master for his mother and sisters.

Algis had written about that story for his paper. It had gotten many approving letters as an example of true socialist restructuring of the peasant family.

Since then, Saulene protected that family and loved Vitas as a son. That's why she insisted, even though he was too old, that he go to school. She dreamed of sending him to the university one day. To help the family along, she gave him the night watchman job, so that he would be free to study in the daytime.

Vitas was a tall, thin boy, with no outstanding features. He wore his old uniform to save money on clothes. He followed Saulene around like a calf, and Algis often saw him at her house, where he helped her as he would have his own mother.

This was the new Lithuania, and Algis sought out every aspect of it, gathered it in his travels around the countryside, feeling, quite rightly, that he had had a hand in it and that it had not been for naught. A peaceful life with no major problems painted itself for the future. Blood, an excess of blood, had washed away the problems. The evening, the sleeping quiet homes, the heady smell of clover all made Algis think along those terms.

He wandered down the road, away from the village. The clover fields stretched all the way to the station. It was quiet and deserted. The only living thing was a one-horned cow, set to pasture in the clover. Once in a while it snorted and its bell would ring. Algis smiled as he thought that Vitas, the night watchman, was in another field, or perhaps had not even started his rounds, and somebody—it wasn't that easy to change people—had set his cow to pasture on the kolkhoz clover.

He walked on. He could make out the station house and the line of telegraph poles. He heard a low whistle. Drawn out. He used to whistle like that when he was a child, two fingers in his mouth.

He looked around and saw the silhouette of a horse and rider in front of a dark little house. The rider was whistling. Shrill and demanding. Standing in the stirrups and his fingers in his mouth. Algis could see only the man's outline in the bright moonlight. He knew almost everyone in the area and would recognize him if he could see his features.

The rider lowered his hand and listened. He was concentrating on the dark house, but there was no answering sound. He whistled again—short, impatient. He listened.

A slender figure separated from the house and ran springily through the clover toward him. The rider dismounted and waited, holding the horse's reins.

Algis felt uncomfortable, being an unwitting witness to a lovers' rendezvous; the two certainly did not wish to be observed. Yet something compelled him to sit down and hide in the clover. He was instantly soaked to his shoulders. He wanted to see who they were. An artist's need. He wasn't planning to expose them or himself.

The silhouettes of the rider and the girl met. He put his arm around her shoulder. He was a head taller than she was. And they went off. Through the clover, each step bringing them closer to Algis' hiding place. The horse stood still for a moment, turned its head, and then followed behind, as it must have done many times.

The fused silhouette of the pair neared Algis and he could hear the swishy sound of clover being parted. There was nowhere to go, and Algis hunched down even more.

The moonlight caught the brass buttons on the lad's shoulders —and Algis realized, without seeing his face, that it was Vitas Adomaitis the night watchman, Ona Saulene's favorite. And the girl, Algis saw when they walked a few feet from him, was none other than Danute, the girl who had tried to sell milk to the passengers at the station.

There was nothing unusual in what he saw. A village romance as old as the hills. Touching in its simplicity and ingenuousness, which is not always available to urban dwellers. And with a smattering of healthy romanticism. Moon, mist, stallion, whistling in the night, a girl running to her assignation through the wet clover.

Her skirt must be soaked, Algis thought with a smile. Even though he was still young, Algis was a married man and felt he could be condescending and paternal toward the scene he was witnessing. The fact that Vitas was not carrying out his duties as night watchman was not so bad. It happens to everyone once in a while. The fellow was combining business with pleasure. Whether he was with Danute or not—he was still in the field where he was supposed to be.

The moon was shining on their backs, reflected in the horse's glossy croup. The horse followed obediently. Algis stood, brushed the mud from his pants, and went on toward the station, in the opposite direction from the young people.

He came back along the same road an hour later. He passed the dark house that Danute had come out of and the turn in the road where the cow had been grazing. It was gone. It was very late, and Algis hurried, knowing that Ona Saulene would not go to sleep until he was back safely.

The peacock's raucous call let him know he was close to the house. The window was lit, and a broad swatch of light fell from the open door onto the porch. Someone was in the yard. Several people. Algis heard their voices from a distance and thought that Saulene had guests. He moved out quietly from behind the shed and stopped in its shadow. Ona Saulene was sitting in the yard in an old armchair with an ornately carved high back and worn tapestry covers. The light fell from the house behind her. She was sitting heavily, like a sack, her head bare. A tired, dispassionate look was on her face.

A scrawny old woman, half Ona Saulene's size, was kneeling before her. She looked pleadingly into Saulene's face, trying to catch her eye, but Ona knit her brows and avoided contact with the old woman. Her skirt was spread on the ground and only her bare feet showed; the skin was deeply cracked and the toes were bent out of shape.

Further back, half in the shadow of the shed, stood the watchman's harnessed horse, jerking its head and warily eyeing the calm black and white cow, chewing her cud, a long thread of saliva stretching from her lips to the ground. A chain glistened in the moonlight from her only horn.

Vitas Adomaitis, long-necked, his bulging Adam's apple sticking out over the military collar of his jacket with brass buttons on the shoulders, stood like a soldier between the horse and the cow. The other end of the chain was in his hand. He looked up at Ona Saulene guiltily, without blinking. Danute's rumpled hair showed over the cow's humped back. Her angry, unforgiving eyes flickered under her knit brows and Algis could see under the cow's stomach how she shifted from one bare foot to the other.

The picture was completed by the two peacocks, who looked like turkeys in the dark, fluffed up on the shed roof. They let out piercing calls from time to time.

The old woman was crying, snuffling, her clasped hands moving in time with her sobs.

"Don't ruin us, Ona . . . Forgive me, the devil made me . . ."

"I've forgiven you before. No more." Saulene spoke through clenched teeth, without looking at her.

"It happens to everyone . . . Please return the cow . . ."

"No."

"I'll starve . . . so will my daughter . . . Have pity."

"And who'll pity me?" Saulene asked hoarsely, with concealed hurt. "You? You have no conscience, Petronele . . . And you never will. It's finished. You are my enemy."

"Me? Have fear of God, Ona. How can I be your enemy? We were girl friends throughout our youth. Have you forgotten? The way I kneel before you now, we both knelt, bending our backs, callusing our knees before the master. You can't have forgotten?"

"I forget nothing. Don't try to crawl into my soul."

"Why are you killing me?"

"Listen, Petronele," Ona said, resting her hands on her lap and leaning forward. "Don't try to get my pity. I've told you many times . . . you didn't listen. You wouldn't join the kolkhoz, that was your choice. But I will not allow you to rob us, to poison our clover at night."

"What then can I do?" Petronele asked, wringing her hands. "You took away our last piece of land. Where can my cow graze? On the roof? We'll die without the cow."

"That's your problem. The clover is ours, keep your hands off. I won't return your cow! If you pay the fine, you'll remember and won't go into other people's things the next time."

"How can I pay the fine? I don't have anything, you can turn me inside out. We'll die . . ."

Petronele started bawling and fell face forward onto the ground, and crawled toward Saulene to kiss her bare feet.

"Spare me, don't kill me . . ."

Saulene shivered in disgust and, bending over heavily, pushed Petronele's head away from her feet.

"That's all. The conversation is over." She was breathing hard, trying to get up from the armchair. "Vitas, you son of a bitch! What are you standing around for? Take the cow and lock her up!"

Vitas shuddered, turned to the cow, and, trying to avoid Danute's eyes, wound the chain around his hand. Danute glared at him, grabbed the cow's horn with both hands and pulled.

"What's holding you up? Afraid of a girl?" Saulene taunted.

Vitas jerked the chain and the cow turned toward him. Danute let go of the horn. She put her hands on the cow's neck, leaned over, and spat in his face.

"That's for you. You kolkhoz bastard!"

She leaped onto the porch and bent over her prostrate mother.

"Get up! Why are you lying at her feet like a dog? She'll pay for all our tears, the viper. Get up. We won't die. They'll all kick off first."

The peacocks shrieked from the roof and the cow mooed in surprise when Vitas led her toward the shed.

"Oh, they've killed us, they've robbed us," Petronele repeated over and over. "What's going on, good people?"

"Choke, you old toad!" Danute spat out the words in Saulene's face. "You'll die alone, like an old witch! Nobody'll give you any water!"

She picked up her mother's shawl, hugged her thin, shivering shoulders, and led her home. Algis shrank behind the corner to avoid running into them.

He came out of the shadows, helped Ona out of the chair, and brought it inside. Vitas came to the house, guiltily standing in the doorway.

"A lover," Saulene smirked. "I entrusted him with that work, and some snotty girl twists him around her finger. A soldier! A Komsomol member! Almost traded in his honor for a skirt."

"But, as soon . . . as I saw," Vitas muttered, "I brought the cow over immediately."

"Found yourself the perfect mate," Saulene yelled, venting her spleen on him. "Aren't there enough girls in the kolkhoz? Where do you go looking? Among the class enemy?"

"What kind of enemy is she?" Vitas began timidly, but Saulene interrupted.

"The enemy! Yours and mine! Everybody's! You're a young fool. A Communist can't sit around and drool. Do you understand? I wouldn't spare my own sister!"

Saulene fell back against the wall, closing her eyes, as though the light from the lamp bothered her, and rubbed her chest with her hand.

"It hurts, damn it all."

And weakly waved Vitas away.

"Go."

Algis' mood was spoiled. He did not feel like eating. And Saulene did not offer supper anyway, forgetting about the hare she had bagged. She went to bed behind the screen, tossing and moaning. He did not go to bed, even though he could have gotten some sleep before the train. He sat at the old dried table scraped white, listening to the ticking of the ancient wall clock with its greened brass weights. He put his things into his beat-up suitcase and decided to wait for the train at the station.

His steps in the yard awakened the peacocks, and their harsh cries made him start.

The sandy road had darkened from the dew, and the fog had settled on the clover, as thick as white snow. The moon was high. It was as light as day.

He recognized the small dark hut from afar. It stood on the edge of the field without a single light. What were Danute and her mother doing there now? Not sleeping, of course. Lying in the dark, cursing Saulene.

The house under its sagging, crooked roof attracted his gaze despite himself, and Algis had the vague sensation that he too was to blame somehow for their misfortune. They were huddled alone with their grief in the dark. He could not reproach Saulene for anything. She was right according to her truths. They were cruel and hard, and would keep her awake till morning. Life had separated the former girl friends, set them against each other like blood enemies. Two miserable women, with the same widow's fate.

A meek, faltering whistle distracted him. Not far from the house, shoulder-deep in the fog, stood the stallion and its rider. Vitas was staring at the house and whistling—pitifully, pathetically, as though begging for forgiveness.

It was quiet in the house. The stork in the flat nest on the roof moved around grumpily and stood to stretch its long, twiggy legs.

The rider whistled again. Hopelessly, like a puppy's whimpering. The door flew open and Petronele, fully dressed, rushed out onto the porch.

"So, you're whistling? Go whistle up your mistress' ass! And don't show your face around here! Get lost! Go find yourself a kolkhoz bitch!"

His horse stamped its feet and jangled its bridle, but Vitas had no intention of leaving. He accepted the woman's curses meekly, without a word. Then he whistled once more, loud and long.

And Algis saw the window open and a girlish figure crouch on the windowsill and jump down.

The rider whistled ceaselessly, while old Petronele, out of breath, quieted down. She said nothing when she saw Danute's head and shoulders floating above the fog in the moonlight, heading through the wet clover toward Vitas.

Algis watched no more, and went on to the station smiling stupidly and shaking his head. He felt light-headed and happy. He was so full of pleasant thoughts that he did not notice time fly or the train pull into the station, letting off steam, the black cuckoo engine in front.

It turned out that he never returned to those parts again. He became famous after his second book of poetry, left the paper, and had no reason for going that way. He found out what had happened to Ona Saulene, Vitas Adomaitis, and Danute, and Petronele from his former colleagues.

Saulene lost power. It could not have been any other way with her uneven temper and her concept of justice. She clashed with the district authorities like a brood hen defending her eggs, and she was disposed of like a used, obsolete thing.

The farm mentality, fair in its own way, of this peasant woman had to come to disagree with the hard-and-fast rules of Soviet power. She made all the deliveries to the government that were required of the kolkhoz, and before anyone else in the district. The rest she put away, dreaming of building new houses for everybody, a clubhouse, a school.

But the state never had enough. The stronger kolkhozes had to make up the deficit of the poor ones, and thus go bankrupt like the rest.

They demanded a second large payment from Ona Saulene. They hinted that she was running a kulak den instead of a collective farm and that it would be a good idea to break it up. Saulene beat up the secretary of the district committee for those words and flatly refused to pay for the drunkards and sloths who could not make their payments. They put her in jail for hooliganism, took away her Party card, and fired her from the chairmanship of the kolkhoz.

They shipped out everything that she had been saving over the years in her granaries and set up a new director, a drinking, evil man, who kowtowed to the authorities. They destroyed what she had devoted her life to. The young people started running away to the city, including Vitas and Danute. People worked without eagerness and started to pilfer and cheat. The men took up drinking again.

They took away Ona Saulene's house, which had belonged to a kulak, and she headed for the station, empty-handed, meaning to go wherever her eyes landed. But she did not leave. She had no one close to her in the entire world.

Petronele, Danute's mother, gave Ona a place to live. They made up in their old age and live together, seeing no one, like lepers. They make moonshine, secretly from the police, sell it to passengers in milk cans, and drink it themselves now and again. They spend the long evenings in their dark little house, and their long sad songs can be heard down at the station.

People also say that they take their one-horned cow, the same one, to graze in the kolkhoz clover. They have never been caught, because there is no night watchman. And no one wants to tangle with two old women whose only means of support is the cow, which keeps them from dying before their time.

And now that same Danute was lowering her unkempt, rumpled head at Algis from the upper berth of his compartment. The same upturned little nose and eyes as gray as the Lithuanian sky. Only her name was Sigita and not Danute. And almost twenty years had passed since those days. The real Danute must surely have children by now, and maybe a girl—the same age as Sigita. Could Sigita be the daughter of Vitas and Danute? He had to find out her surname. Life is stranger than fiction. The most feverish brain could not invent what life can throw your way.

How about the Komsomol button on the lapel of her cheap old jacket? And two police officers taking a young girl with that button under convoy to Lithuania to stand trial and be put away behind the barbed wire of a concentration camp? Somewhere in Siberia, in the Far North? Where you can kick the bucket from the cold alone. And this was happening today in our times. The new generation, Sigita's generation, knew nothing about the past. The young people didn't know that, two decades ago, the population of Lithuania was cut in half and the Krasnoyarsk Region in Siberia was named Little Lithuania.

Hundreds and thousands of little girls with gray eyes were killed by a bullet in the back of the neck, or strangled by a noose, or sent behind barbed wire. And now? Why were they threatening her with camp? What had she done?

Algis wanted to ask the guards and Sigita herself all about it. He was so agitated that he forgot why he had returned to his compartment and with whom. When he saw Joanne's reflection in the window, he realized that he had been unforgivably rude to a foreign visitor. He rushed out of the compartment, apologizing vociferously. He took her back to the dining car, knowing that there would be no opportunity to be alone with her any more and not particularly caring.

Sigita was firmly established in his thoughts, and an artist's healthy curiosity overwhelmed him. But for the sake of politeness he had a few more drinks of cognac with Joanne in the dining car. He answered her questions, treating the experience as an interview, blathering the Party line and not worrying whether she believed him or not. She quickly realized that Algis had changed in the short period he had spent in his compartment and that he was looking for an excuse to get rid of her and return. Joanne was not offended, she wrote it down to the emotionality and inconsistency of the artistic personality. At an appropriate moment she got up, bid him good night, complaining of tiredness, and asked him not to walk her to her compartment. She did not want to arouse the suspicions of her Intourist guide.

Algis returned to his car. Both policemen were waiting for him in the corridor by the open door of the compartment. Each would look in once in a while. Sigita was lying on the top left berth with her back to them. She had not removed her shoes, and the soles of the boy's half-boots she was wearing hung over the edge. The cops were wearing civilian jackets and even ties. But the matching jodhpurs with the light blue piping and the heavy boots left no doubt as to their profession. They introduced themselves to Algis, shaking hands firmly and moving away from the door. The older officer, the shorter one, was First Lieutenant Gaidialis of the Kaunas police force. He had an anxious peasant face tinged with yellow and prematurely wrinkled, witness to his difficult life and long-standing stomach problems, perhaps an ulcer. The other one, Dausa, was some ten years younger and a captain. He was better educated and had more social graces. Perhaps because he had spent most of his life in the city and had quickly risen in the force. That just increased his self-confidence and developed his condescending attitude toward others. He was strong and wiry. He was cheery, and it was clear from the first look that no assignment away from home and family depressed him. On the contrary, he reveled in them.

He took it upon himself to fill Algis in on the passenger they were accompanying to Kaunas.

"A simple thief," Dausa explained, motioning Algis away from the door. "Village girl. Worked in Kaunas as a domestic. In a decent family. According to our information they treated her like one of the family. Didn't skimp on food or clothing. But no matter how much you feed a wolf, he still looks only toward—as we all know—the woods. One day she stole five hundred rubles and left town. So we're taking her back to be tried. You should be informed of the situation since you're sharing the compartment. If anything comes up, we'll work together."

"You think she'll try to escape?" Algis said in surprise.

"She won't go anywhere," Dausa laughed, patting his hip, where he must have had a pistol.

"Here's the situation, comrade," interrupted Gaidialis, wincing from his own cigarette smoke. "Don't be afraid. Everything will be all right. But just in case . . . Anything can happen . . She's got spunk. There's a suicide attempt on her record. Poison. We picked her up at the hospital. So you have to treat her carefully . . . She may try something else. She's got the mind of a child. Not even seventeen yet. My daughter's age."

Algis sensed definite compassion and pity for the girl in the guard's voice. Something unusual in guards, and certainly never expressed. It made him like Gaidialis.

"Let's go into the compartment," Dausa said, laughing. "She's riding in comfort, and we're like the poor relations huddled in the hall."

They went in, closing the door behind them, and sat on the lower berths, carefully moving the bedclothes. Sigita was either asleep or feigning it, and her half-boots still hung over the berth.

The policemen were flattered to be traveling with Algirdas Požera and they did not miss the opportunity to discuss literature with the famous poet. They gave their opinions, which were the opinions of the people who, the Party press had taught them, were the most refined critics of the arts. Algis sat through the usual banalities indispensable to any readers' conference. They were verbalized by Dausa. Gaidialis said nothing, breathing with his charred lungs and chain-smoking.

In order to get away from the obnoxious Dausa, Algis asked Gaidialis if he had served in the strike battalions of the late forties in the struggle against banditry. Gaidialis nodded. The conversation's direction changed. Algis and Gaidialis exchanged memories of those years. Dausa was forced to listen enviously. He was too young to have participated.

It turned out that their paths had crossed several times, and they remembered more than one operation that they had both participated in, without knowing each other. Gaidialis perked up and his eyes, dull and withdrawn until then, brightened with youth.

"Ah, those were the days," he said, shaking his head, gray and balding. "It was terrible, God forbid, but it left something pure in my soul. I even miss it sometimes . . ."

"It's not the horror you miss," Algis said smiling. "It's your youth. We were in our twenties then."

"You're right," he agreed. "I was strong . . . and then I took two bullets . . . and they cut out half my stomach . . . and I signed up into old age immediately. Time to retire and baby-sit with the grandchildren. I don't have grandchildren. But I could be a grandfather to my own kids."

He smiled shyly and sadly at Algis.

"You were luckier. You became a writer, everybody knows your name . . . And I'll just drag on until I die. The bandit didn't finish me off, so some criminal will knife me in the ribs."

"Tell me, Gaidialis," Algis asked, "how many were there in your battalion?"

"It depended," he replied, taking a drag on his cigarette. "Sometimes half a thousand, sometimes a thousand. We would lose a lot of people after major operations."

"No, I mean after the fighting was over. How many bayonets were left then?"

"You mean in 1951? Who can remember?"

"I was doing other things then and don't know how it really was." That loosened the guard's tongue.

"Just like they told it. We beat them, the Green Brotherhood. What's to tell? You must remember, whole districts were empty, without any inhabitants. And our side lost countless numbers, too. I didn't expect to get out alive. In other words, Lithuania was burning and if it had gone on a little longer, there would have been no one left at all. But one wise man managed to out-smart everyone. Do you remember who the chairman of the Council of Ministers was then?"

"Gedvilas." Algis replied without hesitation.

"Right." Gaidialis nodded. "It was Gedvilas. He figured it all out. He had planes fly over the forests, dropping leaflets. All over Lithuania. This is the way things are. Whoever comes to the collection points with his gun in his hands and turns it over without resistance will get amnesty. Get your passport and go wherever you please as a full-fledged citizen. The motherland has forgiven all your sins and will never throw them up in your face.

"We Lithuanians are trusting people. And the men crawled out of their bunkers, dragging their arms, whole arsenals—even cannons. Twenty thousand came out of the forests—everyone who was still alive in '51. Except, of course, for the chiefs. They hid and are still missing to this day.

"They laid down their arms and got their passports. Well, now we can go home, they thought. The war is over. But, they're told, it's too early to go home. What do you mean? You promised that we would be full-fledged citizens. That's right, we promised. Then why can't we go home? Because, they were told, as full-fledged citizens it is your duty to join the Soviet army. Many had passed their recruitment time while they were in the woods. So they had to fulfill their civic duty. They were enlisted all right, but they did not get guns. They were called construction battalions. You heard of 'em? They went off to Siberia to build Communism. I haven't met any who came back."

Dausa, who naturally considered himself politically more mature than Gaidialis, thought these words were careless. He put his finger to his lips and looked at Sigita. Algis also looked up. Her back was to them, but Algis could have sworn that she was not asleep. She was listening intently to every word that floated up to her. He wanted to talk to her. Everything that Dausa had said about her did not seem to go with her face and image. He wanted to hear her version, her confession, to understand what would lead this creature, so innocent at first glance, to commit a crime. And to attempt suicide . . .

He decided to look for an opportunity to have a tête-à-tête with her. Without witnesses.

Gaidialis droned on, paying no heed to Dausa's warning. He was flattered that a famous writer was listening to him with sincere interest.

"Basically, everything was over. Peace came to Lithuania. In May 1951. The Green Brotherhood was shipped off to Siberia. A few were left as decoys, and were allowed to come up in the world. One former bandit, I recall, drove a tractor in a kolkhoz. In Pasvalis, I think. He even got the Order of Lenin. That's a joke. It was obviously propaganda. The others disappeared. In Siberia.

"The authorities thought: the problem is solved, we can rest. But that's not how it was. The bandits were gone. But not the Lithuanian fighter forces who fought on the side of the Communists. What were they supposed to do? They were young, and had no professional training. They were used to living for free, without work. They had food and drink—they took it from the people. If they encountered resistance, they threatened with a machine gun or a hand grenade. It was robbery. And they had lived that way for five or six years.

"They weren't regular people any more. They were a criminal element. Even though they were considered Communists and Komsomol members. Their uniforms and guns were taken away. They didn't like that. They ran off with the arms. Into the same woods where the bandits used to hide from them. They took over. Robbing warehouses and stores. Lithuania was embattled again. They had to send in the troops. Shot them down like dogs. Worse than the Forest Brotherhood. When they finally wiped out the fighters, then there really was peace in Lithuania."

Gaidialis enclosed himself in a cloud of smoke and smiled at his own thoughts.

"Do you want to know how I survived? Easy. I was in the hospital. Wounded."

Gaidialis' words smelled of that horrible, fiery time, and Algis, as he listened, clearly pictured himself in those days . . .

The district committee of the Party was located in a two-story stone building right beyond the church gates, surrounded by old, thick lindens, and their heavy crowns hung over the tile roof. The church warden used to live in this cozy villa, but he had been exiled to Siberia right after the war, and the priest who replaced him, a frightened little man, gladly agreed to move into the shed behind the church.

Typewriters clattered all day at the committee office. Horses of the committee instructors whinnied and neighed by the granite cross out front that served as a hitching post. The instructors, carrying innumerable machine guns and hand grenades, traveled from farm to farm throughout the forested district. The deep sighs of the church organ meekly floated out over the damp earth, sprinkled with yellow linden leaves and pockmarked with hoofprints.

A cold fine rain was falling. Pedestrians quickly disappeared from the few streets of the tiny hamlet. A candle sputtered in the window of an occasional low, damp house. The occupants went to bed early, to sleep fitfully, never knowing what waking up would bring. The arrival of the police looking for a still. The stamp of armed men who give you an hour to pack your things (no more than sixty kilos) and proceed to the station to the cold freight cars that only know the way to one place—Siberia.

The stillness of the night would be broken by single shots and machine-gun rounds, which would make the windowpanes ring. Footsteps running down the street. A hoarse Russian curse. Then silence. Only the rain's whisper in the naked branches and the nervous grumbling of dogs in their kennels. People in their houses would snuggle deeper into their comforters and fall asleep with their hearts racing.

The only lighted windows were at the Party headquarters. Lights were blazing in both stories. Stripes of light streamed into the wet garden and the watchman, armed and dressed in a raincoat with a hood, walked through the stripes, disappearing in the dark and reappearing in the feeble light falling from the windows.

The Party workers stayed in the committee headquarters until dawn. There was usually nothing to do, but no one had the nerve to decide to leave. What if there was a telephone call from the capital? Everybody knew that, in Moscow, Stalin was suffering from insomnia. He made most of his decisions at night. So the enormous Party apparatus throughout the land stayed awake, yawning and fighting sleep in all the offices, whose walls were decorated with large portraits of the leader who stared down at them. They all met the day with bleary, red eyes.

Algis was in the office of the first secretary. There were five of them in the room. The second secretary, the third, the propaganda secretary, and the head of the district Ministry of Internal Affairs, who wanted to see the visitor from the capital. Visitors were rare because the district was considered dangerous. A one-day stopover by a correspondent from Vilnius was an event.

Algis was the youngest man in the group, but they all respected him, an artist, a man from a different world, and they tried to choose their words carefully in conversation so as not to appear provincial. All the district bigwigs were there, every man's fate in the district depended on them, but at night they did not seem particularly awesome. They reminded Algis of boring patients, gathered in a ward because they had the same boring disease. The faces were puffy from moonshine. They had dull, mindless expressions and matching greenish suits with a semi-military cut in imitation of Stalin.

The office looked like the dozens of offices in other district headquarters that Algis had visited in his travels around Lithuania. A large glass-covered desk and another one, covered in green baize, set perpendicularly in a T-shape for conferences. Stalin's portrait on the wall. A metal fireproof file cabinet in the corner. A wooden bookcase, stuffed with red sets of the works of Stalin and Lenin, graying from the dust of disuse. They were a required touch in every office.

Algis sat in the director's chair behind the desk. The first secretary himself and his colleagues were in the chairs around the green table. Business was finished. Algis' notebook was crammed with figures and names they had given him. He was researching education in the political enlightenment network. The figures the propaganda secretary had given him without blinking were inflated. Algis knew that. And they knew that he knew and were glad that he was a regular fellow who preferred to take them at their word rather than go check up, following the wet roads to the cold damp farmhouses, from which there was no guarantee of return.

The whole system of political enlightenment boiled down to groups who met to study a short biography of Stalin. Nothing more. The account the propaganda secretary gave him showed that almost all the adults of the district attended these meetings. The population had thinned out considerably with the latest deportation to Siberia. It seemed an unreal figure, but everything there seemed unreal, and he did not want to pursue it. He only wanted to get some sleep and then get out of there.

They were talking away, happy that their visitor had decided to spend the night there and not at a hotel. It would not be as boring as usual and there would be an opportunity to hear something new. They spoke a strange language that only remotely resembled Lithuanian. They expressed their thoughts in newspaperese, which they had picked up from reading newspaper editorials. Their basic reading. The formulas in the papers were literal translations of the Russian, borrowed from the central newspapers. Algis was saddened by imagining what these people would sound like in five or ten years, if they were not shot. They would completely lose the ability to speak like humans, and communication with them would become impossible.

The first secretary praised Algis' poetry, which had recently been published in the paper, called the verses "actual" with a "high ideo-artistic level," and said that they were an aid in the "struggle in the collectivization of agriculture." He added that his small son had memorized them, and that Algis could hear his recitation if he would only stay on another day. The propaganda secretary also tried to butter Algis up by telling him that he would require the poem to be memorized in the local school for the holiday, and that Algis must definitely come to hear the recitations, and while he was at it, write an article about the teachers, who were very active in the network of Party and political enlightenment.

Algis was uncomfortable. He was about to say good night and go into the next office to nap on the couch until morning, when there was a knock. The watchman appeared in the doorway in his soaking raincoat. His gun was wet, too. Everyone turned to him in irritation.

"Permit me to report," the watchman said with a guilty snicker. "There is . . . a woman here . . . with children . . . who insists on seeing you. I told her it was impossible . . . she put up a fight . . ."

"Throw her out," the first secretary cut him off. "That's why you have a gun . . . Don't bother me with trifles . . ."

"But she's with kids . . . in the rain. She came far . . ." he offered lamely.

"It's obvious that you have forgotten regulations," the director of the Internal Affairs Ministry interrupted. "Watchmen on duty do not enter into the conversations. Close the door."

"Wait," said Algis. "It's really pouring out there. Maybe it's something important. She wouldn't drag the kids for nothing."

The first secretary made a face and gave the guard a severe look.

"Who is she? Did you ask?"

"Bratkauskiene," he answered guiltily. "From Geguchai."

"A familiar bird," the Internal Affairs man said gleefully, smoothing his shaved skull with his hand. He winked at Algis. "Maybe she's come round. Let her in."

The guard shut the door, and they all began explaining who

this Bratkauskiene was. According to them, she was a monster, one of the fiercest enemies of the Soviet state. She lived on a farm ten kilometers outside the district capital. Wouldn't join the kolkhoz. Of course, she had almost no land. And what she did have was all clay. Poverty-stricken. And taxed to death. But the problem was not with her; it was her husband. The authorities had been hunting him for three years, all in vain. Pranas Bratkauskas hid in the woods, a commander of a regiment of the Green Brotherhood. A violent, horrible animal. Several activists' slit throats to his credit. Escaped every trap set for him.

I'm using new tactics on him," the Internal Affairs director confided to Algis, his eyes gleaming with a hunter's cleverness. "We know for a fact that every two or three months he drops by his farm. He's human, even if he is a bandit. Changes his underwear, sees his kids, spends time in the sack with his wife. Can't do without it. That viper loves his wife. We know for a fact. So that's where we should get him.

"We set up a trap at his farm. Ten of the best men. They spend weeks there. She has to feed them . . . and . . . all the rest."

He saw that Algis did not understand, and so he explained.

"The men are young, and she's in her prime. They take her every night. They know how to do that. And, why not? She's an enemy. Let her know the wrath of the people."

He laughed. When he saw the displeasure in the first secretary's eyes, he quickly added:

"But that's not for the paper. Why hide it from one of our own? Man talk. So the troops live with her until they are needed somewhere else. Then he comes to the farm. We know that. Let him be pleased with his wife. Then we send in more troops. That's the game. For a year now. See who has more patience."

He turned to the door. There were footsteps outside.

Bratkauskiene turned out to be a very unattractive young woman. With faded looks. Algis looked at her closely and real-

124

ized that she must have been good-looking once, but now she created an unpleasant, repugnant impression.

Wet hair plastered to her face, colorless, expressionless round eyes, and drenched clothes that looked like dark rags. Two frightened, wet children were holding on to her skirt on either side. The skirt was dripping puddles on the floor.

Something about her made everyone cautious. At first no one noticed the dark, wet package she held under her arm.

She said nothing, but stared ahead at a point above Algis' head. Her frozen straining eyes made them uncomfortable. No one said a word. A chair squeaked under someone.

The sound brought her out of the trance. She placed her hands on the package, which turned out to be a sack containing something round, like a head of cabbage. Holding the sack in her outstretched arms, she moved toward the desk, and the children, holding her skirt, followed. She was headed for Algis, thinking he was the leader since he was sitting at the desk. Algis tensed, anticipating something horrible and not knowing how to avert it.

With a strange detachment the woman began to unwrap the package over the desk. The water silently dripping on the thick glass was reddish. She shook the sack, and a man's head fell with a loud thump onto the glass. He had not had a haircut or a shave in a long time.

Algis shuddered. The head bounced on the desk, turned on its axis and rolled toward the edge. The white vein stuck out from the stump of the neck like a tube.

"Take it," the woman said calmly. There was only exhaustion on her face. "That is my husband and their father."

The children did not take their eyes off the hairy head with the unnaturally white ears. They did not cry; they snuffled rheumily.

"Bratkauskas!" shouted the Internal Affairs director, bending over the head and even touching it. "Pranas Bratkauskas in our hands."

"Now take us away . . . somewhere," the woman said. "Or they'll kill us."

"We'll help you, Bratkauskiene," he told her, his face bright. Reflections from the lamp shone on his skull. "We'll hide you so that they'll never find you. We'll take care of everything. You'll get the thanks you deserve."

"The children are sleepy." She closed her own eyes.

"Right away. Guard, take them into the next office. There are couches there. See you in the morning. Good night. You did well, woman."

She moved with the children toward the door, held open by the respectful guard. At the threshold the boy, who was on the right, looked back at the severed head on the glass top of the desk and sobbed meekly. The mother jerked his arm. The guard, backing out of the door, shut it.

"To our victory, comrades!" the director congratulated them. "There'll be a hullabaloo tomorrow! We have to prepare a telegram. Give me the material evidence!"

He shook out all the papers from his roomy brief case and took the head off the table without a trace of fastidiousness. He wrapped it in newspaper. Algis caught part of a headline: "Long live the Commun . . ." The director shoved the package into his case and shut the lock on the bulging side.

"Bratkauskiene goes to Siberia." He was out of breath. He sat on the couch, the brief case at his feet. "There's nothing more for her to do here."

The men began speaking in agitation, congratulating the director, forgetting or overlooking the horrible brief case by his foot. They forgot about Algis, who sat perfectly still, leaning back in the armchair, staring dully at the reddish puddle that was dripping from the glass onto his lap.

It was night, dark and frosty, outside the windows. The train stopped and the passengers were told they would spend twenty

126

minutes in Smolensk. The policemen jumped up and dressed, hoping to have enough time for some supper at the station. They knew the dining car was closed because of the foreign tourists. As they left, they made signs to Algis not to leave the compartment and to watch Sigita until their return. Algis gave them some money and asked them to bring him a bottle of cognac.

They left, closing the door, and Sigita up in the berth immediately turned over. She turned, looked down at Algis severely with her gray eyes, and threw down a piece of paper folded in four. As soon as she was sure that he had the note, she turned her face back to the wall and froze in her former position.

Algis held the note for a second and opened it. She wrote in an unsteady schoolgirl hand. No grammatical mistakes, except in punctuation.

Greetings my beloved poet!

I decided to write because I am too shy to tell you. You may laugh at me, but I am writing the truth straight from my heart. I love you. For a long time. As soon as I learned to read and the first time I saw your picture. The older I got, the surer I was that you were my ideal. My ideal man and citizen.

I know that you will laugh reading my note. Go ahead! Now that my life is ruined I have nothing to fear. There is no shame in confessing love.

I am sure that THEY told you about me. It is all lies. I am an honest person. I never took anything that did not belong to me. You can believe me. And if you don't, go to our kolkhoz and ask people about me there.

My life is lost in my youth. But I am happy that I got to meet you and tell you that I love you. My name is not Sigita. It's Aldona. I made up a name for them, but I'm telling you the truth.

Farewell.

I wish you success in your personal life and in your work for the good of our Soviet people.

Algis crumpled the note in his fist and felt tears stinging his eyes. The clumsy, naïve child's note gave off an amazing purity. A horrifying injustice had befallen a simple creature, defenseless and meekly accepting her fate. That touching confession of love cost her a lot. Algis was ready to cry. He had to do something fast. Tell her something, ask her something, find out more and then make a plan. Algis had no doubt that he would do something to help her. He had to call her down from the berth and get all the details. How should he address her? As Aldona or Sigita?

"Come on down, Aldona-Sigita," he called, trying to calm himself and smiling because he used both names.

She turned abruptly, like a wound spring. She had been waiting for him to call. She leaped down and sat opposite him, smoothing out her skirt over her knees. She looked up. Her eyes were full of tears.

"Just don't laugh."

"Don't be absurd. Who's laughing at you?" Algis reached out for her shoulder, to stroke her and soothe her. She jumped back, flattening herself against the wall. Angry sparks shone in her eyes.

"There, now, you see, I don't know how to behave around you. I'm old enough to be your father, why are you afraid of me? Tell me everything before they come back. Like at confession. It's very important. Understand? I'll try to help you . . . Everything that I can do. So tell me everything. Talk. I'm listening."

Here is what she told Algis, rushing and stuttering, afraid that he would tire of the story and that he would not understand the essence, what words can't express, what you have to feel.

She was born and had lived her entire short life until very recently in a small village near Zarasai, in a region of countless lakes and sandy hills. As long as she could remember, her mother always worked in the kolkhoz milking cows. Sigita, like her friends, lived in a world bounded by the hills and it was only when she learned to read that she discovered that the world was big and that it had cities and oceans the likes of which nobody in their village had ever seen.

There were big roads, not like the dusty back roads of their district, but wide ones, paved with black asphalt, that circled the globe. Cars ran along them to all ends of the earth. Her dream was to become a chauffeur and drive one of those cars. She studied in school, ran the house while her mother was at work, and read, read, read. Every spare second. At night until the first roosters crowed. She read everything she could get her hands on. But she particularly loved the poetry of Algirdas Požera—the romantic poet of the fighting Komsomol youth, who called upon them to be brave, steadfast, and to meet challenges head on.

Sigita knew Algis' long narrative poems by heart. His picture, a handsome, willful profile, cut out of a book, hung over her bed. Every book of his published in Lithuania stood on the shelf she had built for them.

Reading his fiery verses, the girl was transported to the times described by the poet and fought alongside the hero with the kulaks, died from a bandit's bullet, and built kolkhozes—the harbingers of a happy life. And when she tore herself away from his books and looked around, all she saw was her dull, gray quotidian life and cried that she was born so late, after all the battles were won. Her only hope was the wind of wanderlust, the beckoning road to the unknown.

Sigita ran away from the village to Kaunas to take driver's training, but she was only sixteen and a half. Six months to wait for admission. She did not want to go home, so in order to kill time until she was seventeen, Sigita took a maid's job in a big house on one of Kaunas' major streets. Her employers worked in a store and lived high on the hog, obviously embezzling a bit. But they treated her well, bought her some clothes, and did not hide any of the food from her. All she had to do was live through those six months, watch the child that she had come to love, and everything would have been fine. But trouble was waiting.

Sigita had never taken anything that was not hers. That was how her mother brought her up, and that's what she had learned in books. Theft was tantamount to death for her. In all her seventeen years, it had never occurred to Sigita to steal anything, even though they were poor and every penny counted. And then fate tempted her.

One morning, after the parents had left for work, and the child was fed and asleep, Sigita was cleaning the bedroom. She shook out the eiderdown, fluffed the pillows, and suddenly saw bonds on the floor that had fallen out of the pillowcases. Hundred-ruble notes. Five bonds. Sigita quickly picked them up from the carpet and folded them. They burned her hands. She had never seen or touched that much money in her life.

Her heart beating wildly, Sigita stood in the middle of the room with the money pressed to her breast. Pictures of the exotic, mysterious places she could visit right now, by simply buying a ticket, swam before her eyes. And she would have plenty of money left over for other trips and other roads. All of her dreams, her fate, were in those five pieces of paper.

Sigita had only a blurred memory of leaving the house, not even taking any of her things, just locking the door and leaving the key under the mat, of buying a ticket on the first train that came along, which raced through the country all day and all night and let her off in the Ukraine in a strange and foreign city, where no one spoke Lithuanian (and her Russian was poor). She had not yet thought of the consequences of her action, that the authorities would be looking for her. She wanted to travel and discover new worlds.

But the world did not welcome a village girl with stolen money. Where to spend the night? In a hotel? You have to present your papers. Sigita had none. All the documents she had brought from the village were in her employers' safekeeping.

Sleep on a park bench? This was not the West, where unemployed bums slept on benches under newspapers, as they showed in newsreels. The police would investigate a Soviet citizen without a place to sleep. Sigita wandered around the strange city until morning, and, tired, bought a train ticket. She rested on the train. The same thing happened in the next city. And once more, she found shelter in the train.

The girl started traveling the rails. She was afraid the police were looking for her. She scurried through the streets with her kerchief pulled low over her face. Only in the train, in her berth, turned away from her neighbors, did she find temporary peace. Cities and stations rushed past, the people in the compartments changed, and she was carried across the huge, unfamiliar country, alone and frightened, without any hope of getting off and saving herself. Her future was measured in the money she had left. She was running low.

Her money was stolen. She got out at a station to buy some food at the buffet. She took twenty rubles with her, and left the rest in her purse under her pillow. When she got back the purse and the money were gone. And the man who had been traveling with her, so proper-looking, had disappeared without a trace.

She did not even cry. She realized that the endless flight of a hunted animal was over. The train was headed for Moscow. What she had left would buy a ticket to Lithuania.

Sigita decided to die. She could not begin to imagine being arrested and tried for theft. Better to die. But not in alien Russia. Closer to Lithuania. Perhaps they would take her body to her mother and bury her in the village cemetery by the lake.

The last destination on her itinerary was Moscow. How she had dreamed of seeing it. To stroll along Red Square. To hear the melodious Kremlin Chimes, in person, holding her breath, and not on the radio. To pass in the eternally grieving line through the marble mausoleum and see the face of dead Lenin, whose profile was on the Komsomol button she wore so proudly.

The half day she spent in Moscow, between trains, was devoted to something completely different, her earlier dreams completely forgotten. Moscow became the city in which she pronounced her own death sentence and where she tried to no avail to find a way to carry it out. Of all the methods of violent death known to her child's mind, Sigita chose the simplest and most common, sung in innumerable folk songs about unrequited love. She decided to take poison.

She preferred that. It would not hurt and she would not notice that she was dying. Most poisoned people die in their sleep, and they lie in their coffins with faces undistorted by suffering, but rather transfixed with peace. "She looks alive," the neighbors would sigh when she was taken to the village for her funeral. The local photographer would take her final picture before they shut the coffin. She would look alive in that picture, but with her eyes closed, as if asleep. Her mother would hang it on the wall near the shelves with her favorite books and would look at it every day, year in and year out, until the photo faded and the features became indistinguishable.

But how could a Lithuanian girl who speaks Russian badly get poison in Moscow? You need a doctor's prescription in a pharmacy or a friend working there. Sigita remembered that her employers once bought bedbug powder in a pharmacy and warned her to be very careful with it because the tiniest dose was fatal.

She bought a package of the powder without arousing the slightest suspicions. She then went to the Belorussian station for a ticket; all the trains went in the general direction of Lithuania from there. She had only enough to get her to Smolensk—halfway there. But that did not dismay her. The important thing was to die en route to Lithuania. They would take the body home for free.

She bought a postcard at the station and sent it to her former employers in Kaunas. She asked them to forgive her, because she had never been a thief and this was the first and last dishonest act she had committed in her life. She would punish herself for it. And therefore asked them not to judge her harshly.

The change in her pocket was enough for a bottle of lemonade. She took a free table in the restaurant car, which she had entered with a pale, brave face, prepared to take the poison. She ordered the lemonade, paid the waiter, leaving her last five kopeks for a tip. She poured out half a glass, poured in the contents of the package, gulped it down, and fell on the floor. She had fainted from fright.

That's what saved her. She was removed at the very next stop and taken by the waiting ambulance to a hospital. The doctors pumped her stomach and put her in a private room under the unflagging observation of the nurses and attendants. Sigita came to, cried, and, mixing her Russian and Lithuanian words, told them everything. The staff sympathized and attempted to comfort her, telling her that she would not be tried and sent to prison. Sigita wrote to her employers from the hospital and gave them a detailed account of everything that had befallen her. She asked them not to hate her, because as soon as she got out of the hospital she would take any job so as to pay them what she owed in installments.

And Sigita thought there were kind people in Lithuania who had come to her aid. Those two, Gaidialis and Dausa. They came for her, even brought her candy, calmed and comforted her. They told her that they would get her into chauffeur classes, and that when she went to work she could pay back everything she owed.

She had been worried by the fact that Gaidialis and Dausa were wearing matching jodhpurs with blue piping. Police usually wore pants like that, but the two men convinced her that they had no connection with the police. They said they were simple Lithuanians who had been sent to Russia for her, because Lithuanians must come to one another's aid.

"If they tricked me," Sigita concluded, her eyes growing

bigger and her eyebrows meeting at the bridge of her nose, "and they put me in jail, I won't spend more than one day alive there. I don't know how, but I'll find something . . . I'll cut my throat on the barbed wire. But I will not live in dishonesty."

Algis' heart contracted from the anticipation of the catastrophe that awaited Sigita. Of course, they had tricked her so that she would not harm herself en route. The prison door would slam behind her as soon as she got to Kaunas. She would see the sky through bars.

The room felt stuffy. Algis could not breathe. He opened the window. The frosty air blew into the compartment, carrying voices from the platform and train whistles.

"Close the window." Sigita laughed. "They'll come back and be angry that we let in the cold while they were gone."

Algis closed the window and sat weakly on the couch. Sigita climbed back up to her berth. But she did not turn her back. She smiled down shyly.

What's to be done? What can I do? His brain was buzzing. How can I help her? Save her? She's no criminal. She is one of the purest creatures I've ever met.

In the final analysis, it was he, Algirdas Požera, who was responsible. It was his poetry that had helped shape her character, awakened in her a pure, romantic view of life. And life, which was not at all the way he depicted it in his poetry, had smashed her down at their first meeting. If he did not help, it could be fatal.

He had to do something. He could not leave her alone. To be destroyed. My God, it was time for him to wake up, to come out of hibernation in his sated, carefree, oinking life of a Soviet big shot. He was not a poet. He was an evil fraud with no conscience. His poems lulled people into settling for the filth and lies that surrounded them and led them away from a sober assessment of life. They had created Sigita, totally helpless before the flood of hypocrisy and fraud that was called Soviet life.

134

It was the fault of the schools, newspapers, radio, and television. And of him. Algirdas Požera. A classic in his lifetime, showered with excessive luxuries inaccessible to the average Soviet citizen. At first he believed in it, and then, by inertia, he tried to stay on the slippery road, singing the praises of the life that had become a nightmare for the people. And that old spider Jonas Šimkus, who survived the Siberian camps, was right a thousand times over—his poems were getting weaker with every passing year, because they were empty, no longer animated by faith, and they had begun to stink, like a corpse, of newspaper editorials.

He had been dead as a poet for a long time. And as a man, too. What had his life become? Drinking and overeating. And women. Lots of women. Their faces lost to memory. All with the same face. He sought them like an addict in need of something to still his conscience's anxious voice. He used to be honest and straightforward. He had faced death without a second thought. Because he had believed, and his faith gave birth to his first poems, praised and noted by everyone. Because they expressed the cry of his soul, romantic and honest.

And what was he now? A sated, heartless master who did not even care that everything he once worshiped was a lie. The more sensitive ones ended up badly. In Siberia. Or at home, welcome nowhere, drunk in roadhouses. He had survived. But at what price? And had he really survived if he had destroyed his soul forever?

Was it forever? Couldn't he stop, do something, save himself? Start with a small step. Save the girl. And let that be his first step to spiritual cleansing, to try to return to the sources of his life. Begin a new life. As prostitutes sometimes did when they found a man who loved them purely, without ulterior motives.

"Do you love your wife?" Sigita's voice sounded through his reverie. She was smiling down at him, waiting for an answer.

"Why do you want to know?"

135

"Because I love you and it's very important for me. I'll renounce my love if you are truly happy. I can't live a lie."

His wife. Did he love her? Had he ever loved her? Let's examine the situation. If you're going to pick at wounds—do it thoroughly.

How it all began, Algis could not recall. The district center, where he worked as a teacher at the Komsomol committee. A pile of little gray houses nestled in the sandy knolls, overrun with an evergreen forest, thinned during the war. But two or three kilometers outside town the woods were as deep as in a fairy tale, and led into such dark, secret places that mushroom and berry pickers feared to set foot there even in peacetime.

Way back in the villages in the woods, they had never heard of Soviet power. There was no power. It was the kingdom of the Forest Brotherhood. The Brothers hid deep in the woods living in secret bunkers, raiding the villages for food, a night with their wives, or for a chance to catch and publicly hang a Soviet activist.

Soviet authorities showed themselves there rarely, unexpectedly, without warning, swooping down guarded by drunken fighters armed with grenades and machine guns. They were executives from the finance section, there to collect taxes quickly, or state collectors after potatoes and meat. Or lecturers—often city intellectuals, nervous folks who read the lectures written for them at the Party committee headquarters with trembling lips to the peasants who were brought at gunpoint to the hut to listen to the boring lecture on the wonderful life that Soviet power would bring them.

The drunken guards stood outside the hut and, prompted by boredom, shot off their guns once in a while into the foggy sky or down the street. That did not add credence to the lecturer's words.

Soviet power had a stronghold only in the district center,

where the NKVD, predecessor of the KGB, and the fighter battalion were located. The battalion had several hundred men, hotheads collected from all over, always drunk because moonshine and food were free. They just took it from the locals. They were ready to serve anyone and to hang or shoot their own fathers for the free and wild life. Whatever Communists and Komsomol members there were all lived in the center too.

The Komsomol cell was made up almost entirely of high school students. Some had joined the Communist Youth League because of a romantic urge, common to young people everywhere, born of reading stimulating, inspirational Soviet books in Lithuanian translation. Others had already grasped the benefits that stemmed from having the gray Komsomol-member book with a black profile of Lenin on the cover. They were preparing to break out of their poverty into the new class of masters, with the little book as their passport.

They were not mistaken. Algis often ran into his former charges many years later in the ministries in Vilnius. They had luxurious offices and private cars. They were fat, self-confident members of the Party and state elite. Some of them hardly recognized Algis, who had nurtured them and started them on their path to this sated, comfortable life, because at the time he was only a poet, a good one, but not a famous one yet. Now, they did not take poets seriously. They condescended to him, not trying to hide the fact that their positions were more important and permanent than his. And that they, and not he, could determine his fate by promulgating any legislation they wanted.

There was still another category of Komsomol members in the district. Also high school students. Algis was unsure and suspicious of them. But they were the best behaved and hardest working. They were the sons and daughters of wealthy men—the clerks, storekeepers, and lumber merchants. That stratum of society lived in constant fear of confiscation of their last holdings and of exile to Siberia. So their children, shy and unsure, often

137

forced by their frightened parents, joined the Komsomol in high school, knowing that the membership book could be a letter of protection for the entire family.

They did not ask unnecessary questions, did their work dependably, and were the first to raise their hands whenever volunteers were needed. But when the task was completed, they retreated into their private worlds, behind the shutters of their big houses. Instead of Soviet literature, at night they read the worn books from papa's library, learning about the world that was beautiful and unknown to them, that had no Komsomol meetings, no repetitive, hackneyed speeches, or the uncontrollable fear that was constantly with them. Fear for themselves, their families. It poisoned the best time of their lives—their childhood.

Nijole Kudirkaite was one of them. Plump, with delicate white skin, and dimples. She curled the ends of her flaxed hair. She had soft, questioning gray eyes. A typical provincial young lady. In the upper grades in high school. She was a good student and would probably enter a teachers' college, as her parents hoped, and go live in a big city, where it was safer and which still had remnants of the former culture.

Her father used to be the owner of a store, which had of course been nationalized and turned into a co-operative. He worked there at a miserable salary as a salesman.

In the former life, her mother used to give private piano lessons. Now all her pupils had disappeared with their rich fathers far away into the unknown reaches of Siberia. She took care of the house, a pitiful state compared to their former life-style, but not so bad because they had managed to hide some of their savings. They kept their family budget at a decent level, hidden from prying eyes.

Nijole was one of the many young people that Algis inducted into the Komsomol with a long speech—always the same, but inspired nevertheless—handed a membership card, and wished success in the struggle for the holy work of Lenin and Stalin.

The only thing he remembered about her was the roar of laughter that filled the rowdy room in the Komsomol headquarters when Nijole, pink with nervousness, took the gray booklet from Algis with the tips of her white fingers and not knowing the appropriate response for the momentous occasion, curtsied.

That awkward moment made her stick in his mind. He used to go to meetings at the high school, which he led because he was more educated than the others in the committee, knew literature well, and was beginning to write poetry. At those meetings, which the students liked to attend because they considered him their leader, Algis noticed Nijole several times. She had matured very early. Her full breasts stood out under her school uniform and she had dimples on her white spun-sugar cheeks, which reddened when he looked at her. She was neat and industrious and agreed calmly and straightforwardly to head the literary club at the school. She knew the poetry of Maironis and Salomei Neris and she recited it with feeling at the concerts the Komsomol students gave after district meetings.

Once Algis gave her his own poetry to read and comment on. Embarrassed, he asked her not to show it to anyone else. Nijole was amazed that the tall young man, two years her senior, who was so severe and confident at the meetings, and whom all the girls feared, could become a simple shy lad, like every beginning poet unsure of the value of his work.

She took his notebook home. One day after classes, she came to his office at the committee headquarters, the notebook rolled up into a tube in her hand. Algis recognized his book, got rid of the people in the room, locked the door, and sat in front of Nijole, crossing his legs. He was confident at first, the way he was in this office, but the silence and Nijole's inability to find a way to begin the conversation made him uneasy. He started worrying like a pupil waiting for the teacher to grade him. His nervous blinking elicited a sympathetic smile from Nijole.

Sensing her power over him, she began speaking with assurance. She was tactful and tried not to destroy his ego. She praised a few things and pointed out what, as far as her taste was concerned, was less successful and did not sound at all Lithuanian. In summation, she smiled respectfully and said that he had definite talent and that she envied him because she could never write like that even though she was crazy about poetry. She recommended that he read more of the classics. The wealth of classical Lithuanian to be found in them would protect him from an overdependence on the new, and, in her opinion, vulgar and tasteless expressions in the language.

Algis forgot who he was and thanked her warmly, putting up a very weak argument against her criticisms, and walked her home. She did not invite him in. They stood at the gate. He read her his latest poem and he saw the surprised faces of her parents, glued to the window behind the parted curtains.

Nijole did not arouse any feelings in him. He did not think about things like that then. He had his work, which took up all his time. Women did not interest him as such. And a young lady, from an alien class, was only raw material for creating a future Soviet person. But he valued her mind and the extensive knowledge she had that he lacked.

The senior Komsomol members were being mobilized to go out into the surrounding villages to work as librarians. Even though it had no external political overtones, the job was dangerous. You had to live in the village among coarse and brutal people and agitate covertly, through the choice of reading material, for Soviet power. They called it "straightening out the muzhik's brains" at the committee headquarters. You also had to pick young people carefully and talk with them in secret, preparing them to enter the Komsomol against their parents' wishes. It was not an enviable job, especially for a girl from a cultured urban family. Only God knew how it would end.

Algis had included Nijole's name on the list of possibles. For some reason her name came to mind. To his amazement, she did not turn it down, even though there were big strapping fellows there at the meeting who came up with hundreds of excuses: their sick aged parents, their own poor health, and the fact that they would not complete high school by going out into the sticks and the Soviet Government needed educated builders of Communism.

Nijole went to the village. Deep in the woods. Inaccessible in spring and autumn because the roads and swamps were flooded. She went without complaint, with no pressure. She resigned herself to a bitter life with a kerosene lamp, a dark, smelly roach-infested corner in someone's house, to complete isolation among alien and hostile people, to dangerous nights and gunshots, to coarse swearing, and a constant homesickness for her parents, who were too afraid for their own skins to stop their daughter. She went off into the unknown darkness, from which they feared she would never return.

She left her Komsomol card at headquarters. Algis put it in the safe. No one must know in the village that she was a member. She would not survive if they did. She was just a city girl from a decent family. The peasants knew her father's store, because they used to buy on credit before the war when they came in for the fairs. The daughter of such a man could count on some roughhewn hospitality, respect, and defense from untoward advances. Besides, handing out books to the village children was a harmless job, one even encouraged by the peasants, who hoped that the books and education, which were free, would take their barefooted families into the real world.

It was part of Algis' job to visit the librarians in the villages, take them new books, give them instructions, and comfort and inspire them. He made the rounds alone, without guards, so as not to attract the attention of the Forest Brotherhood and not to give away his subordinates in the villages. If the peasants found out that they were not librarians, they would surely kill them. Algis dressed simply in worn country clothes, hiding his personal weapon. He traveled on an old country nag. A traveling peasant to all appearances, he got to the village he needed to visit.

It was that way this time, too. Leaden clouds, bloated with rain, crawled along the horizon, barely scraping the tops of the pine trees. The wagon wheels rolled over the tree roots, which crisscrossed the path like ribs. The forest disappeared into the cold darkness.

His driver, a taciturn peasant, was wearing a worn leather jacket even though it was summer. It was cold and rainy, however. He was silent the whole trip. It was only after Algis offered him a manufactured cigarette that he expressed interest in whom Algis was visiting so far away from everything. Algis said Nijole. It turned out that the peasant knew her.

"She's wasting herself here," he said in a rheumy voice. "Time for her to be getting married. No match for her in our hole of a village."

He glanced up at Algis through his bushy brows, and asked disinterestedly, without any curiosity: "You here on business? Did the district authorities send you?"

Not about to reveal his hand to the first person he met, Algis answered quickly:

"I'm her fiancé."

The little peasant shot another look at him to see if he was lying. He sighed.

"Well, at least life isn't over for everybody . . . Some of us are getting ready to lay down our bones to rest . . ."

He took Algis to the village, knocked with his whip on the window, and smiled for the first time.

"Hey, library! Your fiancé is here!"

Algis and Nijole sat over a cup of tea in the large empty room the village had designated for the library. There were homemade bookshelves against one of the log walls. The rest of the room looked like a typical peasant hut. A big sooty stove, homemade rugs on the walls, and a niche in the corner for a votive light.

There was no trembling light in the corner, but the flickering kerosene lamp illuminated the crucifix over the niche.

Nijole was ecstatic at his arrival. She laughed uproariously when he told her how he had cleverly duped the peasant by calling himself her fiancé.

She made him take a nap on her bed behind the stove while she slipped on a scarf and ran to the village to tell the young people there would be a party that night. Algis had to meet these young people and discreetly determine which of them could be secretly summoned to the city and taken into the Komsomol without the villagers' knowledge. Nijole had to point out the ones he should have a private talk with in the corner during the party.

As he lay down to sleep, he took the green egg-shaped "limonka" grenade from his coat and hid it behind the stove. He did not travel with a revolver. You could not count on it. And you probably would not have enough time to use it when you needed it. The limonka was much better. You could hide it in your clothes and just pull the pin when you needed it. He did not intend to fall into the Forest Brotherhood's hands alive. Blowing up with a grenade was the best way out. Instantaneous death. Plus you take along a few of the enemy, too.

The library filled with people. Nijole was an authority figure in the village. There were local musicians too. They looked just like the other peasants. A skinny, tubercular old man with an accordion, which he took out of the case to dust its mother-of-pearl sides with a soft cloth. A one-legged, blowsy-faced invalid, who put down his crutch to pluck the banjo. A kerchiefed woman with a toothless mouth, who brought in a huge kettledrum. The musicians sat around the dinner table under the lamp. There was no other furniture, so there was plenty of room for dancing.

Algis looked over the village lads and lasses who had crowded into the room. They were ruddy forest dwellers bursting with good health. Both sexes were wearing men's jackets, which was the fashion then, and they whispered, casting droll looks at Algis and Nijole. That reassured him. No one doubted that he was her fiancé.

The musicians struck up a polka. The country shyness that had overwhelmed the party dissipated as soon as Algis took Nijole by the hand into the center of the uneven floor. They danced smoothly as if they had done it many times before. Other couples swirled around them. Whooping and stamping their feet. Enviously watching Algis and Nijole and determined to dance as well.

It was fun. It got hot. They opened the windows. A bottle of moonshine was discreetly passed around the benches. The men drank, turning their backs so Nijole would not see. Cigarette smoke drifted upward, clouding the light of the kerosene lamp. The girls were squealing from the boys' pinches. They treated Algis as one of their own, and he managed to take a couple of swigs from the bottle, endearing himself completely.

The musicians played continuously, taking a quick stop only for a gulp of moonshine and a chance to wipe their mouths. Whenever there was no music, and, consequently, no foot stomping, the hut was filled with the homey sound of a cricket chirping. Algis, tipsy, felt good. He knew that the evening would go well and that he would not return with empty hands.

The noise and music kept them from noticing that a long caravan had pulled into the village street, even though the windows were open. Strangers, unshaven and dirty, surrounded the house. Gun butts glittered around the necks of several of them.

The Forest Brotherhood traveled along routes known only to them, and that night their path went through the village. They would not have stopped. They had a more important destination. But the music and voices caught their attention.

The door was kicked open, and three men piled in. One was wearing a hooded raincoat. A Soviet army strap with two German grenades with wooden pins bound the coat tightly around his waist. All three had automatic machine guns. Soviet make—PPD, with round black cartridges.

The visitors stood by the door in silence, obviously enjoying the impression their unannounced visit had made. The music broke off and the musicians gaped at the men. The dancers backed up to the walls, tensely awaiting the worst. It grew very quiet. The cricket's persistent chirp and the horses' snorts and neighs outside the window underlined the malevolent silence.

"Why did you stop?" the one in the raincoat asked. He sneered and a metal tooth flashed under his unshaved lip. "Dance. We'll watch."

No one moved. Algis looked back at the stove, behind which he had hidden his grenade. But it was no use. He could not work his way over there without being noticed. He looked at Nijole. She had maintained her outward composure and even managed a weak smile when she saw him. She was trying to reassure him.

Will they turn me in or not? The thought kept repeating in his head. They all think I'm her fiancé. Why should they turn me in? I'm like the rest. Nothing suspicious about it.

"Well, dance," the man in the raincoat insisted. "You'll make us think that you're not happy we dropped in. And yet you're Lithuanians just like us, right . . . ?"

No one answered. Only the accordionist's balding head nodded in appeasement.

"Go on partying. It's just the right time. Lithuania is bleeding to death. A foreign boot is trampling our soul!"

He stopped smiling and dropped each word like a rock into the thick, heavy silence. "And you, you sons of bitches? You're happy, you toads? Want to stay on the sidelines? Well, dance! We want to watch."

Algis, who had instinctively stepped behind someone's back, stealthily observed the speaker's face. He was no peasant. He had a thin, nervous face, and a three-day growth covered skin sallow from exhaustion and lack of sleep.

He must be from Kaunas, Algis thought feverishly, trying to guess whether the man could recognize him. He's one of the surviving intelligentsia . . . He's their leader . . . He runs things in this area . . . And I've appeared at meetings . . . My picture was in the papers . . . I shouldn't look at him . . . He'll remember me, he'll recognize me . . .

"So, the dancing continues!" the man commanded authoritatively. "Orchestra, let's have some music!"

The musicians, grinning stupidly in their confusion, broke into a lame polka. One couple timidly went into the center of the floor and began bouncing up and down, afraid to get near the three men by the door.

"Stop!" The man in the raincoat stopped the music and the dancers with a wave of his arm. "I don't see any gaiety."

A crooked smile crept over his mouth, which had dry white flecks in the corners of the blue lips.

"Everybody dance! Naked! Like the day they were born!"

At first no one believed him. They thought it was a joke and even smiled in answer to his demand. But he touched the barrel of his machine gun and the two men at his sides aimed the dull barrels of their guns right at the crowd.

"I'll count to three. Whoever hasn't undressed will die with his clothes on! Move it! You're not ashamed to dance in a cemetery, over our bones—why are you ashamed to show what your pants cover? You have no shame, you sons of bitches! One . . ."

People who had been hugging the walls came out of their spell. The fellows, never taking their eyes off the gun barrels aimed at them, felt for their belt buckles and began to fumble with their pants. The girls numbly undressed facing the wall.

Nijole did not turn away. She calmly removed her blouse, neatly folded it over the back of a chair, then unbuttoned the side of her skirt and shook it down over her hips, stepped out of it, and hung it on the chair, too. She sat down and took off her shoes, stockings, and garter belt. She still wore white transparent panties and bra.

"Two! Take off everything!"

Nijole, pulling her lovely arms behind her back, unhooked her bra, and it fell to her lap, revealing two firm white breasts, blue veins showing through the skin, and the dark circles of her jutting nipples.

Algis undressed automatically, without thinking about what he was doing. It was only when he was naked that he felt the cold coming from the windows and hugged his shoulders in an attempt to warm up.

The large room looked like the antechamber in a steam bath with white splashes of naked bodies and piles of clothes dropped on the floor.

"The dancing continues! Orchestra, please!"

The orchestra played the same polka. The accordion whined like a beggar and the drum pounded like a heartbeat. Like zombies, several naked people began moving around the room.

"Let's dance." Algis heard Nijole's voice near his ear. She stood in front of him, but her eyes were vacant. As though she did not see him. She put her cold hand on his naked shoulder. He felt the touch of her pointy nipples and then the softness of her breasts on his chest.

They began dancing barefoot as in a dream, feeling the uneven floor with the soles of their feet. They stared at each other above eye level, at the hairline.

"Dance," her lips whispered. "Dance, dance, dance . . ."

The tubercular accordionist quickly got his bearings. He conscientiously stretched out his accordion, keeping the beat with his balding head. His eyes stared out at the naked people who whirled past him, leaping like goats, breasts shaking, the men's organs bouncing like tails between their legs. He roared his laughter. That doomed the orchestra.

"Stop!" shouted the raincoated bandit. "Musicians strip too!"

147

The one thing that was permanently etched in Algis' memory was the one-legged invalid and his soft, wrinkled belly. The banjo rested on his stump, which resembled a rotten ham, scars and seams showing blue and pink along the edges. The stump bounced in rhythm to the polka. Algis was sick.

They danced until they were dropping, covered with a sticky sweat that did not warm them, but tightened the skin with a clammy coldness.

Then they were chased out into the street, into the raw darkness, and they raced through the mud, which hurt the soles of their feet with its iciness. They were chased down the streets by their guffawing convoy. Their bodies glowed white in the dark as they ran past closed houses with darkened windows. They ran past the entire caravan stretched out for a kilometer in the street. Laughter and burning shameful words came from each wagon they passed. They ran in silence. Only the patter of their feet in the mud. Heavy breathing, and an occasional hopeless moan from one of the girls: "Mama, oh, Mama."

There was a wet meadow outside the village. It went right up to the forest, which looked as empty as a cemetery.

They were forced to line up with their backs to the convoy, facing the woods. Nijole was next to Algis again, her cold fingers clutching his, but afraid to look at him. He did not look either. He was not thinking about anything anyway—his head was resonantly empty. Just a skull with nothing in it. The emptiness contained cold air.

Safety catches clicking and low conversation among the convoy. Then the familiar voice of the one in the raincoat hit them in the back of the head.

"Listen to me, you toads. You should all be shot like dogs. But you are Lithuanians, and there are so few of us left. The Russians will kill all of us soon. So we won't spill Lithuanian blood. But we will teach you a lesson. We'll open fire at my command.

Whoever makes it to the forest, light a candle in church. Whoever doesn't, it's your own fault.

"All right, you traitors! Bitches! Lowlifes! Move it! March!"

The line moved, blown by the wind toward the woods. Zigzagging. A line of white blots. Machine-gun fire in their wake. Algis jumped over hillocks, slipping, but never letting go of Nijole. Short of breath, she could not keep up. Bullets whizzed past his ears and he moved his head, not understanding that that would not save him.

Nijole jerked his hand. He looked back and saw her wide-open eyes, her mouth opened in a silent scream, and the dark stream creeping from her cheek to her breast. She did not fall but went on running, heavier and slower, pulling painfully on his hand.

Without realizing it, Algis stopped, picked her up, and carried her as he went on, dreamlike, hearing the slurp of the mud and the last shots dying away.

He carried her through the woods, as the pine branches scraped his face and body. The fragrant pine needles made a soft, springy floor for his feet. He saw a naked figure running through the trees and he wanted to call for help. But it disappeared. Only the whispering of the treetops. They made him sleepy.

By morning Algis stumbled upon a lonely farmhouse. The owner was frightened half to death when he saw two naked blood-smeared people.

Nijole's wound was not dangerous. The bullet had glanced off her chin, scratching her cheek. She spent a short time in the district hospital and left with a meandering scar that became almost invisible with the years. It colored red when she was upset.

While she was in the hospital, Algis visited her every day, and she begged him each time to say nothing to her parents. She did not want to worry them. Algis agreed, avoiding her eyes, searching for words to tell her what happened at her house.

A group of "undesirables" from their district had been sent packing to Siberia and Nijole's parents were among them. Algis had not been there when the list was made up. And he did not have time to save them. He only found out about it several days after the fact. He had decided to pay them a visit to prepare them for the news about their daughter's accident. He was met by boarded windows and a sealed door.

He tried to go through the district channels to rectify the mistake—the deportation of the family of an active Komsomol member who had shed blood in the line of duty. He tried to telegraph and overtake the echelon and have Nijole Kudirkaite's family taken out and returned. But either the telegrams did not reach their destination, or else the authorities could not find the right echelon in the chaos of all the Lithuanians, Latvians, and Estonians being sent to Siberia. His trouble was for nothing. Even the authorities began to disapprove, accusing him of putting his private, personal feeling before the public good. In those days that was a grave sin for a Communist.

Nijole was left all alone. There was no one close to her except Algis. Full of pity for her and fully comprehending his responsibility for the fate of that naïve and gentle creature, already tied to him by invisible but indissoluble strings, Algis took her home from the hospital. She spent days at a time without talking to him, locked up in her world. She spent a week and said nothing in reply to his proposal to legalize their arrangement.

So they became man and wife. And Algis never regretted that he had made his decision so accidentally and quickly. After he became a famous poet, living in the capital, respected and wealthy, he was proud to observe that his wife was much better than those of his new friends. She understood him, knew all his weaknesses and faults, and hid them discreetly from others. She was demanding in private. Algis owed much of his success and position to her, her unerring taste, and the atmosphere she created at home.

She could not blame Algis for her family's plight. She had accepted the system in her husband's footsteps, first against her will, and then reconciled, like all of Lithuania. They both spent years trying to locate traces of her family in the wilds of Siberia. They drew on all their friends and resources. They even traveled there themselves. But they had no success. Her father, mother, and two younger sisters disappeared in the taiga, a dense forest zone in the North, in the barbed wire of countless concentration camps, in the gray huts and sod houses that sprang up like pox on the wild strange beauty of the banks of the Yenisey River. Algis later published a volume called *Songs of the Yenisey*, devoted, however, to the beauty of the countryside, which had amazed him, and to the hydroelectric power stations that had been constructed according to Communist Party desires. Nijole hated those poems and they did not keep a copy on their bookshelves.

After Stalin's death, when the surviving martyrs began to return from exile, Nijole's father suddenly showed up. Without his wife and children. Their graves were in Siberia.

Algis and Nijole comforted the old man, surrounded him with the love and care he had never dreamed of having in his declining years. He was sick and half mad. They took him to the best doctors and health resorts, but he dragged out six months and died without ever telling his daughter what he had experienced above the polar circle. He was afraid of everyone, trusted no one, and did not dare tell her what was on his mind.

They buried him according to his last wishes, in the district capital, where the family had lived. His daughter and son-in-law raised a handsome memorial of dark red marble over his grave. The local cemetery still boasts of the monument, which, according to connoisseurs, is a work of art.

Nijole and the children visit the grave every year, and the town officials greet her with pomp and ceremony, because she is the wife of the famous poet. They decorate the monument with flowers and wreaths at municipal expense.

The train had already started when Dausa and Gaidialis burst in with their packages and a bottle. They were chilled. Frost on their eyebrows and lashes. They stamped their feet to warm up. The noise made Sigita turn to the wall.

"Hey, missy," Dausa called drunkenly. He had had time for a few at the station. "Join us for dinner. Don't look down on us."

"I'm not hungry," she retorted without turning.

"Disrespectful to her elders. That's not nice," Gaidialis noted.

"Leave her alone," Algis interrupted. "Sigita, please. Join us. Listen, comrades, why don't we men leave the compartment. We're in her way. Let her set the table and get everything ready. A woman's touch. All right, Sigita?"

She turned and smiled.

"There's a writer for you," Dausa exclaimed. "He has a way with women . . . We're uneducated and green."

"Let's go," Algis said, urging them toward the door.

He could not wait to be alone with them and talk about her fate. They might be policemen, but they were still human. Gaidialis especially inspired his trust. They must know how to help her. Rather, how to save her from destruction. And knowing how, Algis would take it upon himself.

They were already out the door when they heard her voice:

"What about a knife? Am I supposed to cut the sausage with my fingers?"

"Hah, she wants a knife?" Dausa smirked. "How about a gun?"

"Give her the knife," Algis said.

"We can't. It's dangerous," Gaidialis said. "We have to keep an eye on her."

"Give it to her," Algis repeated. "I'll vouch for her. I'll take full responsibility."

"If anything happens, you'll answer for it," Dausa said gloomily and took a knife from his pocket. He pulled out the blade and handed it to Sigita. Then he scowled at Algis sarcastically. "Humanism . . . empty jokes . . ."

Algis did not argue. He took them both away from the door and told them everything he had learned from Sigita while they were gone. To his surprise, the news affected Dausa as well as Gaidialis.

"What should we do? How can we save her?" Algis asked anxiously. "Give me your advice."

"What advice?" Dausa asked. His long face was serious. "Set up her bail. It's not done very often anymore. But for you, a well-known person, they'll make an exception."

"Do you know anyone important in Kaunas?" asked Gaidialis. "In the city committee of the Party . . . or in the prosecutor's office?"

"The committee's first secretary is my best friend!" Algis shouted.

"Then there's no problem." Dausa clapped him on the back. "Consider the girl in your care. They'll let her go on one word from you. The only thing is to figure out a way to keep the employers from prosecuting her over the five hundred."

"I'll give them the money!" Algis was shouting. "I have it on me. Bank notes! I'll cash them tomorrow in Kaunas and take it to them!"

"Just don't forget a receipt," Dausa counseled businesslike.

"Comrades, you have no idea what a good deed we'll be doing tomorrow!" He hugged them both and saw that they were as moved and excited as he was. "But for now, not a word! Let's go back and have a drink."

"You've got a deal!" Gaidialis perked up.

"It's no sin to have a drink," Dausa supported him. "As my mother would say, it's no sin to wet your whistle after a good deed."

All four had a drink. Even Sigita. Not a whole one. And she

coughed and sputtered. Both policemen laughed and slapped her on the back.

"Oh, Sigita," Dausa yelled drunkenly. "If I were only twenty years younger. When you go take the drivers' courses and go out in the streets and make a traffic violation, it'll break my heart, but I'll have to give you a ticket. Duty comes first."

"So you *are* from the police?" Her eyes narrowed.

"Don't be silly!" Dausa sputtered, realizing what he had done. Gaidialis quickly intervened.

"Child, do you think they take such fools into the force?"

"Then why do your pants have piping like a policeman's?"

"Piping? What piping?" Dausa acted dumb. "Oh, you mean this piping? You're right, my beauty. These are police pants. Do you see how thick and warm they are? We had to go to Russia for you. It's very cold there . . . So they gave us these pants. So that we don't freeze. How else could we get you back home? Is that clear?"

Sigita was convinced and she calmed down.

All three sat opposite Algis: Dausa, Sigita, and Gaidialis. Sigita between them. And sang. An old village song. She had a high, high voice, and they sang bass.

"Where are you running, my little path?
Where do you lead? Where are you calling?
But you won't return the one
I waited for, the one I loved."

Sigita had put her hands trustingly on their shoulders. Her eyes were glued to Algis' face. She was singing for him alone. The two policemen, softened by the cognac and heat, sang deep and loud, their voices framing hers. Their faces made their pleasure and contentment obvious. If you did not know, you would never suspect that she was a prisoner and they were her guards. Just three country Lithuanians singing their hearts out, forget-

154

ting the world, as if they were not on a train racing through frosty Russia, but back home in the village on a soft summer evening.

"A single unified people," Algis thought, touched and moved. "Small, beaten by everyone who has the energy. But still alive and incomparable. There is none closer to a poet's heart."

Algis took up the song. They sang for a long time, until midnight. Until people began knocking on the walls of the other compartments. Then they settled down to sleep. They put out the light, leaving the blue night-light on, climbed under their blankets, and started to fall into slumber, their hearts at peace, and the rails clicking under them.

A sudden braking jolted the car. Algis slid to the very edge of the berth and had to hold on to the table to keep from hitting his head. The buffers between the cars were clanging. The train was slowing down. The buildings of some station floated past the frosty window more and more slowly.

The compartment was flooded with a dead blue light. Gaidialis was snoring above Algis, his foot with a hole in the brown sock hanging down from the berth. Dausa, his head under the covers, was sleeping opposite. Two pairs of boots, swaying in rhythm with the braking, stood in the aisle. Algis caught the heavy odor emanating from them, made a face, and turned his face up toward Sigita.

Her tousled head was hanging down from her berth. She was smiling at him. The car was passing the station's lights, and the yellow pulsating light entered the compartment, flickering over Sigita's plump child's face and her laughing eyes.

Algis smiled back. He put his finger to his lips. Like a conspirator. Don't wake up our neighbors. Sigita nodded and put her head on the very edge of the berth. Her cheek hung over the edge. She looked even more like a mischievous child, absolutely sure that the world was good. She watched Algis with a daughter's trust.

The car stopped in front of a gray station house with cement columns and cold white spots on the frozen windows.

"Minsk." Algis looked at his watch. Twelve-forty. The station speaker's creaky voice penetrated the compartment. All he understood was that they would lay over in Minsk for twenty minutes.

People were shoving in the corridor. Somebody's suitcase bumped into the compartment door. That woke Algis up completely. He sat up, pulled on his pants and shirt, and started tying his shoes.

Sigita watched him from above in silence. Dausa and Gaidialis were asleep. Algis was dressing quietly and swiftly. He was trying not to wake them. As he dressed, he made up his mind.

"The train will be here for twenty minutes. That will give Sigita and me time to get out and take a cab as far away from the station as we can get before they wake up. The important thing is not to wake them."

Algis was not thinking about what he would do next. He had to save the girl. That was important. The rest was a trifle. He would be saving himself as well. His soul. He would make a clean break with the past and begin a new life. No matter how it turned out it would be better, at least, purer than the present one. He was still young. What was forty, after all? A proper Englishman—and the English certainly know how to live—only gets married at that age. He was still full of energy and strength. He had to shake himself up, get organized, and then . . .

What would happen then, Algis did not know. The phosphorescent hand on his wristwatch was moving inexorably. He could waste no more time.

Dausa muttered in his sleep. Algis froze with his hands on his shoelaces. But Dausa did not stick his face out of the covers. Instead, he turned his face to the wall.

Algis looked up at Sigita. She was no longer smiling. Tense, she was watching him, not yet guessing what he had in mind, but feeling the conspiratorial bond that had sprung up between them when he began dressing.

Algis ordered her to dress with a light nod. She had been waiting. She sat up, her knees to her chin in the upper berth. She took out a sweater and pulled it on over her head, smoothly, like swimming through still water.

Algis took his jacket off the hook and put it on, even buttoning all the buttons. Sigita pushed her head through the sweater and nodded to him. She passed down her battered suitcase. Algis took it quietly and put it on his bed. Then he put on his coat and hat. Now he had to raise his bed to take out the suitcase and traveling bag.

Gaidialis' snoring stopped.

Algis stood in the aisle, trying not to breathe. He was eye to eye with Gaidialis' long-nosed face, dead in the blue light. The guard's eyes were shut and his red eyelashes were fluttering.

Mustn't look at him. He will feel my gaze and wake up. Please don't let the berth squeak when I lift it.

He bent over and moved the bedding with his foot, without a single rustle, exposing the gray leatherette top of the berth. He took the edge with both hands, straining his muscles.

The berth lifted without a squeak and Algis leaned it against the wall, while he felt for the luggage with his right hand. He put the suitcase and then the bag on the floor. Then he lowered the berth just as smoothly, replaced the mattress, fluffed the pillow, and pulled up the covers to cover half the pillow.

He took a controlled breath in three parts. Sigita touched his shoulder, and he moved over. She lowered her foot in the man's boot with its crooked worn heel, and felt around for support. She bumped into the tea glass on the table. The spoon rattled in the glass and the saucer jangled. Sigita pulled her foot up.

Dausa stirred in his berth. He stuck his head out. His thin hair was stuck to his forehead. One eye was fixed dully on Algis, who was dressed. Algis could think of nothing else than to bend over him, blocking his view of the luggage, and calmingly wave his hand before his nose.

"Sleep . . . I'm going for some cigarettes," he whispered.

"Oh," Dausa said sleepily, and shut his eyes.

Algis straightened up.

Sigita was sitting in the corner of her berth, staring at him, holding her breath. Algis signaled her to move to the other end of the berth, closer to the door. He looked down at Dausa. His eyes were closed and he was breathing evenly, a gurgle in his snore.

Sigita lowered herself in a smooth, fluid movement. She was hanging by her hands from the berth. Algis caught her and silently lowered her to her feet. She looked up. He understood, felt around the berth until he found her fuzzy jacket, and handed it to her.

They had to leave right away. Without hesitation. And without slamming the door.

Sigita was standing by the door. He was behind her in the narrow aisle. Changing places would be difficult. Even dangerous. They could bump into Dausa.

Sigita was resourceful. She gave him a soothing look, took the chrome door handle into both hands, biting her lip in concentration, and pushed. The door opened slowly. It opened a crack into the lit corridor and immediately let in voices.

Algis' back was killing him. He did not look behind him. Standing in the aisle, he was blocking Sigita from the view of the sleeping men. He stretched his arm and helped her with the door. She squeezed out into the corridor, her jacket over her arm. He passed her the suitcases and bag.

She turned right, out of view.

Then Algis turned. Dausa was wheezing, the blanket pulled over his face again. The only sign of life in Gaidialis' dead eyes was the fluttering lashes. Algis' eyes slid over the table with the unfinished glasses of tea, the uneaten piece of sausage on a scrap of newspaper, and the hill of colored wrappers from the sugar packets. The net bag over his empty berth held an orange soap dish, toothpaste, and toothbrush in a case. In order to prove to himself that he was calm, actually to test himself, Algis stopped for another second and took everything out of the bag and stuffed it into his pockets. Only then did he squeeze out into the corridor and pull the door back very slowly. It locked shut with a light click.

Passengers who had boarded at Minsk were crowding in the corridor, pushing ahead with their luggage under the dull lights of the corridor. The raw cold air was creeping into the platform with them. Sigita was trapped by the flood of incoming passengers and had to shoulder and elbow her way through them, generating angry stares and grumbles. She looked back helplessly at Algis. He smiled, winked to cheer her up, and used his suitcase as a battering ram to get them both out to the platform. They had to hurry no matter what. Dausa and Gaidialis could notice they were gone at any minute.

A sleepy child was crying in his mother's arms. People were exchanging information rapidly and nervously, worried that there would be no seats for them. A fat woman wearing a heavy scarf over her coat pushed Algis up against a wall. She was breathing down his neck. He pushed with his entire body and heard the snap of buttons being torn off.

"I'm crazy," he thought. "What am I doing? I'm running like a kid. Pushing and shoving. Why? Where?"

And suddenly it all seemed funny.

"Pardon, madame," he said, and smiled blindingly. "My button seems to be caught in your scarf."

"Crazy," she hissed at his back, but he was moving away from her, pushing people coming at him, each time laughing and excusing himself:

"Pardon . . . pardon."

It was less crowded on the platform and he got a chance to catch his breath and button his coat. He could see Sigita's head on the platform.

The young conductor in the black coat looked up at Algis.

"Your ticket is to Vilnius. Are you getting off here? I'll mark your space vacant."

Algis' heart contracted. New passengers would take their places and the police would realize they had escaped.

"The young lady is getting off too?"

"No, no," Algis said as calmly as possible. He smiled. "We'll be back. We want to hand over these things. People are meeting us here." He nodded at his luggage.

"Oh," the conductor said with suspicion in her voice. "I thought it was your baggage. Hurry, don't be late. You only have ten minutes."

"Yes, sir, comrade leader," Algis joked. She smiled back.

"Go on, go on, don't block the entrance."

Walking down the steps to the snowy, blustery platform, Algis remembered that he had not paid for the two glasses of tea with lemon. He imagined how she would curse him up and down the train when it was clear that he had disappeared. And not alone. With a criminal who was being transported to Lithuania for trial . . . All the passengers would enjoy the scandal. The police are just as hated in Lithuania as they are in Russia.

Sigita bundled up in her jacket and stood squinting on the platform.

"Let me carry it," she said as she reached for his traveling case. Her eyes were glowing with trust and loyalty.

"You are a lady," Algis said, and pushed her hand with his elbow. "And I'm not that old yet."

Sigita laughed.

"Let's move it," Algis ordered, heading for the end of the platform. "Away from here."

They crossed the large waiting room decorated in marble. People were sleeping on the wooden benches, their luggage and bags piled up around them. It was warm. The air was heavy and stale.

Algis stepped out into the square with relief. It was dark and the streetlights were few and far between. The wind was stronger and attacked their faces with icy needles. The green lights of two free taxis blinked invitingly at them from the end of the square. Algis and Sigita rushed toward them, passing people with baggage also headed toward the cars.

"If we get there first," Algis thought superstitiously, "Sigita will be saved."

Sigita was practically running to keep up with him.

He put the baggage in the trunk, helped Sigita into the back seat, and joined her, slamming the door.

The driver, a young man in a hat with flaps and a fur vest over his jacket, looked at them appraisingly and asked:

"Where to?"

His question stopped Algis cold. Where would they go? He had not thought about it in the excitement. The important thing was to get away from pursuers, but where to go had to be decided at the spur of the moment, without hesitation while the driver stared at him.

Algis had never been in Minsk and he had no friends there. A hotel was out of the question. Documents would be required and Sigita did not have any. Besides, the guards would miss them any minute and start searching. They had to leave the city as soon as possible. Get far away and cover their tracks.

"To the airport," Algis said.

The driver revved up the Volga's motor and sped past the station.

Algis looked out the window for the police. The taxi made a U-turn in the square and dove under a trestle. A train clattered overhead. It must have been theirs.

Algis sighed in relief, leaned back against the seat, and looked at Sigita. She looked as if she were playing a fascinating, breathtaking game and was waiting for her partner's next move. Her partner was none other than Algirdas Požera, famous poet, prizewinner, and paterfamilias, with graying hair at the temples.

"Do you know where we are going?" he asked her in Lithuanian, casting a wary sidelong glance at the driver.

"No," she replied simply and affably.

"Ah, Aldona-Sigita. We're really in a mess . . . Who knows how it will come out?"

"Please call me Sigita. I don't like my name."

"All right, you'll be Sigita . . . But who will I be?"

"My comrade. My older comrade. But keep your name. Algirdas is a beautiful name."

Algis laughed grimly. Lost in thought, he patted her unkempt locks with his hand. Sigita hunched up her shoulders and moved away with a dirty look.

"I'm old enough to be your father, silly. What are you so huffy for? Listen to me carefully and we'll both decide what to do next."

He told her the truth that the police had hidden from her. That trial and at least two years in jail had been awaiting her in Kaunas.

She was scrunched up against the back of the seat listening intently.

"Those dogs," she moaned when he was through. "They made believe they were nice guys, taking me to my mama . . . I felt there was something wrong. Those jodhpurs with the piping . . . Of course, they're the police. How could I have believed them? And you . . . you knew the whole time . . . and said nothing to me?"

"That's why I'm with you now."

"Where will we go? They'll be looking for us."

"They will. But we'll hide," Algis said smiling.

"You, too?" she asked uncertainly.

"I can't very well leave you alone, can I? You're too silly." Algis laughed at her. "You'd be sunk without me. We'll both hide. I have a good reason for it myself."

"You robbed someone, too?"

"Myself. That also happens, Sigita. For many years in a row. And now—no more. There is no more Algirdas Požera. A new man is born. He's seventeen. And he's beginning a new life. Brand new."

Sigita was watching his face doubtfully, waiting for him to break out laughing. But his face was severe and sorrowful. The lines around his mouth were deep and bitter.

Sigita believed him. She took his hand from his lap and threw herself on it, kissing it silently. Algis felt the warm, wet touch of her tears on his skin. He put his other hand on the tousled hair at the nape of her neck. She did not push it away. She rubbed up against it gently and trustingly.

"We're here," the driver said into the rearview mirror, without turning his head. The car stopped, slowly settling on its shock absorbers.

The driver unloaded their luggage, collected the fare, and asked Algis curiously:

"Foreigners?"

"Yes, yes," he replied, without thinking.

"Germans?"

"Yes, German."

"There are a lot of foreigners now. You can't even talk to some of them. You speak pretty good. Just a little accent."

Algis gave him a generous tip, and he helpfully carried their things to the waiting room. He shook their hands.

"Bon voyage."

Algis felt a pleasant, youthful tension, as he had felt when he had a surplus of untapped power in early youth. His powers and youth coincided with the height of the Civil War in Lithuania, when danger lurked at every step. He had been accustomed to living like a wound spring ready to strike out at any second. Algis felt a long-forgotten surge of energy and preparedness for battle.

He was entering battle—battle with the whole world, in which he had lived and prospered. A battle with no backing off. And all for one thing—the salvation of his soul, rather, of what was left in its farthest reaches.

From the moment of his decision, his past was crossed out. Algirdas Požera had to disappear in a puff of smoke, without a trace, so that no one would search for him. Even his family and friends would come to terms with their loss, deciding that he had died in an accident or as a victim of a holdup. That his killer had wiped out all evidence.

He was tying his future to the future of this simple Lithuanian girl who expected help and salvation from him. He would not deceive her, would not abandon her in her hour of need. If only because meeting her had turned his soul inside out and spurred him on to this step, which would let him have some self-respect.

And now he had to act. Carefully. Without mistakes. The authorities were probably looking for them by now. The Minsk police force would be circulating their descriptions, supplied by Dausa and Gaidialis. The airport would be under surveillance. If not right now, then in an hour.

The ticket hall was cavernous, with muted light coming from the chandeliers and wall lamps. A bored-looking policeman was walking around. He was wearing a black overcoat with a leather belt with a brass badge. He had a gun in his holster. He glanced at the new arrivals. Sigita slipped behind Algis. The policeman waddled toward them. Algis stopped, put down his travel bag, and feverishly searched for words that would assuage the cop's suspicions.

The policeman came abreast of them. He was still looking past them. He walked on. Algis looked at his destination. There was a clumsy, clay trash receptacle in the shape of a blossoming flower by the wall. The policeman was going to put out his cigarette. He threw it in, brushed off his hands, and walked over then to some empty leather couches off to the side.

Algis broke out in sweat.

"Don't ever do that again," he muttered fiercely at Sigita. "Don't panic at the sight of a policeman. Remain calm to the bitter end. Otherwise you create suspicion. Got that?"

"Yes. I won't do it again."

"All right, now let's go buy tickets."

"To where? Lithuania?"

"Under no circumstances. An hour there, and you'll be behind bars. We'll fly somewhere so far away that they'll never think of looking for us. Have you ever been in the Crimea?"

"Are you kidding? I've never been anywhere . . . except for that last time."

"Now you will be. You were the one who was dreaming of travel. Consider your dreams come true."

"Thank you."

"It's beautiful in the Crimea this time of year. It's warm, the wisteria is in bloom . . . And we'll be able to go swimming soon. Do you know how to swim?"

"A little."

"I'll teach you. And you'll learn to cook shashlik. And you'll drink wine—muskat . . . massandra . . ."

"Oh, no, I don't drink."

"Silly. Crimean wine isn't vodka or moonshine. Even children drink it. And don't get drunk."

"Then I'll try it too."

"That's a deal," Algis laughed as he set down their things by the counter. "Stay here . . . with your back to the room. Like that."

He looked up at the board behind the counter and found the Minsk–Simferopol flight. It left in the morning, at ten-fifteen.

That was not convenient. He bent down to the oval window in the glass and asked how he could fly to the Crimea without waiting till morning. The girl with the blue Aeroflot uniform over her large bosom suggested the night flight to Moscow. He could get a flight to Simferopol there. There was a flight every hour to the Crimea.

Algis thanked her, but did not take her up on the suggestion. The prospect of spending even a brief period in the crowded Moscow airport did not please him. The chances of meeting someone he knew there were enormous, and that did not suit his plans at all.

"There is another flight," the cashier said, seeing that he was vacillating. "With a changeover at Kharkov. It leaves in two hours. But it's not a turbojet, just a prop. You won't like it . . . It's not de luxe."

It was apparent that Algis' gentlemanly exterior convinced her that he belonged to the upper crust.

"When did you say it left?" Algis was interested.

"At three-thirty. We'll be announcing boarding in an hour."

"Marvelous," Algis said, unable to hide his pleasure. "That's the best option." He started explaining to allay suspicions. "You can sleep in the plane. Instead of hanging around here till morning. And the changeover in Moscow is no picnic either. Two tickets please. I'm with my daughter."

The cashier glanced at Sigita.

"She should have a full fare," she said good-naturedly and coquettishly. "She's big."

"Almost a bride," Algis replied, picking up her manner and acting the proud father. "Will make a grandfather of me soon."

"You're no grandfather," the cashier said, batting her false eyelashes. Her pencil was racing through the forms with practiced speed. "You're still young. And handsome. Turn any young girl's head."

"Ah, it's too late for me."

166

"Tell that to someone else. I have an eye for these things."

"You have two eyes, and they're very pretty."

That rather corny compliment, which made the cashier blush, helped Algis out of an unpleasant situation that he had not foreseen.

The cashier asked his name, and he gave her the first that came to mind, Ivanov, a Russian name.

She wrote down Ivanov and Ivanova on their tickets and asked for the passports. Algis was trapped. But he was in control.

"The passport is in the suitcase . . . In the baggage room." He sounded worried. "I'll have to go get it . . . Where's my stub?"

"Forget it," she stopped him, playfully winking. "We'll manage without it."

Algis relaxed. He paid, put the tickets in his breast pocket, bade a warm farewell to the cashier, and headed for Sigita, sensing the burning look of the cashier in his back. He was used to those passionate looks. But he had really needed one this time. Because it had saved him from a terrible mistake.

He took Sigita from the ticket counter to the general waiting room on the second floor. He found an empty couch in the far corner behind the newspaper stand. They were hidden from people but had a full view of the room.

"Take my scarf," he commanded. "Put your head on my lap and cover yourself with the scarf. I hope you realize why. And I'll make believe I'm napping too. I'll put my hat over my face. Well, my little friend, pleasant dreams."

So far everything was going well. In a little while citizen Ivanov and citizenness Ivanova would fly up into the sky while the police hunted for them on the sinful earth. They would be following the fruitless trail of the Lithuanian poet Algirdas Požera and one Aldona, alias Sigita, a minor, kolkhoz member, former Komsomol member, height 168 cm, gray eyes, hair, light brown, no distinguishing features, who committed a crime, the robbery of an inhabitant of Kaunas, citizen X, in the sum of 500 (five hundred) rubles and liable under article so-and-so of the Criminal Code of the Lithuanian Soviet Socialist Republic.

From this day forth, Algis and Sigita would be outlaws, without papers or a past. All they had was the future. Unclear, with no prospects, but seductive and leading them into its slightly frightening indefiniteness.

But, wait! In order to have that future, they had to eat. Without papers, even though they could manage to hide away, there was not the slightest hope of either of them getting a job. Any job. That was the passport system. Without papers to prove your identity, without police approval for a right of domicile, a Soviet person could not take a step. It was only Algis' masculine appeal that had saved them at the ticket counter. Once. You can't go far on sex appeal.

Algis did not want to spend a lot of time and thought on the future. The important step was already taken. The Rubicon was crossed. They wouldn't starve. It was lucky that he had hidden his publisher's advance and had gotten a letter of credit instead of depositing it in his account. He could cash it anywhere in the Soviet Union. He had done it without any forethought, never guessing how much he would be needing the money.

If they lived frugally, the advance would last them six months or even a year. And he would think of something by then. He would find the one right move. He would not be overcome. It was not like Algirdas Požera to be overcome. Fortune had smiled on him all his life, if you were to believe the many enemies and so-called friends, who fawned on him and tried to get his undivided attention. Everything he had achieved in his former life he had gotten with his own hands and talent, without help or support. And he would not be lost now. On the contrary, he was full of strength. And just recently he had been contemplating his sated, peaceful old age, with dimming will, needs, desires, and passions. And now—no. Enough! He felt that he had had a transfusion of brand-new blood. His organism was reborn. Sitting in the waiting room, with the muffled roar of the jet engines outside, Algis felt as never before every muscle in his body and the dizzying pulsing of his blood.

He thought that Sigita had fallen asleep on his lap. But one wide-open eye was staring at him from under the scarf.

"What are you thinking about?" he asked, a fatherly warmth in his voice.

"About your wife?"

"What do you care about her?"

"I'm sorry for her. She'll be suffering. And it's all my fault."

"Ah, you're taking a lot upon yourself." Algis smiled sadly. "I left not her, but my entire former life, of which she was a part. Unfortunately, she became a victim of my decision, even though she was not guilty of anything as far as I can see. I had to tear, Sigita, do you understand? And when you tear, you rip along the living seam. Let's not talk about it any more. All right? We have nothing in the past. Everything is ahead."

Sigita's lid, with a barely noticeable blue vein, shut over her eye. She was in agreement. Her light lashes, never exposed to makeup, fell on her smooth cheek, untanned and defenselessly pale, dotted with delicate freckles.

Both loudspeakers in the room began squawking at once. Drowning each other out. Algis strained to hear and realized that their flight was ready for boarding.

. . . From the air, Simferopol presented itself in emerald green fields alternating with black plowed ones. There had been no snow since Kharkov. The windows in the white Crimean houses reflected flashes of the bright southern sun. As they stepped onto the heated asphalt of the landing fields, they were immersed in the dry, aromatic warmth of the Crimea. Red roses were blooming on the other side of the fence around the terminal and a crowd of messy women with dark, tanned faces were selling buckets of heaped-up flowers. Algis could not resist and bought Sigita a huge bouquet. Then they waited for the luggage under an awning. For the first time that winter they were happy for the shade. Their clothes were warm and suddenly heavy.

They had to think about a change of clothing. Algis decided to shop in Simferopol. The stores in Yalta would hold some danger for him. The first warm days lured the literary crowd down to Yalta as honey lures flies. He would be more likely to run into friends there than in Moscow or Vilnius. Yalta had become forbidden territory to him, even though he loved that cozy little resort, so unlike the others. Old-fashioned dachas clung to the cliffs of the southern shore like nests. Every spring he would go to spend several months in the House of Creativity of the Writers' Union—a luxurious sanatorium for the elite. Writing went well there. And so did relaxing. As nowhere else. A writer of his standing could choose any of the other Writers' Houses—near the golden beaches of Palanga and Dubulti on the Baltic, in the pine forests of Komarov on the Karelia Peninsula that the Russians had taken from Finland, or in the spicy humidity of subtropical Gagry in the Caucasus.

Yalta had been his second home for many years. He had explored every nook and cranny and the outskirts on foot, as if he had been born and bred in Yalta. That's why he had not had to think for very long in Minsk about where to go. He could not live in Yalta itself, but in the environs, where he and Sigita could hide from prying eyes and still have ties with the exciting corner of paradise that was Yalta. It would be cheaper in the outskirts, and maybe even nicer.

The excursion through the Simferopol stores with heavy winter coats on their arms and a fur hat in his pocket was not fruitful. The selection of goods was so poor and what the stores did have was so unattractive and tasteless, that Algis was finally made aware of the fact that he had been cut off from the realities of Soviet life for many years. He had been in the closed circle of Soviet fat cats who could get their hearts' desires in the special stores closed to the average citizen. And now, even though he had the money and was willing to pay any price, he could not find even the most basic things without which a person's life was unthinkable. Or so he had thought.

Sigita and he both needed bathing suits. At home in Vilnius he had a collection of suits made in Japan, England, and Yugoslavia in the most varied colors and designs. Here all they could find were boring sateen bottoms and bra and they had to settle for that. They could not very well go naked on the beach. He bought two simple sleeveless dresses for Sigita and sandals, clumsy and uncomfortable, for both of them. He also picked up a sun kerchief for her and a cap for himself. It was as flat as a pancake, but at least it was colorful and had a long protective visor. He decided to shop for the rest when they had settled somewhere and made their first forays along the coast.

Sigita would not put down the bouquet he had bought at the airport and kept smelling it as if she could not believe that at this time of year, when it was winter everywhere, she could be holding something that marvelous. She was radiantly happy. All traces gone of the tiredness the night must have brought. Of course, she had fallen asleep quickly in the plane, her head on his shoulder, and she did not wake when new passengers embarked at Kharkov. He did not sleep. He thought about how they would get on in the Crimea away from curious people. And he remembered the perfect place.

Two years ago one of his old flames had taken him there. She was an experienced Kaunas lioness, the wife of a Party ace. They had met on the beach at Yalta. She was vacationing at the Party sanatorium without her husband. Algis was spending the spring at the House of Creativity as usual. He might have known her before and they might have run into each other at receptions, as she had insisted. He did not remember. That did not stop her, a thoroughbred, a spoiled woman, bored by the Party milquetoasts and their primitive wives at the sanatorium. Which was guarded like a fortress, surrounded by a high fence from the world. She clung to him as to a life preserver. Their affair was stormy and wild.

The evening they met she suggested they leave Yalta for a few days to avoid meeting any of their friends. After dark she led him down a road known only to her to a little stone house, smeared with clay, with a flat Tatar roof. The house stood alone high on a cliff over the sea. The mountains with ancient pine trees that whispered at night were behind the house. A narrow path led from the house through the broken cliffs down to the shore, full of rocks and completely deserted. There was no beach. There were no roads leading to the house. The waves lapped and hugged the mighty greenish boulders and bug-eyed crabs warmed themselves on the rocks. Only the distant shrieks and calls from the left and right gave away the nearness of the resort beaches. They had spent two days and two nights there, isolated from the rest of the world. If you did not count the owners of the house. They didn't. They paid for the lodgings and the simple supper in advance without haggling. The place was wild and virginal, unlike the resorts that surrounded it. The owners were also strange. Algis had often thought of them.

They were called Tasya and Timothy. Their surname was Savchenko. Ukrainian. Both over forty. Childless. They lived poorly, far from people, up on a cliff so high that you could not make it up there without taking a breather. It was two hundred meters up. That's probably why nobody visited them. They themselves came down from the cliff only when they had to—either to market or to fish on the rocks. Timothy did not have a job. He puttered around in his tiny three-row garden behind the house, hauling the water for it from the spring that gurgled in a cold stream from a crack in the side of the cliff. There were twenty steps carved in the stone leading to the spring.

Tasya was away all day. She left early. She worked in a sanatorium in Oreanda in the checkroom. She returned at sunset, dragging a basket filled with the leftovers from lunch and dinner, which she got from the sanatorium dining room. It would take her a long time to get to the top. She would stop several times to get her breath. Halfway she would call loudly for Timothy to come down and help her with the basket.

Tasya was an invalid. Her right leg was gone, replaced by a clumsy wooden prosthesis, wrapped in a thick flesh-colored stocking and stuffed into a low-heeled shoe. So even on the hottest days she wore a heavy stocking on her good leg, too.

She had been wounded in the war. She had served, like many young girls, on a landing ship in Novorossisk. She lost her leg there, near the Crimean shore, in the summer of 1944, toward the end of the war. She spent a long time in a hospital in Yalta. She had even wanted to commit suicide on Victory Day, in the glare of the fireworks display, to the tears of the joyfully hugging people around her. Who would need her in her condition? She had no family, no home. There was no corner of the earth where someone was waiting for her, willing to take her as she was. She probably would have thrown herself into the sea if it had not been for Timothy.

Timothy was a sailor and was in the same hospital. He was perfectly healthy, without a scratch. Strong and good-looking. He would spend all day sitting on the veranda with his face to the sea, listening to the waves. He sat alone and talked to no one. He listened intently, waiting to hear something important from the sea.

He was blind in both eyes. Hopelessly blind. His eyes had melted and his temples had caved in, glued together by a red ridge. There were green freckles on his cheeks and forehead—powder burns.

He did not have a place to go, either. So they got married. Right in the hospital. Their wedding was paid for by the state. The administration was not cheap with the food and drink. There was cigarette smoke in all the wards, because many of the patients were not ambulatory, and the party had moved to the wards. At the table, as Tasya would later recall, there were only three legs for every two people, and even fewer arms.

Tasya was so happy that she did not give any thought to a place to live. The Crimea and Yalta itself were full of empty houses. The Tatars had been relocated in Siberia and their homes were being taken by whoever wanted them.

They lived in the hospital at first, eating for free. But the hospital closed and became a sanatorium again. As it had been before the war. They started looking for a roof over their heads. They did not find anything better than the little house on the cliff.

So they remained in the little house, close to the sky, far from people, living on their meager earnings—veteran's benefits and Tasya's salary. They could not even make money from the summer folks who jammed up Yalta every season. Who wanted to climb that far on vacation? Tasya and Timothy were hysterically happy whenever somebody did live with them for a few days. There were not many who did. It gave the couple some extra money. But that was secondary. The guests brightened Timothy's long, lonely days, while he waited for Tasya to come home from work. He would nurse and service the guests so diligently that they became uncomfortable. Algis recalled that they had left on the third day. He and the lady from Kaunas.

Algis remembered the house on the cliff and the owners. It was the best possible course for Sigita and him. He did not doubt that they would be free or that Tasya and Timothy would welcome them. There was one more important plus for the house. Everywhere in the Crimea landlords demand your passport and hand it over to the police for registration. If they fail to do it, the police come around to see why not. Usually at night, when everyone is asleep. They fine the landlord and confiscate the vacationers' passports.

Tasya and Timothy were not experienced. It would never occur to them to take his passport and the police would never come looking for anything at their house. There could be no better place for fugitives like Algis and Sigita.

Algis got a taxi in Simferopol. It took them toward the mountains. Behind them was the Black Sea. Sigita was charmed as a child, craning her neck to see everything on the right and the left. She had only seen this area in the movies. They were riding down a paved highway, first through the plains with the mountains ahead in a purple haze, like scenery in the theater.

Along the road, behind the poplars, they could see the white Ukrainian clay-walled cottages with the blooming gardens, the empty out-of-season cafeterias with chairs piled up on the tables, the occasional tractors in the fields, puffing black smoke into the clear, cloudless sky.

The car was climbing imperceptibly. Yellow rock was beginning to show along the road. The first groves of trees appeared on the slopes, and then the forest, just as in Lithuania, but climbing ever higher, its dark green groves extending up, covering the bald rock of the cliffs with a fluffy soft carpet. It grew colder and clouds filled the sky. The road twisted between the cliffs, opening on new vistas with every turn. Vistas you could only see in the movies or on picture postcards. Sigita was squealing with pleasure, turning to Algis with radiant eyes, begging him to share her joy.

Mount Ayu-Dag, which in Tatar means Bear Mountain, hovered ahead, huge and brown like a bear at a watering hole. The bear's head was stuck in the Black Sea, toward which the car was now speeding. The sea appeared first as a painfully shiny strip of perfect blue, and then grew wider and wider, sparkling and blinding them.

A white ship grew in the horizon, welcoming them to this earthly paradise.

Once over the mountains, they were back in the heat, gulping the heady smell of the flower gardens. The bright flower beds jarred their eyes. Row upon row of cypresses, which Sigita had never seen, rushed alongside the road.

They passed through Yalta. Beyond Oreanda, the bustle and noise of the resort even this early in the season behind them, Algis located the turnoff from the highway. At the foot of the cliff they disembarked. Algis took the suitcase in his right hand. They carried the travel bag together. Higher and higher along the narrow path. They soon saw the small clay-walled and whitewashed house under the pines. It was staring out at the world through its little windows. In a narrow bed marked off by bricks, nasturtiums and hollyhocks were blooming. Fish on a string were drying in the sun, hung from the roof. Small clay pots without handles were drying on poles the way they do in Ukrainian villages. There was no sign of the owners. Only a reddish-brown dog rolled out from under the shed with a thin, harmless bark. In two seconds it was sniffing their luggage and feet, whining joyously.

They felt at home and cozy immediately. All the worries of the past two days were forgotten. The view from the cliff was phenomenal. The sea lay below them, vast and empty, except by the shore, where it was crowded with rocks. The water foamed around them, accentuating the blueness of its smooth parts. Rocks, trees growing with their roots around them, and the sea.

Nothing had changed since the time Algis first saw it. Not even Timothy, who came out when his dog began barking. He came from the spring, balancing two buckets of water on his back. He was wearing the same faded striped shirt, taut across his broad shoulders, and the same tarpaulin pants, a shiny brass anchor the buckle on his belt.

He recognized Algis' voice as if it had been yesterday. His eyebrows were working. It looked as if he were trying to open his eyes and look at his guest. He was smiling broadly and gently, revealing his gapped, but sturdy teeth, yellowed by nicotine.

"Of course, of course, I remember you." He spoke with a lilt, like all Ukrainians. "From Lithuania. You write poems."

And although Sigita had not given herself away with the slightest noise, he turned to her. His face had green powder burns.

"Hello. I remember you, too."

"No, Timothy," Algis said hurriedly. "This is my daughter. A schoolgirl."

"I sensed that she was young." Timothy extended his hand to her. "So, you've come to the Black Sea? To warm up? It's still cold back on your Baltic."

"She does not speak Russian," Algis stepped in when he saw how confused Sigita was.

"Only your own tongue? That's not too bad. We'll go fish for bullheads in the sea. All right? There's no need to talk there. You have to be quiet. Will you be staying long?"

"Long. Until summer."

"How great!" Timothy was ecstatic. "I'll have somebody to talk to. Soon I'll be blind and mute. A total invalid."

He laughed and led them to the house. He gave them the far room of the two in the house. He left the front room, which you had to pass through, for himself. He bustled about noisily, moving furniture and the heavy iron beds, refusing their help, orienting himself perfectly. He quickly cooked up some *kulesh* (a wheat porridge) in a smoky old cast-iron pot over the clay stove in the yard and fed them after their journey. Algis and Timothy drank the cognac they had brought. They drank out of heavy glasses. Timothy belted the brandy like vodka. He did not eat anything with it, but just smacked his lips in pleasure.

"*O tse garno!* Really good! I haven't had any in ages! You say it's Armenian? Oh-ho! Those Armenians know what they're doing. They know how to live!"

The house was poor but clean. The whitewashed walls were

177

cool. Tasya's embroidered curtains billowed in the windows. Rugs, also made by Tasya, hung over the beds. They represented swans in a pond, a cossack and his girl by a fence, and the silver crescent of the moon up in the white clouds, like caps on waves.

The food and drink made Timothy sleepy. He slept in the yard with Tuzik the dog curled up on his stomach. Algis and Sigita lay down for a nap, too. Each on his own bed. They were against opposite walls, but so close that if they had reached out they could have held hands. Sigita was embarrassed to change in front of him, and was going to lie down fully dressed, but Algis talked her into changing and left the room. When he returned she was fast asleep, her skirt, stockings, and blouse neatly hung over the chair.

At twilight, when the sea had darkened and blended with the horizon and dotted lights were sprinkled to the right and left of them along the shore, Tasya climbed up with her basket and bucket. She oohed and aahed with pleasure when she saw her guests. She recognized Algis immediately and was very happy that he had come with his daughter. So lovely—a copy of her father. She was only worried about Sigita missing school. There were three more months of school. Algis invented a story about Sigita's illness during the winter. Doctors' orders to come South.

"Of course, of course," Tasya said, her gentle eyes never leaving Sigita. Tasya had no children of her own. "Perhaps you want to go to the sanatorium? There's plenty of room now. Even in mine. Shall I inquire?"

Algis lied again. He said Sigita would be fine right there. He had a lot of work, he needed the silence and privacy to write. He did not want to see anyone or be disturbed by anyone.

"Well, then you've come to the right place!" Tasya clapped her hands in glee. "This place is like a grave. Even the police won't find you. Great! We'll be like a family. My Timothy was really getting lonely here. I'll bring groceries up for you. There's a goat for your daughter. It's the best milk. She'll be a healthy beauty in no time."

They dined together. In the yard under the stars. Timothy lit a lantern and the moths swirled around it in clouds. It was quiet. The slapping surf against the beach rocks was the only sound. Tasya had the rest of the brandy, flushed, and livened up. She sang a long Ukrainian song with her husband. The cicadas accompanied them. Timothy put his arm around her, she put her head on his shoulder, and sang in a high voice, her eyes closed, smiling sweetly. He sat straight and tall, seconding her voice with his deep mellow bass, not drowning her out, but highlighting her soprano. His empty eye sockets were pointed through the dark to the sea. Far out several lights were moving. A late ship was heading through the night to Yalta.

It was good and peaceful. Algis felt happier and more at peace than he could remember. Acknowledging that it was she who had led him to take this step, Algis watched Sigita lovingly. She was enraptured by the beauty of the Crimean night and the song that was new to her but close to her, because it was being sung by kind, suffering people who made her feel as happy and safe as her own family. The embarrassment and discomfort she had felt had long passed. She was in her element and was watching their faces, trying to mouth the unfamiliar words of their song.

"We're doing all the singing," Tasya realized. "Are your songs worse than ours? Come on, Sigita, sing one of your Lithuanian ones. Timothy and I will listen."

Sigita did not need coaxing. She smiled shyly at Algis and began the song, quietly and unsure at first, that they had sung with the policemen in the train.

"Where are you running, my little path?
Where do you lead? Where are you calling?
But you won't return the one
I waited for, the one I loved."

179

Tasya was listening to the unfamiliar words with her mouth open in surprise.

"But that's our song too," she exclaimed. "Only with different words! So, it's sung in Lithuanian and Russian."

Sigita understood Russian but spoke it with difficulty.

"No," she said stubbornly. "It's our song, Lithuanian."

"How can that be?" Tasya turned to Algis for support. "It's ours. I remember in our village before the war every girl sang it. And the words were nice . . . Not like today."

She stared up at the stars and tried to remember the words.

> "Far away, behind the blue grove
> Where he and I used to walk,
> The moon floated by—love's helper,
> Reminding me of him."

"It's so soulful," Tasya said, sighing.

Timothy was smiling and shaking his head.

"Why argue?" he said conciliatorily, patting Tasya on the head. "If a song is good, everybody sings it. In Lithuania and Russia. People's souls are the same everywhere."

Sigita sang on. In Lithuanian. Tasya, her prosthesis squeaking, pulled up her stool closer to her, put her arm around Sigita, and took up the song in Russian. Timothy, who did not know the words, just sang the ends of phrases.

Algis sat with his eyes shut and listened to the Russian and Lithuanian words intertwine. He thought enviously that not a single one of his poems had become a song like that. Simple and moving. As necessary to man as bread and water. Composers set his poems to music and they were sung on stage and on the radio. For a couple of months. Then they were forgotten. But the people remembered and loved this one. And nobody knew the name of the lyricist or the composer. A folk song. Living among the people. Not gathering dust on tape in the archives of the radio committee or as yellowing sheet music in somebody's trunk.

Yet he could still write as honestly and sincerely as he had in the beginning of his career. He would write such a poem. He really would. Here, in this hiding place. As he had never written before. Without a thought for the editor or the royalties. Just like that song. Let it pour from his heart. For nobody. For the stars, for the sea. For Sigita and her weak, unplaced voice. For Timothy and Tasya, for whom a good song may be the only pleasure and solace in their pathetic, empty lives. He would write about them—two souls tortured by the war, needed by no one. They had left the world and found a refuge for themselves on this cliff under the southern stars. About their love, gentle and human, the support of their life.

Somewhere below, in the invisible sea, a ship's horn sounded deep and long, and two little lights blinked at them.

"Headed for Kerch," blind Timothy said. Tasya noted the time from the horn and said that it was late. Bedtime. She had to go to work early in the morning. Algis did not want to get up. But the blind man was already clearing the table by touch, and Algis rushed to help.

"It's not necessary," Timothy said with a snicker. "I'm used to it. I'm better off at night than you. You might as well be blind in the dark. It's always the same for me. I see with my feet and hands."

He carried the stack of dishes in his outstretched hands, confidently putting one foot before the other along the path all the way to the door. He pushed it open with his knee and disappeared in the darkness. Algis tensed, waiting for the sound of broken dishes. He could not wait, and followed the blind man in. Timothy was crouched in the dark kitchen over a basin washing invisible dishes.

"Timothy," Algis asked, "please let Sigita do the dishes. It's women's work."

"I can see right off that you were never in the navy." Algis guessed at his smile in the dark. "How could any woman compete with a sailor at this? For Sigita to do the dishes would be a loss of time and money. She would have to light the lamp, use up the kerosene. You economize with me."

Tasya arrived, her leg squeaking, and started chasing Algis out of the room.

"You're our guests and you're supposed to be resting. Off to your beds!"

Algis and Sigita closed their door and undressed without putting on the lights. The starlight was streaming into their room through the window, falling in dull spots on the rock-hard clay floor. There was a bitter smell of wormwood in the room. Dried bunches of the poisonous grass were hung from the rafters to guard against fleas.

Even in the dark, Sigita undressed with her back to him. Algis noticed that when they were alone she tensed up, waiting for something to happen.

"Listen, daughter," he said when he was under the covers. "Are you uncomfortable with me in the same room? I can go sleep in the shed on the hay."

"What about me?" She sat up on her bed and Algis imagined that he saw the glimmer of her eyes. "I'll be alone?"

"Then don't be embarrassed around me. We've got more than one day to be together."

"How many?"

"I don't know. How long would you like?"

"Me? For . . . forever."

"What do you mean?"

"Without you, I'd be lost."

"Well, that's not true. You're young. Your whole life is ahead."

"Nothing is ahead. Except you."

"But I'm old."

"No . . . You're the most perfect man in the world. Except I'm no match for you. How could I be?"

Algis said nothing in reply. Sigita sat on the bed, her knees under the blanket pulled up to her chin. Silence. Then he heard soft sobbing.

"Sigita," he called in a whisper.

She did not reply, but stopped crying. She sighed deeply and sorrowfully.

"Do you really love me?"

"Very much." Her whisper carried from her bed.

Algis got out of his bed and bent over her. Her head was bowed. He put his hand on her hair.

"Don't touch me," she said angrily. "Leave me alone."

In their room, Tasya sighed and Timothy coughed.

"They can hear everything," Algis thought. "But—we're speaking Lithuanian. They don't know what the hell we're talking about."

"Sleep, my daughter," he said louder in Russian and tiptoed away from her. "Good night."

As he fell asleep he promised himself to keep his distance with Sigita because her unstable personality and her rapid unexpected veering from docility and gentleness to aggression and anger could lead to trouble. Only God knew what a girl like Sigita was capable of, with her primitive concepts of honor and decency and the complete and total chaos in her silly head, thrown off the track by the sudden changes in her life.

He had to be strict and careful with her, like a father. That's all he was fit for—being her father, anyway. It would be an education for her to live near him and pick up a few manners. She would think of him in a kindly way later. This might be the only good deed he'd ever do in his life.

What about poetry? No. He would do his own thing too. He would work like an ox. Until he dropped from exhaustion. He would take his second wind. Tell the truth. Without censorship.

Just as he thought and saw fit. He would tell the world about Lithuania, the tragedy, the stubborn, almost crazy, heroism the authorities had tried to hush up. Let people find out and shudder. They'd take off their hats before this tiny but great people. No one could tell their story better than he.

But who would hear it? Read it? Who would publish it? Nobody in this country. He was fated to silence and obscurity. Writing for his desk drawer. All his life. But after his death? Who knows? Things change. Nothing is permanent. Only beauty is permanent. His poetry would be found. It would go to the people. When he no longer existed. So what? That is the fate of the true creator, who steps beyond his own time. Please God, that's the way it would be, and he would leave something behind. But no more thinking about the future. That was petty conceit. He would write as long as he had the strength. And read it aloud to Sigita, his pretty and wild "daughter." That was perfect. He was not alone. He had a reader. What else could a poet want?

Algis woke up late. The sun was pouring in through the window. Algis opened both shutters without getting out of bed. The other bed was empty and neatly made. The old cover was tight and the two pillows puffed up and placed on top of each other. There were no voices. Only the sea's sighs. Algis remembered everything. Where he was, and how he got there. And laughed. Feckless, carefree laughter. He laughed out loud. Bare footsteps in the next room headed for the door and he saw Sigita in the sleeveless dress he had bought in Simferopol. The dress was very short, stopping at mid-thigh. Her thighs were thin, but firm and very feminine. Sigita smiled, wrinkling her short nose. Her smile was no longer shy, but open and childishly kind. In the bodice, Algis could see the roundness of her small breasts. She was not wearing a bra, and that surprised him too. There had been many changes in her overnight. She felt at home here, out of danger, and she looked at Algis without her former frightened respect.

"Get up. Breakfast is ready."

"You're using the familiar 'you' with me?"

"How else should a daughter address her father?"

"That's right. But we're speaking Lithuanian and no one can understand."

"There's no one home at all. Tasya's at work and Timothy went fishing."

"I'll get dressed."

Algis expected her to leave the room. But Sigita sat on the edge of her bed and watched him. Without any embarrassment, with undisguised curiosity. He was the one who got uncomfortable, and he turned his back to her.

Then out in the yard she poured water from an iron pitcher onto his hands when he was washing. Algis caught her expression—grown-up, gentle, and concerned, like that of a mother helping her son wash up.

After breakfast, he suggested they go for a swim. She shook her head stubbornly.

"Why not?"

"I don't want to see anybody. We're alone here."

Algis looked into her eyes, still and waiting for an answer, and he realized that she was feeling the same arousal that he had been experiencing for a long time. His heart contracted in sweet anticipation. He looked away. Stood and went into the room. Sigita followed him, closed the door, and hugged him, locking her fingers around the back of his neck, clumsily kissing him on the cheek.

"Stop . . . Sigita . . ." he whispered gruffly and hotly. He felt the warm smell of her hair and the tickle of her eyelashes on his cheek. "Why? I'm older . . . You're still a child . . ."

"I love you."

"You'll be sorry."

"No. Stop talking. There will never be anyone better than you in my life. Do I please you?"

"Very much. But . . ."

"Then, that's all!"

She stepped back. She took the hem of her dress in both hands and pulled it up over her head, exposing her body, and threw it in the corner. When she saw the passion in his eyes, she instinctively crossed her arms over her small breasts. Then she lowered them.

"Well, how do you like me?" she asked in a hoarse whisper. "Too skinny, huh? Not a woman yet? You don't like looking at me?"

"You are a goddess. You are enchantment itself. There's not a woman who compares to you."

"That's not true," she said, shaking her head, but she was so unsure of herself that Algis realized how important it was for her to hear those words. He talked on, constantly, a stream of love words, while he struggled with his buttons. Sigita stood before him, white, untouched by the sun, thin, her ribs showing, unconsciously rubbing her thin strong thighs.

He threw the mattress off his bed on the floor, and then pulled down the one from her bed.

"Why?" Sigita asked in surprise.

"Too narrow. We won't fit."

"That's right." She got on her knees and helped him make the bed on the floor. Her small breasts with their dark nipples hung down swaying firmly. Algis could not wait. He put his hand under her stomach and grabbed them, like two balls in his hands. She gasped weakly and fell on her side.

After, he lay still and smoked, flicking the ashes in his palm. Sigita was gone. The sound of running water came from the kitchen. She was washing out the bloodstain from the sheet. Algis heard her purring and humming to herself. He was impressed by her restraint and grown-up independence. He was her first man. She had known no one else, all this was new to her, yet she gave herself to him without fear and instinctively knew

186

how to behave. She did not moan or push him away, even when he knew and could see that it hurt and she wanted to scream. Instead, she watched his every move with compassion and pity, trying to help him, and patted him on the back with her hot, sweaty palm, as though she wanted to encourage and calm him. And now, as if this happened every day, she was busily washing the sheets, removing all evidence of her sins, and singing.

He smoked until she came back. She saw the ashes in his hand, took them into hers, and threw them out the window. With utter simplicity and country reasonableness. She did not flirt, or try to catch his eye, or look for compassion, as it usually was with the older women Algis had known. She was natural in her every movement and felt no shame in parading around naked. That was the way she was, and she did not know how to pretend. After their intimacy, her body belonged to him as much as it did to her and it seemed as incongruous to cover herself and feel shame before him as it would have before herself.

Algis felt relieved. She took the burden of responsibility from him. She became an equal partner. He was infinitely grateful to her that everything was going so well. They were truly together now, tied not only by their flight, but by their desire.

"Get up," she said, treating him like a child. "I'll make the bed and we'll be able to go for a swim."

They went down the path to the sea in their sateen suits from Simferopol, towels over their shoulders. The rocks on the shore were warm. The sea was foamy around the rocks and smooth and still beyond.

They could see Timothy's back on one of the far rocks, in his striped shirt, his bamboo fishing rod arched in front of him. He heard the pebbles under their feet and said hello without turning. He informed them that the water was cold and it was too early to swim. They could take a boat ride. His was moored over there. They just had to get the oars from the shed. They thanked him, but did not feel like going for a ride. They chose a large, flat rock within a yard of Timothy and lay down on its hot, rough surface.

Timothy still had his back to them. He was happy for an opportunity to talk. He pulled a reed basket out of the water. There were a dozen bullheads bulging their red eyes and splashing about and a large pike perch. Sigita and Algis praised his catch. Timothy promised them a fish stew the likes of which they had never had.

The sun was high, but the heat was not bad near the water. There was not a soul around, not even a sea gull. Algis put his hand on her stomach, and she put her hand over his. His fingers climbed higher toward her bra. He lifted it and felt the smooth softness of her breast. He got as far as her nipple, pinching it slightly, when he felt a surge of desire, sharp and irrational.

He quickly took off his suit, bent over her, and started undressing her.

"What about him?" she asked in Lithuanian.

"He can't see." Algis laughed, casting a sidelong glance at Timothy's striped back.

"But he can hear."

"We'll be quiet."

Sigita did not resist. She spread her white legs on the warm yellow rock, took his head in her hands, and held her breath.

"How do you say 'bread' in Lithuanian?" Timothy asked. Algis was still for a second and then answered.

After a bit, Timothy was interested in the word for "sky" and then "water."

"What are you laughing about?" he suddenly asked, turning and fixing his empty sockets on them. Algis and Sigita burst out in raucous laughter.

She jumped from the rock into the cold water and washed herself up to the neck. She splashed Algis, like a mother washing a child, and then dried his legs and stomach with the towel.

Sigita and Timothy made supper in the yard. Algis sat in the room writing. It was coming easier and faster than usual. He put it down to his mood, the elevated spirits and good health he had felt since morning. Sigita would come in once in a while, look over his shoulder at the page, holding her breath. He would rub his head against her breasts and try to catch her hand with his lips.

"Write, write. I won't bother you." She would pat him on the head like a child and tiptoe out.

A week passed. Algis did a lot of writing. Every morning he spent naked on the rocks at the shore, and, even at home up on the cliff until twilight and Tasya's return, he walked around undressed, trying not to bump into the blind Timothy.

They lived on an uninhabited island. Like aborigines. Their bodies acquired a soft even tan that can only be gotten in the Crimea in the spring. The tan was even all over their bodies, without any white areas, because everything was exposed to the sun. They only pulled on their shorts toward evening, when they were expecting Tasya.

Timothy was always around, doing work around the house and talking non-stop, making up for all the lonely hours he had spent. Their life had a special piquantness from the fact that there was a stranger near them who did not realize they were naked. Algis would talk to him while he held her breast in his hand and she ran her fingers through his pubic hair. A sensual desire was always with them, and they would throw themselves upon each other's bodies with abandon at a single look, whether they were at home or down by the beach. And Timothy was almost always an unknowing witness to their love-making.

Behind the house the slope of the mountain rose ever higher, overgrown with forest. The Judas tree was blooming with deep violet blossoms—not on the branches, but right from the gnarled stump. It was a Crimean attraction, as old as a fossil, from biblical times, brought here by the Greek colonists from Palestine.

Sigita and Algis would go into the forest. Naked as the day

189

they were born, their clothes bundled up in a strap slung over their shoulders. They went high into the mountains, crossing the peak, getting as far as the Uchan-su Waterfall that cascaded dozens of meters down the slippery cliffs. They would dress here and walk out onto the road, full of tourists with knapsacks on their backs and Yalta taxis. They would have a charcoal-broiled shashlik at the cafe by the waterfall and go home through the forest.

Algis stopped shaving and his tan cheeks were overgrown by a soft blond stubble. The first signs of a beard gave him the idea that he had changed enough to risk an excursion to the inhabited shores of Simeiz and Alupka. He still avoided Yalta.

They went into Alupka, which was full of vacationers. They went to a bank and withdrew enough cash for two months from the letter of credit. Then they strolled through the luxurious parks planted by the Russian tsars and walked along the parquet floors of palaces converted into museums. Algis explained everything like a conscientious guide, and Sigita, wide-eyed, took in the generous beauty, so sincerely exhilarated by it that he saw it all for the first time again.

Algis led her to a bronze bust on a large marble pedestal in a meadow at the Vorontsov Palace. The statue represented a military man in an army cap, epaulets, with many orders and medals on his chest. They were topped with two five-pointed stars. He had an Asiatic face with high cheekbones. Algis explained that he was a two-time Hero of the Soviet Union, the pilot Sultan Kahn, born in Alupka. According to Soviet law any citizen who had been awarded the two gold stars that go with being a Hero had a monument raised in his honor in his hometown. That's why the Crimean Tatar Sultan Kahn, cast in bronze, was staring down from his pedestal at the vacationers, for the most part Russians. There were no more Tatars in the Crimea, they had been chased from their homeland to Middle Asia by Stalin's decree. Sultan Kahn was the only Tatar in the Crimea now. And he was bronze and not alive. Even the little house they were living in with Tasya and Timothy was Tatar. At one time there were only Tatars in the Crimea. It was their homeland. Catherine II had conquered the Crimea and annexed it, just like Lithuania. Stalin cleaned the Crimea of Tatars. He didn't finish up with Lithuania because his death interfered.

Sigita frowned and took him by the hand.

"Let's get out of here. I don't want to look. It's all stolen stuff anyway."

A month later, when his beard had grown out fully, they went into Yalta. Algis took her to the Oreanda restaurant, frequented mostly by foreigners. Algis used to like to spend his evenings there.

The French steamer *Renaissance* had docked in Yalta that day, letting off swarms of European tourists. They immediately filled up all the cafes and souvenir shops along the dock with their noise and bright clothes.

Sigita and Algis had seen the white monster that morning, with its French tricolor flying in the breeze over the stern. She wanted to see the ship up close, and Algis, who was looking for some way to give her pleasure, to reward her in some way for giving him his youth and making him happier than he had ever been, decided to throw caution to the winds. He suggested they get a cab and try to catch up with the *Renaissance*.

They did beat it into port, and had time to sit and watch it in the glassed-in cafe of the Oreanda. They had a marvelous view of the port. They stuffed their faces with ice cream and watched the *Renaissance* go through its paces, which it could have been doing just for them, until the tugs brought it in to its mooring.

The cafe with its solid glass wall opening onto the sea used to be a favorite haunt of his and of other writers. They would come down from the mountains, from the House of Creativity, after hours of banging away at the typewriter, to clear their brains, sip some wine in pleasant company, and eye the women—resort

191

beauties, seductive and available, if you're a big spender and have a famous name. This was the very spot where Algis picked up women—the beginnings of short-lived and senseless resort affairs, forgotten forever as soon as he bought the return ticket home.

He recognized several women's faces in the half-empty cafe with the cool moist floor. He tried to remember whether he had slept with any of them or whether he had merely spent time with them in the cafe. They looked him over with interest but did not recognize him either. The reddish-blond beard confused them and so did the large sunglasses. Then two Moscow writers dropped in. Algis did not tempt fate. He turned his back to the room. He did not turn around again.

He walked Sigita along the bustling quay to the port terminal. They ran into a lot of friends along the way, including some Lithuanians, even heard the language spoken. It elicited an exited nostalgia. They felt very keenly that they were aliens who dared not reveal their identity or speak their native tongue. They were comforted by one thing. No one recognized Algis, his beard had changed him enough.

Because a foreign ship had docked, the entrances to the terminal were closed to Soviet citizens. They could not see the *Renaissance* up close. Sigita was so saddened that Algis again waved caution to the winds and took a step that was unbelievably dangerous for them. He led Sigita by the hand to the enormous doors where two guards were dispersing the crowd of gapers. He muttered a few phrases in Lithuanian, which sounded like a foreign language to the Yalta guards, and they let the two of them pass, taking them for tourists.

Sigita was in a rapturous state, and laughed gleefully as they walked along the pier toward the great white sides of the ship, with its countless shining portholes. Her laughter made them seem even more like foreigners, because the only people who are that carefree and unguarded in Russia are foreign tourists, who

192

do not give a damn about Soviet customs and the all-seeing eye of the KGB.

Cameras and elegant bags hanging from their arms, the tourists in shorts and miniskirts were milling around on the gangplanks, carefree and excited. At the foot of the gangplanks, as still as the iron posts to which the ship was moored by cables, border guards stood in pairs. Green caps over their inscrutable, officially frozen faces.

"If we could only get on that boat," Sigita whispered.

"What if we could?"

"We'd be saved."

"Who needs us there?"

Sigita looked up at him in surprise.

"I need you, and you need me. Who else do we need?"

Until that moment it had never occurred to Algis that they could escape abroad to put an end to their uncertain position. Truly, it was the only way out. They would be out of reach of their persecutors. They would find peace and security. A touchstone for their new life, which they could live openly, without hiding from anyone. And freedom . . . The freedom to write the truth, without holding anything back. Freedom to shout at the top of his lungs. The iron hand of the censor would be taken from his throat.

Algis tried to shake himself loose of the thought. It was impossible to leave Russia without the permission of the authorities. You could only leave when they decided you could. People did not travel from the Soviet Union, they were sent from it. Only madmen would attempt to escape. The border was locked, as the song goes, and the beefy border guards on the gangplank were proof of it.

That evening Algis took Sigita to the most expensive restaurant in town. It was full of bronze and crystal and antique mirrors in ornate frames. He wanted to live it up and to show Sigita the other side of life, the one she had never seen. Where money was no object, where the lucky ones drank and ate, where they managed by hook or crook to get a fatter portion of the poor pie that was officially designated as the general wealth. After all, Sigita believed what she had been taught, what had been drummed into her head—not without the aid of his poems, by the way. Now she was gaping like Cinderella at the ball. At the fat, chewing mouths, at the glitter of jewelry on the ladies' necks, and the lust and satiety in their eyes, at the arrogant servility of the waiters.

For her, a kolkhoz girl, taken from her primitive, poverty-stricken way of life, brightened only by dreams and hopes for Communism like heaven after death, for her this unbridled bacchanalia seemed blasphemous and unbelievable. She could not even eat. She chewed with difficulty, crushed and destroyed by the spectacle. Algis was sorry that he had brought her here and had subjected her to this ordeal. He was disgusted by it himself, and he understood what changes he had undergone since the day of his flight. His tastes and habits had changed completely. It was a joyous discovery. He was becoming a different person. He was shedding all his former values, all the things that had seemed like necessities. Excited by his discovery, he dragged Sigita out onto the crowded dance floor. The couples were jiggling in the middle of the room to the wailing of the jazz band.

Sigita was shy but there was no need to know how to dance. Only sway and shift from foot to foot, taking care not to be trampled. Someone's purple face with rabbity eyes flashed by. But when Algis tried to look at him, all he could see was the back of his head with two pink folds in the neck over a white nylon collar. The porcine folds looked familiar, particularly the shock of red hair. Algis felt a creeping chill. The face floated out over someone's shoulder and bugged its eyes at him. He was recognized, and recognized by a man who knew him too well to be confused by a beard. It was Sniukas, the director of the publishing house in Vilnius, the editor of Algirdas Požera's books, a friend of the family, present at countless family occasions. Sniukas was staring at him, unable to believe his eyes. He stopped dancing. It was clear that he, as many others in Lithuania, had already buried Požera, had accepted that the poet disappeared in mysterious circumstances. And suddenly he saw Algis alive, bearded, in Yalta, in a restaurant, as if nothing had happened, dancing with some girl, a mere child.

There were a few couples between them, and this gave Algis an opportunity to run off, dragging Sigita after him, rudely pushing into shoulders and backs. He did not need to explain to Sigita. She guessed that Algis had sensed danger and hurried after him without looking back. They did not go back to their table, but rushed out as if there were someone pursuing them. Without paying. They ran down the street toward the taxi stand. And calmed down a little only when the lights of nighttime Yalta disappeared behind the turn in the road.

Back home on their cliff, sitting by the open window and listening to Timothy's snores, looking out at the moonlight tracking a broken path along the sea up to the horizon, Algis figured out the meaning of what had happened. Sniukas would immediately, perhaps right now, call Vilnius and breathlessly announce what he had seen. Algirdas Požera was alive! Changed his face with a beard. Ran when he was recognized and hid somewhere. He was seen with a young girl, sixteen or seventeen, resembling the reports of the girl who escaped from under armed guard in the Moscow-Kaliningrad train. Escaped with the aid of Algirdas Požera.

The entire Crimean police force would be alerted by tomorrow. It was too late to run from the peninsula to somewhere like Siberia or Central Asia. They would be recognized by the first policeman they ran across at the Simferopol airport, the only airway gate from the Crimea. Even if the cop had only skimmed the report on the fugitives.

His wife would definitely fly down here. With responsible comrades from the Writers' Union. It would be a free trip south for them, a serendipitous pleasure, but would look like a moral act on their part. They would pretend that it wasn't easy to unglue their rear ends from their writers' chairs, drop their half-finished manuscripts, and embark on a search for the mysteriously vanished colleague.

They would trap him like a wolf, and he would be unable to escape from the trap that the Crimea had become.

There was only one way out. To wait out the alarm here on the cliff, where no one would think to look. Never go down. Not even to the beach. Find an excuse for Tasya and Timothy. Both got food poisoning, or some disease, whatever, but they both needed bed rest.

The sudden illness of their guests did not arouse suspicions in Tasya and Timothy. The blind man cursed restaurant food thoroughly and roundly and reminded them in a huff that it would be a lesson to them—not to scorn the home hearth. Tasya brought them medicine from the sanatorium. She mentioned in a casual aside to Algis that she had met the local policeman down there, and he was interested in him and Sigita, and wanted her to bring their papers down to the precinct.

That was all they needed! The noose was tightening.

Algis tried to hide his anxiety and explained calmly, much too calmly, why it was not worth the trouble to register them with the precinct. Then Tasya would be hereinafter a landlady, and would have to pay taxes on the rent she collected. And she would have almost nothing left from all the money Algis was going to pay her. And she and Timothy were not so rich that they could turn away an honest living. That was why she should tell the police that the tenants had gone. Algis and Sigita would go on living there, disturbing no one. And when they did leave, Tasya would get all the money.

The argument convinced her. The next day she told Algis, her eyes twinkling, how they had believed her down at the station. And she would not have to pay taxes.

Disaster struck late that evening. Timothy and Tasya were cooking supper in the yard when the policeman climbed up to the house. Algis was in his room writing. Sigita had just gone down for water.

Algis turned out the light and climbed out the window. Hoping to catch Sigita on the way out. But he was too late. Sigita was coming up with two pails balanced on a pole over her shoulder. She did not see the stranger with Tasya and Timothy in the twilight. The cop wanted to know who she was. They began to lie lamely, that she was the daughter of a friend here to spend a day or two. Sigita blabbed something in a feeble attempt to help them out, and her Lithuanian accent made the policeman more suspicious. He asked for her papers.

It was over! The trap sprang shut. One more minute and the policeman would detain Sigita and take her down to identify her. Algis could still save himself. Timothy's boat was tied to the rocks below. The oars were in the shed. He had to climb back in through the window, roll up his manuscripts, wrap them in the plastic he had stored away, stick them in his shirt, and run for the oars.

And Sigita? She would perish in a camp. That was her fate. Algis could not help her with anything any more. As God was his witness: he had tried to do everything he could, but she had stepped into the trap herself. He would perish saving her. This way he would escape at least. And he was saving more than his own skin. He was saving his poetry, the most precious thing he had. Poetry the people needed.

He took his manuscripts and left everything else for Tasya and Timothy, crept over to the shed, and put the oars over his shoulders. The policeman was walking down the path with Sigita in front of him. The old couple were standing in amazement by the open fire in the yard. Sigita turned to them and waved. The sight of her face, smiling and overly calm in view of what was happening to her, made Algis lose control. He caught up with the policeman in a few bounds. The slipping gravel under his feet and his heavy breathing alerted the policeman and Sigita. The policeman reached for his gun. Sigita shouted and bit his hand. Algis, no longer thinking, raised the oars in his hands and brought them down hard like an ax on firewood. There was a sickening crunching noise. The policeman sat down on a rock. Blood, intolerably red, streamed down his eyes and nose. He fell softly on his back, extending his straight, unbending legs, nails showing on his mended uniform boots.

Algis took up the oars and started down the path. Sigita bounded after him like a goat. Tasya and Timothy were shouting down after them:

"They killed him! Murder! Stop them!"

Without looking back, Algis could tell from the sound of their voices that the two were running after them, trying to catch them. Tasya with her wooden leg, and blind Timothy. The voices fell back, gasping. They must have both fallen.

Algis and Sigita splashed past the rocks, raising streams of seawater, to the boat. He put her in, handed her the oars, untied the chain, and pushed off from the rocks, clambering aboard at Sigita's feet.

The oars were in the locks, Sigita moved over to make room for him next to her on the seat. They rowed together, rhythmically, and the boat skimmed along the dark water toward the shimmering moonbeam.

Sigita was smiling gratefully and loyally at her savior. He was concentrating and gloomy, feverishly thinking how not to get lost and how to get far from the shore into neutral waters, where, if there was a God in heaven, they would be picked up by a foreign ship by morning.

They did not speak, but rowed silently, pointing the bow toward the moonbeam disappearing into the clouds. They scanned the horizon for the silhouette or the smoke of a ship. They heard the put-put of a motor. It howled and screamed into their backs. Blinding floodlights fell on the water over their heads.

All that they saw was the blinding circle of the lamp on the bow of the border patrol cutter, which had quickly caught up with them. The light was so strong that it was painful even with their eyes shut.

The cutter loomed up above them, and nosed their little rowboat. Algis was sharply thrown overboard in one direction, Sigita in the other. Cold water engulfed them.

Algis uttered a muffled cry, suffocating, and woke up. The quiet blue of the night-light illuminated the compartment. The train was swaying and shuddering, picking up speed. Lights from some city flashed past the frosty window. His heart racing, and still not completely sure that he was in the train on his way home and that all the rest—the flight with Sigita, the Crimea, their death at sea—was only a nightmare, a terrible dream, Algis stared dully at his neighbor. Dausa, the Kaunas policeman. His heavy boots were swaying on the floor, smelly underwear sticking from the tops. Slowly Algis relaxed, catching his breath. He felt as if he had been running.

A sweet feeling of relief, of uncontrollable physical happiness spread through his entire body, to his fingertips. Pouring, drowning him. He realized he would not sleep any more. And he did not want to lie there, either. He had a need to move, to talk to somebody, to find an outlet for the stormy happiness that was gathering in him. The happiness one feels after a brush with death.

He threw off the covers and sat up on the bed. Across the way in the upper berth, he could see Sigita's head. A few ringlets of hair were hanging over the edge. She was asleep. Algis was glad. He did not want to see her eyes just then. He almost felt as if his happiness was betraying her.

Gaidialis groaned above him and hung down his frowzy, sleepy face.

"Can't sleep?"

Algis shook his head and put his fingers to his lips. He did not want to wake the others.

"I thought I heard a scream," Gaidialis whispered hoarsely, lowering his head. "Everything is all right, then? Nothing happened?"

"Nothing."

"Then let's have a smoke."

Gaidialis climbed down, in his not so fresh underwear and sat down on Algis' bed without asking permission. He pulled on his dark-blue jodhpurs. He went out into the corridor barefoot and shirtless. Algis followed, almost fully dressed. No tie or jacket, though.

The long corridor ended with curtained windows. There were only two lights on. It was cozy and Algis' cigarette tasted good. He usually did not like to smoke on an empty stomach. It gave him a bitter taste in his mouth. He was almost completely relaxed and stood next to Gaidialis by the window, puffing two streams of smoke in unison, staring into the impenetrable, lightless night.

The corridor, carpeted and chrome-shiny, was filled with a sleepy warmth. A conductor walked past them, suspiciously checking out the two late-nighters. Algis asked her if they had just passed Minsk.

"What Minsk?" she laughed. "You slept through everything. We're almost in Vilnius. There's no point in your going back to sleep."

She went to the service car.

Gaidialis beamed.

"I'm glad she reminded us. Your ticket is only to Vilnius. We have to extend it to Kaunas. Or you'll lose your seat in Vilnius. I'll go ask her to reserve it all the way to Kaunas."

He pulled up his pants and went to the service car. Algis was left alone. He suddenly felt irritation at the fact that the policeman was taking charge of him, deciding for him. And yet, it was Algis who had decided to interfere in Sigita's case and go to Kaunas with them. Just recently, when he was falling asleep, he felt as alert and inspired as before battle. What had changed? The dream? But that was no reason for a bad mood.

The policeman returned and winked at Algis.

"All taken care of. Your seat is good till Kaunas. You can go back to sleep in peace."

"Go on ahead. I'll stay here a bit."

"Why? Worried?"

"No . . ."

"Go to bed. You have to be fresh tomorrow. You have to go to the authorities. We'll take Sigita to my house from the station. Can't take her to the police station. She's crazy, she'll do something crazy. Let her think she's visiting me. My daughter's her age. We'll wait for you. Like our liberator . . ."

He laughed and winked again. As if they were buddies. Algis did not like that.

"So, Comrade Požera, a person's fate is in your hands. You have a lot of power. That's enviable." Suddenly he grew serious. "What if the first secretary isn't in town? What if he's on vacation or on a business trip? I didn't think about that. Huh? You don't know the prosecutor, do you?"

"No. But I hope my name is familiar to him." Algis wanted him to leave. He was getting angry. "Of course, I'm not as omnipotent as you think."

"No, wait a bit." The policeman was anxious. "We have to think this through, be prepared. If the first secretary is out of town you won't be able to handle the prosecutor without him. And that's the end of the girl. They'll send her away. And it'll all be over. She'll kill herself. That's for sure. Who else in authority do you know in Kaunas?"

"What is this? An interrogation?" Algis laughed irritatedly. "Go to sleep. If the first secretary is out, we'll find the second or the third, or the secretary of propaganda . . . I have enough influence to take care of this matter. Go rest . . ."

"Well, I can get some rest now that you've promised. We'll do everything that we're supposed to do. I just hope everything goes well for you."

He went into the compartment. He left the door open, and Algis could see him taking off his pants and climbing up to his berth. He tossed and turned for a bit under his blanket and then was quiet.

Algis flipped down the folding chair by the window and sat down. He was alone in the corridor with no distractions.

"It looks like I'm getting involved in a messy situation." He lit a second cigarette. "All right, so we get to Kaunas. It will be late in the morning. The workday will have started. I'll go to the city committee headquarters. If the first secretary is out, and that's very possible, the whole thing takes on an official character. It's a snap with the first secretary. A word from him and it's done. Without leaving his office. A phone call. He wouldn't even ask why I want it done. He'll laugh and take me to his house for drinks and then drive me to the station for the night train."

If the secretary was out of town, a whole bureaucratic mess would begin. Of course, no one would refuse Algis the favor. They would be polite and helpful, but he would have to write out a request, explain his motives, and go to the prosecutor's office and explain there again. It would be maddening. He would lose the entire day. And most importantly, he would be put in the position of asking for something, and some old, gray, boring Party fat cats would pretend that it was only their respect for his name that made them bend the law and do him a favor. Which he hated. What did he need all that for? Then the rumors and whispers would start. Algirdas Požera is taking the responsibility for a little thief. A young girl. He's no fool. Knows what he's doing, the stud. And Algis would have to justify his action, make a joke out of it. What the hell!

The train would be in Vilnius in an hour. It was still night. They were not expecting him at home. He did not wire or write. Algis liked arriving home unexpectedly. Not because he did not trust his wife. Heaven forbid! But just to keep his hands untied. He could spend a day or two in Vilnius, away from prying eyes, and his wife would still be sure that he was in Moscow.

Just recently he had discovered a treasure in Vilnius—a little actress, Irena. Lovely and sexy, with her own small apartment on Antokole, right by his house, but on the other side of the river. Evenings, Algis could see the lights of his house from her window. She made no demands, was comfortable, and never said no. But he could not swear that her bed was empty when he was away. This did not worry him. Whenever he dropped in, of course not during a play or rehearsal, she was always there, in her quilted robe and nothing on underneath. She did whatever he wished with alacrity, as though that were the meaning of her life: to wait for him and do whatever he wanted. She babbled all the time, even in bed. But Algis learned not to listen to the meaning of her words, only their melodious sound, the smoothness of her actress' voice.

He rested at her place, and went there when he was tense and exhausted.

Algis thought of her. Her small warm breasts, her thin ribs, and her concave stomach. The soft, dyed tresses with the dark roots. She was probably sleeping rolled up in the corner of her wide bed. The mirror on the wall was angled so that you could watch everything you were doing in bed. Algis often caught her staring into the mirror, watching with curiosity as he puffed over her.

He wanted to go to Irena's. To see the stupid, acquiescent actress. To sleep on her bed. Give her money for a good dinner with lots of cognac. And then arrive in the evening at his house, saying he was just off the train. Put on a tired haggard face. Complain of insomnia on the train. His family would soothe and comfort him, serve him. Help him don his fresh pajamas and leave him alone in his study to relax after the trip.

So what was keeping him from having his pleasure? The business with Sigita. The necessity of going to Kaunas, wasting the day there, begging, talking to people whom he never liked to spend any time with anyway. And then he would still have the problem of what to do with her. The little fool seriously thought that her fate interested him. And the police, both dull sentimental dummies, who hoped to expiate their sinful black lives with a good deed. Go ahead, expiate. But what did they need Algis for? What if he had been traveling in a different car? Or even the next compartment? Would they have thought to help that little fool? Not on your life. They would have delivered her, signed the warrant, and never asked how the trial had gone, and how many years she got.

She threatened suicide if they put her in jail. Nonsense. She was lying. Worse ones than she had gone behind bars and barbed wire. They threatened, wept, and then got used to it. Did their time and got out with a rich vocabulary of Russian curses. Their lives went pretty well after that. Sigita was not yet seventeen. Maybe she would get three years. No more. She would get out when she was twenty. The best age for beginning a new life. And she would be wiser, without book nonsense in her head. She would know what was what and would never stray again. She would marry, have a bunch of kids, and tell the neighbors about the time when she was a girl and shared a compartment with the famous poet Algirdas Požera and even wrote him a love letter. No one would believe her and in time, she would think she had dreamed it herself.

Occasional lights flashed by. A small rural station hurtled past. The wheels clacked at the junction. Then it was dark once again. The wheels clattered rhythmically.

Vilnius was coming up. That idiot Gaidialis had told the conductor Algis would not be getting off. Who asked him? What was this plebeian manner of insisting on doing unnecessary favors? And who had given the policeman the right to decide for him? He would get off at Vilnius. Because that was what he, Algirdas Požera, wanted, and nobody, especially no policeman, could tell him what to do.

What was the best way to go about it? It would be best to leave quietly. Seen by no one. Otherwise there would be questions and cajoling. He would have to lie, invent excuses. It was decided: he would get off at Vilnius. The others were sleeping soundly in the compartment.

Algis peeked in. He could see Gaidialis, whose nose and cheek were hanging over the edge. Gaidialis was asleep.

Algis silently opened the door and it clicked into place. Sigita was curled up in a corner of her berth, and Dausa was sleeping on his stomach, his face turned sideways, and snoring with a cramped sound.

Algis had to collect his things. He climbed up on the stepladder and took down his travel bag and suitcase. Noiselessly. Straining every muscle. He opened the travel case and put the things from the table into it: the shaving kit, soap, toothbrush, toothpaste. He tried to estimate how many cups of tea he had had in the evening by the number of sugar wrappers on the table. He gave up and left a ruble, much more than was necessary.

He looked out into the corridor. It was empty from right to left. He put the suitcase and then the case on the carpet runner. Then he took his velour coat off the hook, stuffed his fur hat on his head, and left, shutting the door after himself. Slowly, until the lock clicked.

Suddenly he felt uncomfortable. He was alone with his things in the empty corridor under the sleepy yellow light of the two lamps. Looking around like a thief. With a pounding heart.

What could he say to the conductor if she looked out of the service compartment? She definitely would and soon. And worse, what if Gaidialis and Dausa noticed he was gone?

He could not hang around the corridor in full view. He had to hide somewhere until the train pulled into Vilnius. It came to him. The toilet. Not the one opposite the service compartment, but the one at the other end of the car. He took his luggage and ran down the carpeting. The sign under the door handle said *Vacant*. He breathed a sigh of relief and went in. He put down his things, hung up his coat, and locked the door, so that it would read *Occupied* outside. Still in his hat and without removing his pants, he sat on the plastic seat.

The window was frosted and he could not tell if they were approaching the city. He had to depend on his hearing.

He saw his reflection in the mirror on the door. He looked ridiculous. The fur hat was the final touch. It was very uncomfortable. There was nothing to lean against. His back stiffened.

"God, what am I doing?" he thought, trying to laugh at himself. He smiled at his reflection. "Nobody would believe it even if I told them. Serves me right. It's stupid to travel in second-class cars. Or embark on conversations with the people, the masses. Have to make reservations for the soft-class cars and learn how to appreciate the privileges you have and that others only dream of. So here you sit, cowering in the bathroom like a rabbit. You'll be smarter next time."

He heard footsteps and asthmatic breathing. The door handle turned before his tense eyes. The door was locked. Then there was a knock.

Algis was at a loss. The passengers were waking up, they were near Vilnius. The one banging on the door of the toilet would not go away, and, if he sat there without replying, would go for the conductor to open it with the passkey. Algis stepped on the flush button and heard the roar and rumble of the plumbing.

That was a tactic to let them know the room really was occupied by an animate being.

There were voices outside. Not one, but several. There must already be a line. Sweat broke out on his upper lip. He had to leave. Otherwise they would knock and shout. Then he would have to deal with the conductor and maybe with Dausa and Gaidialis and maybe even Sigita, who would be awakened by the ruckus.

Algis coughed loudly and opened the door. The people in the foyer platform, a few sleepy unkempt creatures, moved aside politely for him to pass and did not even react to the sight of a man in a fur hat leaving a toilet with all of his luggage.

It would be dangerous to go back into the car. There were people in the corridor already, dressed and waiting for Vilnius. Algis dragged his luggage in the other direction to the noisy platform between cars. He went into the next one. The overheated platform was crowded with disembarking passengers. He pushed into the crowd eliciting several scornful looks, and stood, leaning on one foot, swaying with the group, waiting for the train to stop.

His heart was pounding. He felt like a schoolboy who had broken a rule and was waiting to be punished. He was sweating. He was overjoyed when the train lurched to a stop, sending all the passengers flying, and the doors were flung open. Letting in fresh cold air. A barrel of passengers and luggage rolled out onto the platform. Algis was pushed along, but ended up on his feet with his luggage intact.

"Vilnius" the sign over the station entrance said in Lithuanian and Russian.

"Vilnius," Algis read lovingly, and felt happier than he had in ages about coming home.

He headed for the open doors of the station with the other passengers, hoping to run through the hall and grab a cab before the lines got long.

"Comrade Požera," a familiar Russian voice said. He turned to find Tamara, the Intourist guide. She was smiling meaningfully and intimately through her large eyeglasses. She was neatly dressed like a doll again, as she had been at the station in Moscow. Wearing something foreign, powdered and made-up, her hair giving off a dull sheen after its ration of hair spray.

"Comrade Požera, I hope to run into you in Moscow the next time you're there. Here's my office number. I'd be happy to hear from you." She gave him the paper she had prepared. Both his hands were full, so she stuck the note in his pocket.

"Of course, definitely," he muttered. "Good-by, take care."

He wanted to go on, following the stream of passengers, but he was surrounded by the tourists, the tall, well-fed American Lithuanians in their fur coats and boots, with the same white-toothed smiles. He saw Joanne and nodded.

"Mr. Požera!" she called. "How do you do? Please sign this picture I bought of you at the station. Here."

"And mine. And mine." The American Lithuanians set up a hue and cry, waving the picture postcards of him, his profile looking dreamy and lost in thought, leaning on his fist. Poet, thinker, engineer of people's souls.

"Doleful Viking," Joanne said looking at his portrait.

Algis set down his things and began giving autographs. Joanne was first. He wrote nervously, looking over at the station doors and nodding with an artificial smile at the tourists. What if they woke up in the compartment and came running after him? That was all he needed.

He finished signing and picked up his things.

"Farewell, Viking," Joanne said, touching his sleeve. "I'm glad I met you."

"So am I . . . very . . . Good-by."

He ran out of the station, saw the long lines at the taxi stand, cursed, and went off on foot, weighed down by his baggage. He breathed the frosty air deeply. The joy of relief ran through his body.

He was walking fast, almost running. Lightly, effortlessly. Feeling every muscle.

The streetlights were yellow in the dawn's fog. He could make out the familiar shapes of Vilnius' houses in the frosty haze.

Algis Požera, as strong, sturdy, and handsome as a Viking, was entering the city with the fast springy walk of a trained athlete. He was surprised at the ease with which he could run and carry his heavy luggage. He had forgotten that the road from the Vilnius station into town was all downhill. At first the slope was imperceptible. It got steeper and easier.

R18